The Last in Love

An Ardent Springs Novel

The Last in Love

An Ardent Springs Novel

Terri Osburn

Published by Montlake Romance, Seattle

www.apub.com

Amazon, the Amazon logo, and Montlake Romance are trademarks of Amazon.com, Inc., or its affiliates.

ISBN-13: 9781477848517
ISBN-10: 1477848517

Cover design by Michael Rehder

Printed in the United States of America

For Kim. Thanks for everything.

Chapter 1

If Abigail Williams didn't know any better, she'd swear that the universe really didn't like her. Until tonight, she'd thought herself simply unlucky. Maybe even a little cursed. But attempting to bake one harmless cake should not result in nearly burning her house down.

"It isn't so bad," mumbled Clifton Graves, who lingered beside her, watching smoke billow from her roof.

"It isn't so good, either," she replied.

A less jaded person would probably be more upset about setting her kitchen on fire. And on the inside, Abby *was* freaking out. Somewhere. Deep down. Under the cynicism and defeat. The fact was, once a woman had endured losing a husband to a roadside bomb in a foreign land, losing something as piddly as a house didn't hit all that hard.

Clifton had been ordered to keep Abby company while the rest of the Ardent Springs volunteer fire department extinguished her stove. The stove she'd replaced just last week. This was what she got for upgrading. And for attempting a new hobby. What the heck did she know about baking anyway? Absolutely nothing.

"I've seen worse," he assured her, determined to cheer her up. Bless his heart for the effort. Clifton had been part of the volunteer fire squad for as long as Abby could remember. He'd retired from the post office more than five years ago and should have been home enjoying one of Mildred's hot meals on this chilly Wednesday night, not freezing his fire pants off in Abby's driveway. She felt terrible about taking his coat, but he'd refused to let her shiver.

"The kitchen's secured," announced a deep voice from out of the darkness.

The lack of daylight combined with the soot marring the man's face made it difficult to pinpoint his identity. Nonetheless, a flutter of awareness prickled along Abby's skin as the man grew closer and removed his helmet. Full lips split into a sexy grin that revealed a perfect row of pearly whites, while hazel eyes looked her up and down, sending the flutter migrating through her limbs. The heavy gear looked cumbersome, but his wide shoulders, evident inside the thick jacket, bore the weight with ease.

When the mystery man stepped closer, Abby tilted her head back to see his face and nearly sighed aloud. Even covered in soot he was gorgeous. High cheekbones. Strong jawline. Eyes the color of burnished gold.

"Are you all right, Abby?" he asked.

She continued to stare for several seconds, struck dumb by the smudged beauty before her. And then the lust fog cleared and she realized he'd used her name. How could a man she'd never met before know her name?

"Clifton, did you make sure she got checked out?" Without awaiting a response, he leaned closer, bringing his perfect lips mere inches from hers. "Abby, are you breathing okay?"

Her name sounded good on those lips, and she almost reached out to touch them. Nodding, she struggled to regain her composure. "I'm fine. Really." Brushing a hand through her windblown hair, she said, "Do I know you?"

"You remember the Donovan kid, don't ya?" Clifton asked. "Ken and Karen's boy." The old man clipped his fellow firefighter on the arm. "Went off to the big city to make his mark, but he's back where he belongs now."

The reality check hit Abby like a blow. She remembered him all right. As the boy she used to *babysit*. And that added pervert to her other credits of the night. The universe definitely hated her.

"Chief said to have you help Ronnie with the hose, Clif. I can handle things here."

By the looks of him, Justin Donovan could handle Abby six ways from Sunday. And sixty seconds ago, she'd have let him.

"Roger that," the older man said, shuffling off to his assigned task.

Silence loomed as Abby reined in her raging hormones.

"Are you really okay?" Justin asked, voice heavy with concern.

"Yeah," she answered, tugging Clifton's yellow coat tighter across her front. Why couldn't she have grabbed a jacket on her way out of the house? They'd let her pack up a few things from her room, but everything on the coatrack in the foyer had been tainted by smoke. "Cold, but okay. I didn't know you were back in Ardent Springs. Your parents must be happy to have you home."

Whenever Abby would run into Karen Donovan around town, the older woman never failed to brag about her successful son living up in Chicago, but the conversation always included her wish that he would come home to Tennessee more often.

"They are," he said, as if uninterested in small talk. Gold-green eyes traveled from her head to her toes, igniting traitorous little fires along the way. As if he'd missed the lack of makeup and the dirty coat covering most of her body, he said, "You were always pretty, but now . . ."

Clueless how to respond, Abby ignored the compliment and changed the subject. "I can't believe I nearly burned down my house. How bad is the kitchen?"

"Oh," Justin replied, sparing a glance at the house behind him. "I've seen worse." Clifton had said the same, but Abby didn't believe either one of them. "And you didn't do anything. It was an electrical short in the stove."

"But that's a brand-new stove," she said. "I must have done something wrong."

"You didn't do anything wrong except end up with a bum stove, which you couldn't have known by looking at it. The fire didn't get far beyond the appliance and cabinets above it, but you're definitely going to want to stay someplace else tonight. I have a comfortable couch if you need it."

Though her hormones screamed *yes!* Abby declined the friendly offer, certain that the younger man didn't really want his old babysitter invading his space. "I appreciate that, but I've called my brother. I'll stay with him or at my mom's house tonight."

"I don't mind." Justin tucked the helmet under his arm. "I've been meaning to look you up."

Perhaps he'd forgotten their previous connection. "Wouldn't that be . . . weird?" she asked.

Justin tilted his head. "Why would it be weird?"

Slipping her arm through the front of the coat, she waved a hand between them. "There's an age difference here, remember? I was your babysitter."

"I'm not a kid anymore, Abby." She could see that. Boy, could she see that. "Nothing wrong with two adults getting to know each other."

When he put it that way, the situation seemed slightly less pervy, but kids or adults, five years was five years. As she grasped for a response, a pickup truck whirled into the driveway and a blonde bolted from the passenger side before the wheels had slammed to a halt.

"Oh my God, are you all right? Are you burnt? How are your lungs?" Abby found herself pulled into a bear hug before she could respond. "I've been holding my breath since Cooper called me at the hospital. I can't believe we almost lost you."

Haleigh Rae Mitchner, an OB/GYN by trade, wasn't normally the drama type, which made this reaction all the more confusing.

"You didn't almost lose me," Abby muttered against her best friend's shoulder. "But if you don't loosen your grip, you're going to suffocate me right now."

"Let her breathe," Cooper said, but pulled his sister hard against his chest the moment his fiancée let her go. Despite the fact that they were twins, her brother stood a solid ten inches taller than Abby and was built like a brick wall. "You scared us half to death."

"Scared me, too," she mumbled, fighting back tears. The fear and love pouring off her brother made Abby take her close call a little more seriously. What if the smoke detector had failed? What if she'd nodded off on the couch after putting the cake in the oven? What if she hadn't gotten out in time? Cynicism aside, Abigail Williams preferred to live for many years to come.

"She did the right thing by getting out before calling nine one one," Justin said, reminding Abby that they weren't alone.

Releasing the hug but keeping his sister tucked tight against his side, Cooper said, "Thanks for taking care of her."

"My pleasure," the younger man replied, his eyes locked on Abby. "If you want help dealing with the insurance company, let me know. I'll be glad to come over and walk them through the damage. There should be no issue proving you weren't at fault here."

Having been a widow for two years, and a military wife before that, Abby was used to handling a variety of situations on her own. But fire damage and insurance companies were beyond her experience. Accepting a little professional assistance couldn't hurt. No matter what he looked like.

"I'd appreciate that," she said. "I called my agent a little while ago. I assume they'll send someone over tomorrow."

"Do you have your phone handy?" he asked.

"I do, but why?"

"So I can give you my number."

Abby wiggled out of Cooper's grip and handed Justin her cell phone. A few seconds later he handed it back.

"Use it anytime," he said, lifting the helmet back onto his head.

Abby fought a blush. "Thank you. I'll be in touch about the insurance."

Justin tapped the brim of his hat before disappearing into the darkness toward her house.

"I wouldn't normally recommend setting your house on fire to meet a hot guy," Haleigh said, "but you go, girl."

"I did not set my house on fire to meet a guy," she defended, knowing exactly where Haleigh's mind was going. "This is a serious matter."

"And that is one seriously hot fireman."

"I'm standing right here," Cooper said.

Rising on her tiptoes, Haleigh gave her man a quick kiss on the mouth. "I know, baby. I'm only looking for Abbs. Not for myself."

"That's good. Because I'd hate to have to break that dude's legs."

"That dude is Justin Donovan," Abby informed them.

Haleigh's mouth dropped open. "The kid you used to babysit?"

"Yes. Which makes him way too young for me."

"I don't know." The blonde chewed her thumbnail. "We're only talking, what, four years?"

"Five," Abby corrected, determined not to consider what Haleigh was suggesting. "Now can we go? Am I staying with you or with Mom?"

"Mom's staying at Bruce's place, so we're taking you home with us," Cooper answered.

Abby removed Clifton's coat and laid it over the back of the fire engine. "I can stay at Mom's alone."

"Don't be silly," Haleigh said. "We aren't leaving you alone tonight."

Too tired to argue, she nodded. "Fine. I'll stay with you guys." She lifted her overnight bag off the curb. "They won't let me open the garage because it shares the wall that caught fire, so you'll have to bring me home in the morning."

"No problem," Cooper said as they crossed to his truck.

As Abby waited for Haleigh to climb up and slide into the middle of the bench seat, she turned back to her house one more time. Justin lingered at the corner of her garage, where a light from the fire truck shone bright. As he peeled the stained yellow coat off his shoulders, providing a full view of the man beneath the uniform, Abby's mouth went dry.

Why had she turned him down again?

"Abbs, are you coming?" her friend asked, one brow riding high on her forehead.

Busted. Dang it.

"I'm coming," she replied, climbing into the truck. When Haleigh sent her a knowing look, Abby said, "He's off-limits."

"If you say so, girlfriend. But you'd have to be dead not to at least consider that."

"I can hear you," Cooper chimed as the truck slid into gear.

Haleigh patted his knee. "Think of your sister, honey. Her girlie bits are withering away while a cure is standing right over there."

"For heaven's sake," Abby muttered as Cooper increased the volume on the radio.

"No more talking," he ordered. "Especially not about parts of my sister that I don't need or want to know about."

Haleigh laughed, but she held her tongue, which Abby appreciated. Even if the statement about her girlie bits was true. Two years was a long damn time for a woman to go without. Her eyes once again strayed to the young fireman as the truck rolled out of the drive.

A long damn time.

Justin watched the taillights of the old Ford pickup fade in the distance, wondering how Abigail Ridgeway—or Williams, now—had remained single for two years. Either she loved her husband too much to move on or the men in this town were dumb and blind. Justin was neither, and though he would never be thankful that a soldier had lost his life, he saw no reason to pass up the opportunity presented.

He'd been too young to appreciate her when she was helping him with homework, letting him stay up an extra half hour, against his parents' strict orders, to play one more video game. But an encounter during his senior year had been his wakeup call.

After taking a fastball to the temple during a baseball game, which knocked him out cold, Justin woke to find an angel peering down at him. Her soft voice soothed as she gently brushed a lock of hair off his forehead. The words he no longer remembered, but her touch, combined with caring green eyes and a reassuring smile, had hit like a revelation. He never did find out how she'd happened to be in the stands that day, but by the time Justin was back on his feet, Nurse Abby Ridgeway had become the girl of his dreams.

Literally.

Justin's seventeen-year-old brain had kicked into overdrive, and for weeks his nights were filled with detailed, often erotic dreams about the gorgeous brunette with emerald eyes and more curves than any teenage boy would know what to do with. Desperate to get close to her, he took a delivery job with the local florist and paid the other drivers to let him have all of the hospital deliveries.

The week of graduation, mere days after his eighteenth birthday, he'd worked up the courage to ask her out. Carrying an obnoxious arrangement of red roses, Justin marched into the hospital, ready to win his girl, only to find her gushing over the tiny rock on her left hand.

Another man had stolen his dream. Lingering at the nurses' station, Justin eavesdropped for details. The guy was older. Almost thirty, which was ancient from his teenage perspective. A soldier. They'd done a quickie wedding over the weekend because the groom would be shipping out any day for the Middle East.

Heartbroken, Justin had left the flowers on the desk and walked away. That day he vowed never to think of Abigail Ridgeway again. A vow he never managed to keep. Ten years and she still stepped into his dreams every now and then. Sometimes not for a year or more, but she was always there. The girl that got away.

"We're ready to load up," barked Chief Wolinski. The older man stopped next to Justin on the sidewalk. "I didn't think you were on call tonight."

"I wasn't," he replied. "But I figured another set of hands couldn't hurt." In truth, he'd heard the address on the scanner and knew exactly who owned the house on Sunset Lane. "Good thing I did. I don't see Sammy anywhere."

"He's covering at dispatch. Maxine's got two sick kids, Daphne is out with strep, and Doug is visiting his grandma up in Louisville." The chief pinched the bridge of his nose. "It's a good thing we don't get too many emergencies around here."

"I'd forgotten how quiet this town is." Between his years at Northwestern and six years in downtown Chicago, Justin had fully acclimated to city life. He'd still be there now if it weren't for putting his credibility in the wrong hands. "You want me to come back to the station?"

Chief shook his head. "No need. But don't forget about the fundraiser this weekend. Saturday morning, ten sharp, Ruby Theater."

"Got it." Justin tossed his fire coat over his shoulder. "Have you guys done this auction thing before?"

"Nope. This'll be a first for all of us." Stomping off, he yelled for the others to get on the truck and then climbed into the driver's seat.

Grass crunched beneath Justin's feet as he crossed the yard to his car. After climbing inside, he pulled a cell phone from the console. One missed call that he would not be returning. Victoria Bettencourt had been leaving messages for the last two weeks, insisting that if Justin would only give her a chance, she could explain everything.

"You burned that bridge when you screwed my friend," he muttered into the silence, tossing the phone on the passenger seat. "Now you can both go to hell."

Chapter 2

"I can go in there," Abby said aloud. "It's only a little smoke damage, right? Nothing that can't be fixed."

And yet she couldn't make her feet budge. The insurance adjuster would arrive in half an hour, but she'd wanted to survey the damage on her own first. Cooper had offered to go in with her. Insisted, really. But she'd sent him on to work. This was Abby's mess and she'd clean it up. Or at least sign the paperwork to have it cleaned up.

Late April wasn't normally this chilly in middle Tennessee, but then March had felt like May, so who knew what to expect anymore. Bundled in a borrowed coat from Haleigh, Abby forced her body into motion, reaching the edge of the sidewalk before coming to a halt when the smell hit her nose. Smoke and something more putrid. Burnt metal and plastic, she assumed. The cabinet over the stove had held all of Kyle's large plastic cups. The ones he'd carried while running or taken to the gym. Now they were gone. Melted due to her stupidity.

No. Justin said this wasn't her fault. There was no way she could have known that stove had faulty wiring. Accidents happened. Stoves caught fire. Roadside bombs destroyed innocent lives.

"It's safe to go in," Justin said, coming up behind her and scaring Abby out of her boots. He steadied her as she jerked around. "I didn't mean to startle you."

The heat of his grip penetrated the soft material of the thin coat. "I didn't hear you pull up," she said, easing away from his touch. A long night of no sleep provided plenty of time for Abby to come to her senses about this young man. Regardless of Haleigh's goading and Abby's neglected libido, Justin Donovan was entirely too young for her.

Not to mention way out of her league. Men who looked like Justin dated model types, not boring widows.

"Sorry about that." He tucked his hands into the pockets of his low-slung jeans. Though she'd been on the verge of shivering, Justin wore no protection from the cold over his hunter-green button-down, which turned his eyes almost sage. "Do you want to go inside?" he asked.

She took a deep breath and then let it out. Might as well be honest. "I've been trying to do that for the last five minutes."

Picking up what she didn't say, Justin dropped into a voice reserved for timid two-year-olds and cowardly grown women. "It's going to look worse than it is," he assured her. "And I'll be with you the whole time." Stepping closer, he flashed a supportive smile. "You can do this."

Karen Donovan often described her son as a good man. Looking into Justin's caring face, Abby knew the words to be true. With another deep breath the apprehension melted away. "Okay," she murmured. "Going in."

After unlocking the door, she led Justin into the house, lungs protesting the moment they crossed the threshold. Hand over her nose and mouth, Abby hesitated in the foyer.

"Worse than it looks," Justin repeated. "And smells. Opening the windows will help."

His determination to help her through this brought a smile to Abby's face. They weren't sneaking up on the boogeyman, for heaven's sake. Time to woman up and stop acting like a wuss. Within minutes they had every window in the house thrown open, and as Justin had promised, the smell receded.

Unable to put off the inevitable, Abby finally stepped into the kitchen and gasped at the sight before her. The back wall looked as if someone had taken a spray gun and painted the middle four feet coal black from the backsplash to the ceiling. The microwave rested in a melted heap on the damaged stove top, and the doors of the upper cabinets swayed on their hinges.

And then there was the water damage.

Forcing herself to remain standing, she said, "You lied. This is very bad."

"I promise it really isn't. Some sheet rock. A new stove . . ."

"New cabinets. New flooring. New countertops," she added. "The only things I can save are the sink and the fridge." Abby crossed to the farm sink she'd always loved. "Thank goodness for cast iron." Swiping a finger along the blackened granite, she barely left a mark. "This is going to cost a fortune."

Justin leaned a hip on the center island, heedless of the blackened surface. "The insurance company should cover the majority. You also might want to consider contacting the manufacturer of the stove. Mention the word *lawsuit* and you'll likely get immediate action. An upgrade on the stove, if nothing else."

Abby didn't want to contact, let alone sue, a manufacturer. Nor did she want to deal with insurance companies and a construction crew in her house. All she'd wanted was a flipping cake. Smothering the urge to wave her fist at the sky, she instead walked to the fridge and beat her forehead against the stainless steel surface.

"Come on," Justin said, turning her around. "I know this sucks, but in a month you'll have a great new kitchen, and this will all be a bad memory."

She snorted. "I have enough bad memories. When am I going to get some good ones for a change?"

Though her question had been rhetorical, Justin still offered a solution. "I could take you out for ice cream after this. Won't undo the problem, but a frozen treat can help you forget for a while."

Such a tempting offer. Too bad he wasn't five years older. Shaking off the pity party, Abby pushed the hair out of her eyes. "Thanks, but I'll have to pass."

"Why?"

"Because, as I pointed out last night, I'm a little too old to be running around with a twenty-something."

Justin didn't hold back. "That's the dumbest thing I've ever heard."

Annoyed, she said, "You have your opinion and I have mine. If you want to date an older woman, that's your prerogative, but that woman will not be me." She would not embarrass herself by believing she could hold his attention for more than a few days, at best.

Justin opened his mouth to argue when a knock at the front door cut him off. "Hello?" called a female voice.

"We're in here," Abby said. Eyes still locked with his, she lowered her voice. "There are plenty of girls in this town, Justin. Don't waste your time on me." She stepped around him to greet the adjuster.

Damn stubborn woman. What did a few years have to do with anything? He was a grown-ass man with an MBA, a sizable stock portfolio, and the skills to make any woman see God. Twenty-something his ass. If she thought this conversation was over, she was wrong.

The adjuster, a Ms. Dilburgh, seemed friendly and even supportive until the word *culpability* came up and she suggested that human error had caused the fire. Abby's troubled expression shifted Justin's temper to a new source. Dragging the insurance rep to the blackened stove, an area she'd oddly avoided, he pointed out the real culprit, insisting she take pictures of the faulty wiring to include in her report.

Accepting the fact that her company *would* have to pay, the adjuster agreed that the cause was obvious, concluded the inspection, and gave final instructions. A remediation team would arrive in the morning, and Abby needed to submit an inventory of damaged items. Once received, the company would determine the cost of the repairs, and a check would be cut.

One important step hadn't been mentioned.

"What about a structural inspection?" Justin asked.

"Excuse me?" said the adjuster.

"There could be damage in that wall. Unless repaired, Abby could have major issues down the road. It needs to be checked by a professional."

Hugging her iPad to her chest, the woman replied tightly, "I don't think that's necessary. We can see that the wall is still standing."

Justin gritted his teeth. "A professional would tell you that a standing wall isn't necessarily a stable wall. As an insurance adjuster, you know that."

With a huff, Ms. Dilburgh lowered the iPad and began tapping away like a hen pecking for her dinner. "I'll have to do a search to locate a structural engineer in the area. There's no guarantee that I'll be able to find one."

Abby offered a solution. "I know the owner of a construction business in town. He should be able to check the wall, right?" She looked to Justin for backup.

"A man who builds houses qualifies as a structural expert in my book," he said.

"Fine," the pissy insurance lady growled. "What's his name?"

"Mike Lowry," Abby replied. "L-O-W-R-Y. He owns Lowry Construction."

Dilburgh typed in silence for several seconds before flipping the cover on the tablet. "I'll see if he's available, but until then I suggest you put together the inventory list as soon as possible. Regardless of what an inspector determines, the claim can't be processed until that list is submitted and reviewed."

Abby nodded. "I'll start today."

"Good." The adjuster handed Abby her card. "I'll be in touch as soon as I contact Mr. Lowry, but if you need to reach me before then, you can use my cell number." Ignoring Justin completely, she bid her client farewell and marched toward the exit, apparently happy to show herself out.

Staring at the card in her hand, Abby sighed. "Do you really think the wall is damaged?"

"No," Justin answered. "But you can never be too thorough."

"I wouldn't have known to ask about that," she said, glancing up from the card.

"That's why I'm here—I know things about fires that you don't. You're going to want to include furniture, carpet, and curtain cleaning on that inventory list. Sometimes the smell doesn't come out of fabric, but it isn't overwhelming in here, so I think you'll be okay with a good scrub."

"Overwhelming?" Abby muttered. "That smell isn't overwhelming?"

"Not even close." Rubbing his hands together, Justin looked around. "Do you have a notebook on hand?"

Stuffing the business card into her pocket, she crossed to a desk in the corner of the living room. "You don't have to stay," she said.

Stubborn as a mule, this one. "I'm here. I might as well help."

"Don't you have to work or something?"

If she'd been searching for the right button to push, she'd found it.

"That's one of the benefits of being unemployed. Nowhere to be."

He'd expected a look of sympathy. Or maybe pity. Both of which he'd seen enough from his parents. To his surprise, she reacted with honest curiosity.

"Is that why you came home? Because you lost your job?"

"Partially, yes."

"Partially?" she asked, dark brows arched high.

He had no intention of discussing his recent mistakes. "We should start on that list."

Abby fanned herself with the notepad, presumably to ward off the lingering smell of smoke. "Chicago is a big city. Surely you could have found another job. What exactly did you do up there?"

"I worked for a property development firm as a project manager," Justin replied, keeping his answer intentionally vague.

"What kinds of projects?" she asked. So much for vague.

"High-rises, mostly. Some hotels, and others offering new office space."

"Wow," she murmured, appearing adequately impressed. "That sounds like a lot of responsibility. Why did they let you go?"

Because I'm an idiot. "There were . . . complications."

Abby laughed, sending a jolt through his system. Oddly, she looked as surprised by the sound as he was.

"I'm sorry. I don't know why I laughed at that."

Seeing her smile made the blow to his pride worthwhile. "I don't mind. You have a pretty laugh."

The smile disappeared. "You should go."

He'd never met a woman so allergic to compliments. "Abby, I'm not letting you poke around that stove by yourself. It isn't safe. We can keep arguing about this or we can get to work, but I'm not leaving."

A toe tapped on the hardwood as she attempted to stare him down. Justin stood his ground. She wasn't the only stubborn ass in this room.

"You can stay, but this is a onetime thing. And no more flirting."

He couldn't have heard her right. "No more what?"

"You heard me. Save the flattery and that sexy grin for a woman your own age."

Once again, Abby walked away as if the subject were closed. Watching her stroll into the kitchen, Justin pushed up his sleeves. Time to get this age crap out of the way.

"Let's get a couple things straight right now," Justin said, following Abby into the kitchen. "You're going to be dealing with this mess for weeks to come. Whether mine or someone else's, you need to get over this super-woman crap and accept some damn help." She spun to respond, but he kept charging, backing her up against the island. "Second, I will not be disqualified on a technicality." Strong arms locked on to the island behind her, and his voice softened as his eyes dropped to her mouth. "I've waited too long for this chance. I'm not walking away until I get a fair shot."

Flushed, Abby stared into olive-gold eyes, utterly speechless. Desire warred with anger, and both caused her to miss the meaning of his words. Two years since she'd been this close to a man, which she'd begun to think might never happen again, caused a rush of endorphins into her brain, muddling her otherwise practical nature.

Shaking hands gripped the soft, green cotton of his shirt, and for a second she nearly gave in to temptation. One afternoon of sex couldn't hurt anything. Except her pride when he saw her naked. Abby had put on weight since Kyle's death and wasn't as comfortable in her own skin these days.

But beyond her insecurity loomed the guilt. *'Til death do us part* sounded good on paper but turned out to be much harder in practice.

"Are you finished?" she said, voice breathier than she liked.

"Are you going to stop throwing this age thing around?" he asked.

Abby stood her ground. "I'm five years older than you are, Justin. That's a reality."

"I'm not arguing the number." He leaned forward until she could feel his breath on her cheek. "I'm saying that number doesn't mean a damn thing. You're a single woman. I'm a single man. *That's* the reality."

If only things could be so simple.

"For you, maybe," she replied, finding the strength to push against his chest. He barely budged. "But like it or not, that number matters to me. I need you to respect that."

She'd finally gotten through to him. Justin rose to his full height. "I respect you, Abby. I always have. But that doesn't mean I'm giving up. I won't make the same mistake twice."

Justin stepped past her and reached into the cabinet above the blackened stove while Abby struggled to regain her composure. Five mostly melted bottles nearly fell onto his head, but he caught them with ease. Six months ago, she'd parted with Kyle's clothes after Haleigh had convinced her that giving them away would be cathartic. Her fear that removing his things would somehow remove him from her memory had proven to be a shortsighted notion. But then grief didn't always make sense.

And so she told herself that this would be the same. These were bits of plastic, not priceless monuments.

"Do you want to put these on the list?" Justin asked.

Shaking her head, Abby said, "No. I don't need to replace those."

Though a small achievement, the act of letting anything go felt heroic, and Abby would take a win wherever she could find one.

Chapter 3

"Dammit," Abby muttered, not for the first time since they'd begun assessing the damage. "This was my grandmother's serving platter. It dates back to the 1940s."

The three pieces of porcelain in her hands didn't look like much to Justin, but he offered sympathy all the same. "Sorry about that. Think you can find a replacement online?"

"I don't know." Her shoulders fell. "If I could, it wouldn't be the same."

"Do you want me to do some research to find a value?"

"You can try." She flipped the pieces to find a hallmark. "The maker is Pfaltzgraff, but there's nothing else to go on."

They'd brought her laptop into the kitchen more than an hour before. Once Justin had handled the area directly above the stove, Abby took over going through the rest of the cabinets. Thankfully, most items had been salvageable, but the force of a fire hose always took some victims of its own.

"I'll pull up some pictures and we'll see if any look similar." Typing into the search engine, he said, "Can I ask you a question?"

Squatting in front of an open cabinet, she said, "You just did. Why do people do that? If you have a question, just ask it."

"I don't remember you being this grumpy." The Abby he knew had always been ready with a smile and a kind word. The modern version barely smiled at all.

"That's an observation. Not a question."

An observation she didn't contradict.

"Why are you still here?" Justin asked.

She stood up. "Shouldn't I be asking you that? This is my house and my mess. I have to be here. Why are you still here?"

Refusing to start that argument again, he said, "I mean, why are you still in Ardent Springs? You always talked about seeing the world. I thought you'd be living in some exotic location by now."

Abby shrugged. "Kyle had seen enough of the world before he met me that he didn't feel the need to see any more. After we married, he preferred that I stay here at home, with family and friends, instead of relocating to wherever the army sent him."

"Are you saying that you never got to travel because your husband wouldn't let you?" Justin couldn't imagine giving up a dream because someone told him to.

"I didn't say he didn't *let* me. He just didn't want me to go."

"And the difference is?"

"The difference is that staying here was my choice." Abby scratched her temple with the back of a soot-stained hand. "I'm not going to lie. I grew to resent it towards the end, but since he died I've realized that he had enough stress in his life without having to worry about me, too. Saving the world, which is essentially what our poor military is being called to do, takes a toll. If knowing I was safe gave him a moment of peace, then I'm glad I honored his wishes."

Justin had never been to war, let alone saved the world, but he had been in some life-and-death situations during his time fighting fires. He wouldn't want anyone he loved in harm's way, but Abby taking a trip to London or Paris or even Canada didn't sound very dangerous. At least no more dangerous than anything else these days. Europe wasn't as safe as it once was, but a person could just as easily die on a backcountry road as in the streets of some foreign city.

Opting not to point this out, he instead jumped to the next obvious question.

"But you're still here. I don't mean to sound harsh, but you're free now. So why stay?"

Dark lashes flitted over jade-green eyes. "Where would I go?"

That one was easy. "Anywhere you want."

"But who would I go with? And don't go volunteering for that, too."

He'd go anywhere Abby asked him to go but preferred to point out something she'd apparently never considered. "Go by yourself."

Abby dropped onto her bottom as if he'd flung something at her. "By myself? That's crazy."

"Why is it crazy? If you want something, go get it. If you want to see the world, go see it."

"I—" she started, seemingly at a loss for words. "Huh."

As she leaned against the sink, her eyes dropped to the floor, and Justin could see her mind processing his suggestion. Full lips opened and closed, while green eyes sparkled at the possibilities.

Looking up, she said, "Do people really do that?"

"Probably not everyone, no. But then not everyone has your intelligence and sense of adventure."

Her snort took him by surprise. "My sense of adventure took a hike a long time ago."

Justin refused to believe that the girl he once knew wasn't still hiding in there somewhere. "Nonsense. You are who you are, and that doesn't change. The summer before I left for college, you had a collection of travel pamphlets. I bet you still have them."

A pretty pink clouded her cheeks. "You remember that?"

"I remember everything," Justin assured her. "Where are they?"

The half grin lifted one corner of her mouth. "In a shoe box in the top of my closet. But gosh, I haven't thought about those pamphlets in forever."

"The world is still out there," he said, fingers poised above the keys. "Where do you want to go first?"

Abby rolled her eyes. "I couldn't take off on a trip right now."

The woman was too literal for her own good. "I'm not buying you a plane ticket for tomorrow. Just tell me where you'd go if you *could* fly off tomorrow."

"A pretend flight, huh?" One slender finger twisted a dark lock in circles. "I don't know if I can pick one."

"Come on," he urged. "First city that comes to mind."

"London," Abby replied as if the answer had been hovering near the surface and suddenly burst through. "My great-grandmother, who died the year before Cooper and I were born, came over from England when she was twelve—alone, if you can believe it—and I've always wanted to find out more about her. Maybe even see where she grew up."

Encouraged by her enthusiasm, Justin tapped a few keys. "London it is. A little search for popular attractions and here we are." He spun the laptop to face her. "Your potential destinations all on one page."

Like a child approaching a toy store window, Abby stepped closer to the screen. "There's King's Cross," she said, green eyes bright. "I saw a picture once of Nanny Lill standing in front of the station doors. She was just a little girl, and I've often wondered if that wasn't the day she took the train to Liverpool to catch the boat that brought her here. Which would make it the last time she ever saw London."

Justin let her scroll through the other images, watching her smile widen. This was the girl he remembered. Seconds later, she whispered, "There's so much to see."

"You should go," he said. "Maybe not tomorrow, but soon."

Abby stepped back, pushing the computer his way. "I can't."

"Why not?"

She returned to the open cabinet. "Because I'm not a kid to go gallivanting around the world."

"I'm pretty sure that no one uses the word *gallivanting* anymore," Justin pointed out. "And what does your age have to do with taking a trip? Adults take vacations all the time."

"Spending money on a trip to London would be frivolous."

"What's wrong with frivolous? No one is suggesting you stop paying your bills and run away forever. Take a week for yourself. You said earlier that you want some good memories for a change. A trip to London is the perfect place to make some."

Dragging a small, waterlogged box from the cabinet, she said, "I'm not promising anything, but I'll think about it." Abby opened the box and the lid crumbled in her hand. "We need to add a hand mixer to the list. This one is a goner."

Just like that, the practical Abby returned. But the blush remained high on her cheeks. There might be hope for her yet.

Three hours into her twelve-hour shift, Abby already needed coffee.

"You look pretty happy for a woman who spent the day dealing with fire damage," Haleigh said, sneaking up on Abby in the hospital cafeteria. "What gives?"

Abby added French vanilla creamer to her cup. "What makes you think I'm happy?"

"The humming, for starters." The OB doc filled her own mug.

"I'm not any different than I was yesterday," she claimed, lying through her teeth. Yesterday she'd been mad at the world and dreading the future. Today, thanks to Justin, she was considering getting a passport. "Have you ever thought about taking a trip?"

Haleigh reached for the sugar. "What kind of a trip?"

"I don't know." Abby picked a couple of places on her list. "To New York to see a play. Or London to visit the queen."

"Aren't those two of the trips you talked about incessantly back in high school? Are you seriously thinking about going now?"

"You're right," Abby said, brushing the idea away. "I don't know what I was thinking."

"No. This sounds like a great idea. This is something you've always wanted, but I assumed you'd given up ever doing it."

Abby *had* given up. On a lot of things. "Nothing is set in stone. The subject came up with Justin today, and—"

"Wow," Haleigh said, brown eyes wide. "That boy is good."

"What do you mean?"

She clicked a lid onto her cup. "Yesterday you were adamant that he was too young for you, and now you're talking about going to New York together."

"I am not!" Abby defended, drawing attention from the other patrons. She cleared her throat and lowered her voice. "He remembered that I used to talk about traveling and asked me about it. *If* I book a trip, and that's a big *if*, the plan is to go alone."

"Do you think that's wise?"

Bringing this up had clearly been a mistake. "Wise?"

"Traveling alone sounds kind of dangerous." Her friend shrugged.

Abby's teeth clenched. "If I were a man, would you say that?"

Haleigh cringed. "Good point. But it's a reality, whether we like it or not. In most cases, a two-hundred-twenty-pound douche bag is going to come after *you* before he'd go after another guy. Why don't you take Linda with you?"

Taking her mother on her first real travel adventure didn't sound all that fun. Not that Abby didn't love her mom, but a mother/daughter trip was not what she had in mind. However, Haleigh had a point. A single woman in a strange city by herself came with a daunting list of possibilities. Many exciting, but many downright dangerous.

"Like I said, nothing is carved in stone. Just something I'm thinking about."

"Well, I think you should do it. And if you manage to score tickets for *Hamilton*, you aren't getting on that plane without me."

Abby nodded, doubtful that would ever happen. "Agreed."

"Did I hear someone is getting on a plane?"

Sipping her coffee, Abby turned to find Carrie Farmer holding her daughter, Molly, on her hip. The child squirmed like a baby seal but her mother held tight.

"Abbs is thinking about taking a trip."

"Really?" Carrie said. "With who?"

Justin had clearly been mistaken about the travel alone bit. "Not sure yet," she answered. "What are you doing here this late?"

Carrie shook her head. "Hope stepped on Noah's foot. That pony may be small, but she's heavy."

The single mom had found love the fall before with her neighbor, Noah Winchester. Since Christmas, the pair had been inseparable, the threesome making an adorable little family. Abby was happy for the younger woman, who'd suffered much more than she had, but couldn't help but envy her at the same time.

"Is he okay?" Haleigh asked.

"He will be," Carrie sighed. "Despite insisting that he was fine, he couldn't even put weight on it without moaning in pain."

"Ouch. But that's a military guy for you." Abby remembered Kyle's absolute refusal to show any weakness. Noah had been Special Forces with the navy, which likely made him a tougher case than her infantry husband. "They could get run over by a tank and try to walk it off."

"Exactly," Carrie agreed with a laugh. "Oh, listen to me going on without even asking about your house. How are you doing? That had to be scary."

"I wouldn't want to do it again," Abby confirmed, "but the fire department put it out right away, and a team will start cleaning up tomorrow morning."

"That reminds me," Haleigh said. "Are you staying with us again tonight?"

Abby shook her head. "I dropped a bag at Mom's on the way here. A couple more nights and I should be able to return home. I won't be cooking anything for a while, but I'm looking forward to sleeping in my own bed."

Carrie's daughter, Molly, let out a squeal and nearly did a back bend out of her mother's arms. "I'd better go before she gets to the floor and takes off," she said, switching the child to her other hip like a pro. "And I promised Noah I'd bring him back something to drink. When I left he was still in X-ray, but they may be back by now."

"Let us know if there's anything we can do," Haleigh offered, ruffling the little girl's hair. "And good luck keeping him off that foot."

Mother and child headed for the cooler on the other side of the cafeteria as Carrie shared a parting wave over her head.

"She makes that look easy, doesn't she?" Haleigh said.

"It comes with practice," Abby replied. "Remember how clueless Jessi was when Emma was first born?" A homeless, pregnant teen that Cooper had stumbled upon last spring, Jessi and her baby, Emma, had spent their first several months together living in Abby's house. The young mother had since moved in with her boyfriend, Ian, leaving Abby once again alone in a house too big for one person. "She's an expert now."

Her friend sighed. "I think it's a gift. You're either born with the maternal instinct or you aren't. You were. I wasn't."

Cooper had always wanted to be a father and would be a good one, given the chance. Surely Haleigh didn't mean to take that option away from him. "What are you trying to tell me? That you're never having children?"

"Of course not," the blonde replied, sounding more resigned than a potential mother should. "But what if I turn out like my mom? I could never inflict that on an innocent child."

For lack of a better word, Meredith Mitchner's mothering skills were nonexistent. She was cold, unaffectionate, and overly critical of her daughter, while Ryland, Haleigh's younger brother, could do no wrong. Since Haleigh and Meredith were nothing alike, Abby couldn't imagine her friend ever repeating her mother's offenses.

"You can get rid of that notion right now," she said. "When you and Cooper get around to having kids, those little ones are going to be very lucky to have you as their mother."

Brown eyes softened. "Do you really believe that?"

"With all my heart. Now when am I going to get a little niece or nephew?"

Haleigh chuckled. "Let me get through the wedding first."

Abby gripped her best friend's wrist. "Did you set a date?"

"We're talking about it, but nothing definite. It's been nearly a year, and Cooper is running out of patience."

Her twin had loved Haleigh Rae since they were clueless teenagers, and he'd love her until the last breath left his body. But that didn't mean he wouldn't nag her to make things official. The problem wasn't that Haleigh didn't *want* to get married. She simply dreaded planning a wedding with her mother.

"Unless you think he'll wait another thirty years or so, you're going to have to deal with Meredith being involved. In the end, it's *your* day, and your mother will have to take a backseat."

A blonde brow shot up. "Have you ever known my mother to do that?"

She had a point, but still. "I'll be there to help, and you know that Mom won't tolerate her causing trouble." Dropping an obvious hint, Abby added, "A Christmas wedding is always nice."

"You're as bad as your brother." The phone in Haleigh's pocket began to buzz. Checking the screen, she said, "Duty calls. Don't forget about the fundraiser on Saturday. I'll pick you up at nine thirty."

"I may have to work that day."

"Already checked your schedule. You're off on Saturday."

"All right, but I'm not bidding," Abby called as Haleigh shuffled toward the exit.

"Never say never," her friend called back before disappearing through the swinging doors.

Abby didn't care what Haleigh did to her. She would not lower herself to buying a man's time. Even if it was for a good cause.

Chapter 4

Though Justin hadn't seen Abby since Thursday, he'd heard from her via text. The remediation team had moved in as scheduled, and Mike Lowry, the contractor Abby had suggested to the insurance adjuster, had completed a structural inspection. The wall was sound, and the water from the fire hoses had caused more damage than the fire itself. Which couldn't be helped.

What made him smile had been the final bit of information. Abby had ordered a guidebook for Europe thanks to him. A good sign that she'd warmed to him, if only a little.

Now if she'd drop the age crap, they might get somewhere. The few seconds against the kitchen island had shown promise, when her eyes darkened and her breath hitched as she licked her lips. He'd given her enough space to make the next move, drawing the line at forcing his case. And then she'd pushed him away.

Not the result he'd wanted, and though patience was not Justin's forte, her reaction gave him hope.

"You're up next," said Vivi Fontain, her eyes locked on a clipboard as she adjusted her headset. With the push of a button, she spoke into the microphone attached to the earpiece. "Get the Nelly song ready. It's about to get hot in here."

A CPA and veteran EMS member, Vivi handled the finances for the volunteer fire department and had put together this unorthodox auction to raise money toward a new ladder truck. She'd supposedly gotten the idea from an annual women's show put on in Nashville.

Lowering the mic, she said, "Don't let me down, Donovan. You're the prettiest face we've got. I'm counting on a triple-digit bid, at least."

Feeling like a prize bull, Justin attempted to retain some of his dignity. "You realize that's sexist, right?"

"Welcome to a woman's world, sweetheart."

Applause and loud whistles filled the theater, echoing through the makeshift backstage area where Justin awaited his turn on the auction block.

"Who's all that for?" he asked, his competitive nature roaring to life. Embarrassing as this was going to be, his pride would accept nothing less than ending the event as the highest earner.

"Clifton," she said as they both peered through the curtain to see the old man unbutton his shirt, revealing curling wisps of gray hair. "Good Lord. He's doing a striptease."

Staring in awe, Justin said, "I'm supposed to follow that?"

"No backing out now, honey." Swinging her fist over her head, Vivi yelled, "Go get 'em, Clifton!"

Zac Harwick, a local DJ serving as MC for the event, appeared completely dumbfounded.

"He isn't taking bids," Vivi murmured. Opening the curtain wider, she waved her arms furiously to get the DJ's attention. When he finally noticed, she reminded him to do his job.

"Right," Zac said, dropping the stunned expression and turning back to the loudly cheering crowd. "Ladies, this man is working hard for your money. Who will give me fifty dollars for a date with Firefighter Graves?"

A slew of paddles went up, and so did the bids. A minute later, the DJ yelled "Sold!" at the three-hundred-dollar mark, and a tiny, silver-haired woman climbed onstage to claim her prize.

"Isn't that his wife?" Justin asked.

"Yeah. She said she wasn't going to bid because she could have him for free anytime she wanted."

"Looks like she changed her mind."

Vivi laughed. "I bet Clifton did it on purpose. He knew Mildred wouldn't tolerate some other woman spending time with him. Not after that little performance."

Justin chuckled. "Gotta give the man credit. I wouldn't dance around like that." When the redhead didn't reply, he turned to see if she'd walked away only to find blue eyes boring into him. "You cannot expect me to do that."

"A ladder truck, Justin. Do you know how long we've been saving? We're *this* close," Vivi said, holding two fingers an inch apart. "I can almost smell the fresh red paint."

She could smell whatever she wanted, but he was not about to make a fool of himself. That swivel thing was cute coming from Clifton. Justin would look like a drunk walrus trying to twirl a ball on his, well, not his nose.

Vivi crossed her arms. "You agreed to do this."

"I agreed to walk out on that stage, endure the humiliation of being auctioned off like a 1965 Roadster, and then spend an hour with the highest bidder. I did *not* agree to shake my ass for anyone."

"I'll make sure you don't get truck-washing duty for a month. And if you bring in the most money, you'll have bragging rights for the rest of the year."

He worked his jaw, processing the offer. She just had to go and mention bragging rights, didn't she? Damn his competitive nature.

"Fine. But I'm not taking anything off."

"Take it off!" called Haleigh over the cheering crowd around them, mortifying Abby.

Otherwise rational women catcalling men they'd known for most, if not all, of their lives might be the most ridiculous thing she'd ever witnessed. This was supposed to be a civic fundraiser, not a male revue.

Admittedly, Clifton *was* kind of adorable, shaking his hips and blowing kisses to the crowd. A performance that would go down in history, and at least Abby could say she'd seen it with her own two eyes. To her relief, the noise level dropped to a more tolerable decibel level once Mildred dragged her husband off the stage.

"Have we seen enough yet?" she asked Haleigh.

Without sparing her friend a glance, the normally reserved doctor said, "Don't be silly. The main attraction is up next."

Abby hadn't bothered to pick up a program so had no idea who this main attraction might be, but she didn't have to wait long to find out. A familiar song blared over the crowd as Justin Donovan sauntered onto the stage.

"Get your paddle ready, girlfriend. This one's for you."

She should have known. "You're out of your mind if you think I'm bidding on any man, especially that one."

"But he's so pretty," Haleigh replied, dancing to the music as if they were in a club instead of an old movie house. "And he likes you. Why not have a little fun?"

The obvious answer, one she'd already given Haleigh more than once, died on her lips when Abby spotted Justin tugging the hem of his shirt from the waistband of his hip-hugging jeans. A wicked smile combined with a quick flash of defined abs sent the audience into a frenzy.

"Oh my," she whispered before Haleigh dragged her forward, pushing through the crowd.

"We need a closer look," her friend shouted as they forged ahead.

When they reached the front of the stage, Justin locked eyes with Abby. She couldn't have looked away if she'd tried. Three buttons opened on the shirt and her mouth went dry. Two more and she forgot her name. When the last button gave way, the buzz in her ears had nothing to do with the screams echoing off the rafters. The word *glorious* came to mind. As a nurse, Abby had seen her fair share of the human form, but she'd never seen anything like this.

After flashing her a wink, he turned around and swung his hips from side to side. Distracted by the perfect ass in front of her, Abby almost didn't notice the vibration happening in her own back pocket. Reaching for the cell, she spotted the name Eliza Dilburgh on the screen.

Grabbing Haleigh's arm, she yelled, "I need to take this," and handed over her paddle before scurrying to the exit, answering the call as she burst into the theater lobby. "Hello? Ms. Dilburgh?"

"Mrs. Williams, I'm sorry to bother you on a weekend, but your claim has kicked back in the system due to an issue with your policy. Our files show that your husband, Kyle Williams, signed the original documents, but you did not. We'll need a form from Mr. Williams making you a fellow beneficiary before a check can be cut."

Locking down her emotions, Abby closed her eyes. "Ms. Dilburgh, if you check your records again, you'll see that my husband was killed in combat nearly two years ago." Silence came from the other end of the call.

"I'm very sorry," Ms. Dilburgh said. "I assumed you were divorced."

"No," she said. "I'm a widow." The last word never got easier to say.

"I'll work it out," the other woman replied. "You have my sincere condolences."

More than eighteen months later and Abby still had no idea what the hell she was supposed to do with *condolences*.

"Thank you. Please let me know if you need anything else. I'd like to put my house back together as soon as possible." Bouncing between her mother's and her brother's homes, watching two deliriously happy couples enjoy what she longed for, was making this already crappy situation even more depressing.

"I'll be in touch," Ms. Dilburgh answered, and the call cut off.

Shaken, Abby slid the phone away from her ear. She couldn't be angry with the adjuster. It was an honest mistake, and one Ms. Dilburgh no doubt regretted. Abby knew a thing or two about regret. Remembering her recent commitment to moving on, she shoved the phone back in her pocket and pushed through the theater doors. Justin's shirt hung off his shoulders as bid paddles waved in the air. In their excitement, the crowd had tightened to the point that Abby couldn't possibly reach Haleigh again. She couldn't even see her.

Lingering at the edge, Abby enjoyed the show from a distance. The MC, a local DJ who looked overwhelmed by the audience reaction, called out dollar amounts. Three fifty. Then four. The bidding jumped to five hundred, and then six, which appeared to be too rich for several previously determined participants. Only two paddles continued to battle it out until the final number of eight hundred fifty dollars.

Abby whistled to herself. Justin might turn out to be worth a pretty penny, should the lucky woman reel him into more than an afternoon date, but anyone willing to pay that much for a man had to be desperate.

"Congratulations to the winning woman," Zac Harwick announced, "with paddle number four twenty-two."

Still on the fringe of the excitement, Abby applauded with the others, waiting for the lucky girl to hop onstage and claim her prize. And then she realized why the paddle number sounded familiar. That was *her* paddle.

Haleigh Rae Mitchner, I'm going to kill you.

Before she could sprint for the exit, her best friend leapt from the crowd and grabbed her arm. "I got you a present!" she hollered, smiling like a cat who'd just liberated a goldfish—with its teeth. The woman didn't even have the decency to look guilty.

"I'm not going up there. You bought him. You go get him."

Ignoring the order, Haleigh towed her to the stairs beside the stage and physically forced her to climb, leaving Abby to wonder when her best friend had gotten so damn strong. She'd planned to scurry right back down again, but Justin met her at the top with an extended hand, wearing a smile that kicked her heart into overdrive.

"I was hoping you'd be the one," he said into her ear, the scruff along his cheek tickling her temple.

Abby had no intention of going through with this ridiculous date, but she wouldn't embarrass him, either. Planting a fake smile on her lips, she gave a quick wave to the audience before shuffling them both out of the spotlight.

Once hidden in the wings, she spun to face him. "I'm sorry."

"Sorry for what?" he asked. "You just made me a legend."

"I didn't make you anything. That was Haleigh."

Hands on his hips, Justin frowned. "What was Haleigh?"

"The bidding," Abby explained, struggling to focus with so much mouthwatering flesh on display. "She used my paddle, but it was Haleigh doing the bidding."

"Are you saying your brother's girlfriend just bid on a date with me?"

"Not for herself," she clarified. "For me. A date with you *for* me."

"That's a relief. I could probably hold my own against Cooper but would rather not test the theory."

"I'm trying to tell you . . ." But the words *I'm not going out with you* stuck in her throat. Haleigh had been right about one thing. Justin sure was pretty. In a biscuits-and-gravy, I-bet-he-tastes-good kind of way. "Would you please button your shirt?"

Leaning on a beam beside her, his smile returned. The wicked one that muddled her senses. "Why? Don't you like what you see?"

The man's ego knew no bounds. "Because I feel ridiculous having this conversation while you're half-dressed." Betraying her true thoughts, she added, "It's freaking distracting."

Justin finally cooperated. "You're cute when you're distracted," he said, closing the blue button-down. "Where do you want to go today?"

"We aren't going anywhere."

"If you have to work, we can move the date to tomorrow."

"We aren't going on a date." Though why not, she couldn't remember. He needed to button faster.

"You just bid over eight hundred dollars that says otherwise."

"I told you. Haleigh did the bidding." And someday Abby would get her back for creating this awkward scenario.

Stopping with two buttons to go, he repeated her earlier statement. "To buy a date for you. With me. What part of this am I missing?"

Rubbing her forehead, Abby felt herself weakening. Why couldn't she spend a few hours with him? They'd been together two days ago, and truth be told, she'd enjoyed his company. All she had to do was set some ground rules.

"You aren't missing anything," she said, accepting defeat. "I'll spend a few hours with you, but on one condition."

"Name it," Justin said.

"We don't call it a date."

He paused in the process of tucking the shirt into his jeans. "You do realize that the definition of a date is two people spending time together?"

Mere semantics. "Take it or leave it."

His deep chuckle sent tremors down to her toes. "You paid, so you make the rules. Now tell me where we're going on this non-date."

Picking the least man-friendly venture she could think of, Abby said, "I know just the place."

Chapter 5

Someday Justin would have to thank Haleigh Mitchner for her interference. When Vivi shoved him through the curtain, Justin felt like a fool. He'd done some crazy things in college, but always with the help of liquid courage. Shaking his moneymaker for a hometown crowd, which included his eighth-grade math teacher and at least three women from his maternal grandmother's bridge club, had taught him the true meaning of humiliation.

Until the spotlight had veered left, allowing him to lock eyes with Abby in the front row. Then he had a reason to keep shaking.

The light had blinded him for the rest of the auction, so he'd had no idea whether Abby was bidding or not. As the dollar amounts increased, his confidence grew and, though he'd deny it to his dying day, Justin had enjoyed the hoots and hollers. In the end, his efforts had paid off in more ways than one. Vivi grew closer to her goal, and Justin landed a date with Abby.

Not that he could call it a date, of course. Nope. They were simply two people spending time together. Buying flowers.

"You can buy the petunias if you want," he advised, "but I'm telling you, they're high maintenance. I'd go with a hardier perennial. Like these coneflowers."

As part of his civil engineering degree, Justin had studied landscape design and worked part-time with an Evanston company during the fall and spring of his junior and senior years at Northwestern. Thanks to a childhood spent helping his mom in the garden, he also possessed a green thumb.

"Why are their petals limp?" Abby asked. "They look sad. And grumpy."

Who the heck called flowers grumpy?

"They aren't grumpy," he defended. "They're cone shaped. That's why they're called *cone*flowers."

Her nose twitched. "I don't like that color pink, either."

"That's purple."

"They're pink."

Justin pulled the info card from the pot, holding it up for her to read. "Purple Coneflowers."

"Fine," she conceded. "Then I don't like that shade of *purple*."

Heaven help him. "What colors do you like?"

"Happy colors. Yellow, red, orange, blue."

Voice droll, he said, "So anything other than pink and purple?"

Fluttering her eyelashes, she said, "If you don't like what I've chosen for our date, Mr. Donovan, feel free to bow out at any time."

She wouldn't win that easy. "I thought we weren't supposed to call this a date."

"Slip of the tongue, I assure you." Strolling down the aisle, she asked, "How do you know all this stuff anyway?"

"I did landscaping work in college. As I'd hoped, the experience came in handy on a couple big projects later in my career."

"That brings us back to your job situation. How does someone like you end up unemployed and back in his hometown?"

Curious, he asked, "A guy like me?"

Abby toyed with one of the coneflowers. "You know. Smart. Driven. Talented."

"How do you know I'm talented?"

"Because your mother tells me so every time I see her." Glancing up, she asked, "Do you have any idea how proud she is of you?"

While he loved the Donovans more than anything, Justin's ambition to be the best, to be *worth* something, had more to do with the parents that gave him up than the ones who'd raised him.

"She's mentioned it a time or two." Or maybe twenty. Oddly enough, his dad had never uttered the words.

"Anyway, what gives? Why are you here instead of in Chicago?"

Still reluctant to share the details of his epic professional failure, Justin tried a different tack. "I told you. Things got complicated. I didn't leave my last position on positive terms."

"Okay. Chicago is *one* city," Abby pointed out. "Why not get a job somewhere else? Denver. Pittsburgh. Seattle. You should be using your talents."

"I *am* using my talents," he said with a grin. "I'm consulting on your flower bed project."

Abby lifted one delicate brow. "And I thought I was good at evading touchy subjects." Returning to her shopping, she continued down the row, stopping in front of an abundance of red-and-yellow blooms. "What are these?" she asked. "They're gorgeous."

She was gorgeous, Justin nearly corrected but kept the thought to himself.

"Blanket flowers," he replied. "Good in the summer heat *and* they attract butterflies."

"I like butterflies," she cooed. "Now we're cooking." Turning the corner to the next row, she stopped again. "Please tell me I can have the blue ones." Abby bent close and breathed deep. "They smell wonderful. Subtle, but I like it."

"Those are delphiniums. Good choice." Pointing to a display farther up, he added, "I'd throw in hydrangeas and several Soft Touch holly shrubs while you're at it. You'll need the green to break up all the color, and the Soft Touch don't have the sharp points of a regular holly bush. Add a nice border and you'll have a flower bed that your neighbors will envy." When he met Abby's eyes again, a sense of foreboding prickled up his spine. "What does that look mean?"

"You need to start your own business," she said.

She clearly didn't know much about property development. "I'd need investors, and there aren't many millionaires looking for development deals around here."

"No, I mean a landscaping business. You have the knowledge and experience, would be the only such service in Ardent Springs, and I heard the downtown planning committee is searching for someone to dress up the square. I know it isn't the same as transforming the skyline of a big city, but there's something to be said for being your own boss and doing something you enjoy."

Truth be told, Justin had planned to live off his substantial savings until another development opportunity came his way. All he had to do was wait out the industry gossip mill and hope that someone would give him a second chance. But there was no telling when that day would come, and considering his lack of other options, Abby's idea held merit.

Churning the details over in his mind, Justin made a mental list of what he'd need. Equipment, a trailer, a name for the business. And a truck, since shovels and bags of dirt would never come within a hundred feet of his Infiniti. Pop might let him use the old Chevy if he asked nicely.

"I haven't done residential work in a long time. I'm not sure I could convince anyone to give me a shot without showing them an example of what I can do."

Abby lifted a delphinium plant and shoved it at his chest. "There's a house on Sunset Lane in dire need of attention. Have at it."

"Are you serious? You'd let me use your house?"

"Sure," she said. "You get your sample garden, and now I won't have to get dirty."

Tucking the plant under his arm, Justin said, "Every landscaper needs a good assistant."

"Then I suggest you take out an ad, flower boy, because I already have a job."

"Sticking your hands in the dirt can't be any worse than what you do at the hospital," he pointed out.

Abby picked up another delphinium plant. "Don't remind me. Now let's wrap up this shopping spree so you can buy me a pizza."

Justin grinned as she strolled back to the blanket flowers. No matter what Abby claimed, this little excursion was quickly becoming the best date he'd been on in months.

If Abby wasn't careful, she could get used to this. A man opening her car door. Pulling out her chair. Making her feel beautiful and desirable as he hung on her every word. More than once, she'd had to remind herself that (a) this was not a date, and (b) Justin was too young for her. Though she struggled to maintain the second argument. In fact, as the afternoon progressed, age became less and less of a factor.

Justin Donovan was more than a pretty face. He was intelligent and informed. Considerate and thoughtful. Open-minded and down-to-earth. She'd have to be dead or blind not to notice the gorgeous packaging, but she was beginning to think his mind and heart were the real draw. By the time she'd finished off her first slice of pizza, Abby knew the smart thing to do would be to end the date as soon as possible. And yet she continued exchanging smiles and enjoying the moment.

"What did you mean earlier?" Justin asked, dabbing sauce off his chin.

Because Main Street Pizzeria only served takeout, they'd settled on a downtown bench to eat their meal.

"What did I mean when?" Abby said, careful not to lose the pepperoni teetering on the edge of her slice.

"When I mentioned the stuff you see at the hospital and you said not to remind you. That didn't sound like a comment from someone who loves her job."

Eyes focused on the twirling barbershop sign across the street, she shrugged. "I used to love it, and I wish I could say I still do, but . . . I don't know. I sometimes wish I could do something else."

Justin reached for the bottle of soda at his feet. "What else would you do?"

Excellent question. "I have no idea."

"You must have thought about it."

"No, I haven't." Turning to face him, she said, "How have I never thought about this?"

He shook his head. "Think about it now. If you could do anything else, anything at all, what would it be?"

Abby said the first thing that came to mind. "Be a mom."

Twisting the cap off the bottle, he said, "You'd be good at that, but I hear the pay isn't great and the clients can be demanding little assholes."

"How can you say that about children?" She chuckled.

"Hey," he said, holding up his hands, nearly swishing Coke onto his shirt. "Don't shoot the messenger. I'm only passing on what I've been told."

A couple of little ones from Abby's church leapt to mind. They often sat behind her, kicking the pew throughout the service. One had driven a toy car into her hair during the Christmas service the year before. Of course, her future brood would be perfectly behaved little angels, or so she liked to delude herself. That was, if she ever got around to having any.

"At the rate I'm going, I may never have that job, anyway."

Justin nearly choked midsip. "Why do you say things like that? Abby, you have your whole life ahead of you, with plenty of time to have a family."

She dropped the half-eaten slice onto her paper plate. "I'm sure it looks that way to someone still in his twenties, but facts are facts. I'm a single woman in my midthirties with no prospect of getting married anytime soon. At this point, even my biological clock has given up hope. Instead of ticking, it clucks like a dejected goose waiting to die."

After staring at her for several seconds, Justin put the cap back on the soda, set it on the ground, and brushed off his hands as if preparing for a fight.

"First of all, that might be the weirdest metaphor I've ever heard. And secondly, you are not in your *midthirties*. You're barely thirty-three. Lots of people have done great things when they were way older than you are now."

Feeling contrary, she said, "Name one."

Amber eyes cut from her to the sidewalk at their feet as the wheels turned in search of an answer. With a loud clap, he pointed at her. "Neil Armstrong. He was thirty-eight years old when he walked on the moon. Hank Aaron was forty when he set his home run record. And Tolkien was sixty-two when he first published *Lord of the Rings*."

Slightly impressed by his memory, Abby said, "You realize those are all men, right? And all actions that didn't require a set of cooperative ovaries."

"I'd suggest that all of those things required the male version of ovaries, but I get your point. Still, you aren't out of the baby game yet. That's all I'm saying."

Lest he start volunteering to *help* her in her baby endeavor, Abby returned to the original question. "As for a different career, I'd want to do something that doesn't involve people."

"You might want to think about the moon walking, then."

She shot him a pointed look and continued. "Something creative. A job that changed every day, and when I finished a project, I'd have something tangible to show for it."

Seemingly intrigued, Justin leaned in. "Do you do anything artistic?"

Abby shook her head. "Sadly, no. I'm limited to stick people, and even those are rough."

"Sew?"

"Not a stitch."

"Cook?"

"I set my kitchen on fire while baking a cake. I'm going to say that's a definite sign to stay away from the food industry."

Justin rubbed the thin growth of stubble along his chin. "Do you play an instrument or sing?"

"No musical ability whatsoever." This conversation was making her feel like a loser. "Guess I'd better stick with nursing."

"You're willing to give up that easy?"

Brushing off the question, she gathered their plates before lifting the lid of the pizza box. "Do you want to take the rest of this home?"

"You don't want it?" he asked.

"Not a fan of cold pizza."

He snagged the box. "That's heresy. Cold pizza is always good, especially for breakfast."

In a few years, he'd be singing a different tune, but Abby let him keep his illusions. The wind picked up, whipping her hair into her eyes. "Looks like rain is coming," she said, clearing her face. "We'd better get going."

Catching a stray napkin on the sidewalk, Justin threw it and the rest of their trash into the can at the corner. With soda in one hand and pizza box in the other, he fell into step next to Abby as they headed back to the theater, where they'd left her car.

"I'll pick up the stuff you bought at the nursery in the morning and get to work. Offer is still open for the assistant position."

"No can do," she said, happy to have a valid excuse. "My shift at the hospital starts at seven."

They walked on in amicable silence until Justin said, "Thanks for buying me. I had a good time."

Abby rolled her eyes. "I didn't buy you. Hal—"

"Haleigh did. Yes, I know." They reached her car and Justin set the box and bottle on the roof before turning to face her. His scent blended with fresh pepperoni made her wonder if this might be what sexy Italian men smelled like. "I'll thank your friend when I get the chance," he said. "Right now, I'm thanking you for spending the day with me. This has been my best non-date, hands down."

This man could charm the paint off a picket fence. "Maybe we should call it an extended job interview. I did kind of hire you as my gardener, though it's more of an unpaid internship, really."

"I know what you're doing."

Abby tried not to smile. "What am I doing?"

"You're avoiding telling me that you had a good time, too."

"I had a perfectly nice time," she assured him, sounding like an elderly librarian. When Justin shook his head, she added, "I didn't have a nice time?"

Justin moved in closer. "This was better than nice. Admit it."

Pushy man. "I laughed," she said, toying with a button on his shirt. "Bought some flowers. Had pizza. I'm not sure it was worth eight hundred fifty dollars, but who am I to complain?"

"Then we'll have to spend more time together. To make sure you get your money's worth, of course." Long fingers fondled a lock of hair hanging over her shoulder. "I never want to leave a lady unsatisfied."

"That would be bad," Abby murmured, leaning in as her eyes dropped to his mouth. The world fell away and every fiber of her being vibrated with anticipation. Just one kiss . . .

The heavens chose that moment to open up, dousing them both like a cold bucket of water. Abby squealed and dug in her purse for her keys, while Justin, in a moment of impressive quick thinking, held the pizza box over her head. But it was too late. By the time she located the keys, they were both soaked to the skin. Looking up at him, she couldn't help but laugh. As if sharing an inside joke, Justin joined in.

Abby unlocked the car and let him open her door, but before she could climb inside, he planted a quick, hard kiss on her lips.

"The next time, that'll be a lot better." Without awaiting a reply, he nudged her inside, slammed the door, and took off running.

Breathless, she watched him disappear around the corner of the theater, her fingers pressed to her tingling lips. Had she just flirted with and nearly kissed Justin Donovan? As water rolled off her chin and a puddle formed on the floorboard, Abby let out a deep sigh. *Yeah*, she thought. *That definitely happened.*

And she wanted it to happen again.

Chapter 6

An hour into her shift, Abby had fought to secure an IV on a patient with few viable veins, cleaned up another patient who'd defecated in his sleep, and been scolded by an elderly man's wife for interrupting his sleep to take vitals. An act required to keep her husband alive. If the rest of the day went this well, she'd be picking up a bottle of wine on the way home.

Home. Thank goodness she had *something* to look forward to. Tonight, Abby would happily be back in her own bed. Not that she didn't love her mother, but she needed her own space.

"You wanted to see me?" she said, tapping on her boss's door.

Iva Bronson glanced up from her desk without her usual smile. "Yes, please come in and have a seat."

Iva rarely bothered her nurses during the busiest time of the morning, but Abby took a seat and told herself not to be paranoid. This was probably nothing.

"I'm afraid I have bad news," the head nurse said, mouth grim. "The hospital is making cuts."

Abby stopped breathing.

"I'm being forced to eliminate at least two from my staff."

Though she'd been with the hospital for more than ten years, Abby had been with the neurology department less than two. Landing her squarely on the chopping block.

Failing to maintain eye contact, Iva said, "I have to let you go, Abby. Your layoff is official immediately."

Just like that, Abby's world turned upside down. Stunned into silence, she fought the buzzing in her ears in order to make out Iva's next statement.

"I'll need your badge and locker key as soon as you've gathered your things."

No notice. No warning. Just get your things and go.

"I'll be happy to write you a reference," the older woman said, finally looking Abby in the eye. "You're a good nurse, Williams. Another facility will be lucky to have you."

A nice sentiment, except there were no other facilities within fifty miles.

Rising to her feet, Abby replied, "Thanks." Which seemed an odd thing to say to someone who'd just fired her.

Less than five minutes later her badge and key rested in Iva's inbox while Abby awaited an elevator. To her relief, none of the other nurses seemed to notice her leaving. Or perhaps they'd all known this was coming and were being kindly discreet. Letting her leave with dignity. There were several things in the little box tucked against Abby's chest, but dignity was not among them.

When the doors opened, she stepped inside the rose-scented car, nodding blindly to the gray-haired gentleman carrying a large bouquet.

"I went up too many floors," he said with a self-deprecating smile. "I was supposed to get off at two."

"That's maternity," she said. "Are you sure that's where you want to go?"

Even with her own world on tilt, Abby couldn't help but take care of someone else.

"My granddaughter gave birth to a little angel last night," the man said, his smile widening as tears brightened his blue eyes. "She named her after my wife, Sophie."

"Your wife must be very proud to have a namesake."

His shoulders dipped. "She passed away three months ago." A gnarled hand brushed away a tear. "I wish she could be here to see her. Little Sophie is beautiful, just like her great-grandmother."

If Abby had ever needed a reality check, this was it. Suddenly, losing her job didn't feel quite so catastrophic.

Skipping the usual *I'm sorry for your loss*, she said, "I bet your wife is smiling down on you right now, proud of these handsome flowers you've brought for the child who bears her name. And she knows you'll make sure that little girl hears all about her."

The smile deepened the creases around his watery eyes. "Thank you, my dear. I needed those words today." Giving Abby's hand a squeeze, he added, "I bet you're a wonderful nurse."

Now it was her turn to tear up. "I like to think so," she said.

A bell dinged and the doors opened to the second floor. As her traveling companion stepped off, Haleigh stepped on.

"Hey there," her oldest friend greeted, pressing the button for the ground floor, which Abby had forgotten to push. "Whatcha got there?" Glancing into the box, she pulled out a picture from Abby's wedding day. "This was hanging in your locker, wasn't it? Are they moving you?"

They were definitely moving her. "Iva let me go."

Haleigh pulled out another picture. This one of Abby with Cooper and their mom. "Let you go where?"

Wiping her cheek on her sleeve, she snatched the picture back into the box. "She didn't let me go anywhere. Thanks to budget cuts, I no longer work here."

"Wait. What?" Haleigh stuttered, following Abby out of the elevator. "You got fired?"

"Laid off is the official term, but it all means the same thing. I'm out of a job."

Though the house had been paid off when Kyle died and she received a monthly check from the military, Abby still needed an income to support herself. Her family would never let her starve, but the idea of depending on Mom or Cooper to pay her bills was unacceptable. Her savings might carry her for a few months, but she'd rather not use any more of it than she had to.

Taking long strides to keep up with Abby, who'd progressed from shock to anger, Haleigh said, "But you've been at this hospital forever."

"Not in neurology I haven't."

A hand gripped Abby's shoulder. "Would you stop walking and talk to me? I'm getting shin splints trying to keep up with you."

Stopping in the middle of the parking garage, Abby spun around. "Then maybe you should leave me alone." Haleigh drew back, and the guilt hit immediately. "Aw, geez." Abby carried her box to the curb and sat down. "I'm sorry. I didn't mean that."

Her friend took a seat next to her. "I get it," she said. "First the fire, and now this. You're having a rough week."

True. The only bright spot since Wednesday night had been her afternoon with Justin. In fact, if she really thought about it, their non-date had been the highlight of her year so far. Not a great commentary on her life.

"I don't know what I'm going to do."

"You're a fabulous nurse, Abbs. You'll get another job."

The conversation from the day before came to mind. "I think I jinxed myself."

"How did you do that?"

"I told Justin that I don't enjoy being a nurse anymore."

"Okay," Haleigh said, drawing out the word. "Is that true?"

Exhaust fumes swirled around them as a car drove by.

"Yeah," she admitted. "It's true." Abby had been going through the motions for far too long, settling for a paycheck over being happy. "But it isn't as if there's anything else I can do."

Haleigh tapped the box. "Why didn't you tell me this before? There are all sorts of things you can do. Pick something."

"Thirty-three is a little old to change my mind about what I want to be when I grow up."

"Nah. I had a friend back in California who changed careers all the time. She believed that no one should do the same thing for more than five years in a row."

Abby hugged the box tighter. "That doesn't sound like a very secure life."

"She never went without," Haleigh assured her. "Patty believed a new opportunity would come along when she was ready, and it always did."

"Are you making that up?"

"Nope. All true." Another car passed by. "Can we get up now? My lab coat is starting to smell like Cooper after a long day in the garage."

Waving a hand in front of her nose, Abby said, "Good idea." The blonde rose first, taking the box so she could follow suit. "I'm sorry I snapped at you."

"I'm sorry you lost your job. What are you going to do now?"

Brushing a leaf off Haleigh's coat, Abby weighed her options. "I guess I'll go home and check on my new gardener."

Brown eyes narrowed. "Since when do you have a gardener?"

"Since I convinced Justin to start his own landscaping business and then agreed to let him use my flower beds as an example to potential clients. By the way," Abby said, "what were you thinking, bidding like that in the auction?" She no longer minded that Haleigh had bid against her wishes, but the dollar amount had gone way too high.

"I was bidding against Becky Winkle," she replied. "No way was I letting her near that hot tamale. Not when you saw him first."

Jealousy flared through Abby's blood. Becky Winkle had been hunting for husband number four since number three ran off to Vegas with an exotic dancer he'd met in Nashville. After finding out Jessi was her half sister, the spoiled harpy had been horribly mean, calling the new mother everything from a gold digger to a white trash tramp.

Though the girls' father took Jessi's side, putting Becky in her place during a rather public scene, Abby still wanted to rip every teased piece of hair off her head.

"In that case, I'm glad you saved him."

"Technically, *you* saved him," Haleigh said, slipping her hands into her lab coat pockets. "If you'd refused the date, he would have gone to the next-highest bidder."

"Then *we* saved him," Abby insisted. "I'll pay you back as soon as I can."

Haleigh tapped the box. "You're out of work, remember? Anyway, it's all paid for."

Brown eyes twinkled as a satisfied smile split her friend's face. Abby knew that look.

"What aren't you telling me?"

"I hate that I can't keep secrets from you." After chewing on her lip for half a second, she confessed. "We took up a collection before the auction. I had a thousand dollars to spend."

Doubting her ears, Abby said, "People gave you money to buy me a man?"

"When you put it that way . . ."

"What other way is there to put it? A bunch of people decided that I'm so lonely and pathetic that they pitched in to win me a date? A date I expressly told you *I did not want to go on.*" Furious, she charged off toward her car.

"Come on, Abby!" Haleigh yelled after her.

Abby kept walking.

Justin nodded along to Fall Out Boy playing in his earbuds while digging up his fourth monkey grass plant of the morning. Eight of the things dotted the front of Abby's house and had likely been planted when the place was built. Her enthusiasm for color seemed to be a new development, if the neglect he was about to repair was any indication.

He'd already loaded three bags of ancient mulch and winter debris into the Chevy's truck bed, working up a sweat even in the cool April air. After more than a month of unemployment, he appreciated the work more than expected. Not as exciting as closing a multimillion-dollar deal, but respectable all the same.

As Justin turned the earth, familiar smells filled his head. Fresh dirt. Wet grass. A hint of pine from the cones littering the flower bed. He'd saved three snails and two slugs so far, and would likely find several more before the day was out. Choosing a nice spot on the side of the garage, he relocated the first two monkey grass plants to create a new home for the displaced wildlife.

On his knees and his back to the street, Justin failed to see Abby's car pull into the drive or hear her slam the car door, thanks to the music blaring from his iPhone. Which, when she smacked him on the shoulder, resulted in the least manly scream he'd ever emitted. Heart racing, he dropped onto his ass and snatched the earbuds from his ears.

"What the hell, Abby? You just scared the shit out of me."

"I yelled your name twice."

He waved the white cord. "I had music playing. Jesus." While struggling to catch his breath, a realization dawned. "What are you doing here? I thought you had to work."

"So did I." She shook the box tucked under an arm. "But now I'm in the same boat you are. Freaking unemployed."

Without explanation, she stormed into the house. Justin remained on the ground for several seconds, feeling as if he'd been caught in the swirl of a tornado. Did she say unemployed? Leaping into action, he jogged into the house after her.

"What do you mean, unemployed?" he asked, locating her at the island in the kitchen, which sported a temporary plywood top. "They fired you?"

"Why does everyone keep saying it that way?" she snapped, removing two bottles of wine from the box and slamming them onto the plywood. "They'd need *cause* to fire me. No, I got *laid off*. Iva says the hospital is making cuts. She's really sorry. Yada yada yada."

"Man, Abby, that sucks."

"Doesn't it, though?" She crossed to the drawer next to the fridge and whipped out a corkscrew.

Aware of the delicacy of the situation, Justin kept his tone calm as he asked, "Isn't eight thirty in the morning a little early to start drinking?"

"Look," she snarled, pointing the utensil his way. "In less than a week, I've set my kitchen on fire." A hand waved wildly toward the missing stove. "Lost my job. And now I find out that my *friends* care so much about me that they felt the need to *buy me a man*. I don't care what time it is, I've earned a damn glass of wine."

The cork gave way with a dull pop, and Abby took a swig straight from the bottle. Carrying the wine with her, she barreled past him into the living room.

Once again staring after her, Justin murmured, "Bought her a man?" He didn't like the sound of that at all. And then the truth dawned. They'd bought *him*.

"Can we rewind for a minute here?" he said, attempting to piece things together. "Let's start with the job. Tell me what happened."

Abby slouched on the plastic-covered sofa, bottle at her side, free hand over her closed eyes. "In the middle of unclogging a catheter, I got a message that my boss wanted to see me."

Justin suppressed that mental image. "Is that unusual?"

"No." She rolled her head from side to side. "They kink all the time."

"I meant, is it normal for your boss to call you into her office?"

She snorted. "Iva *never* takes anyone off the floor during morning rounds."

"So you knew something was up."

"Nope. Walked in clueless."

Damn. At least he'd known the ax was coming long before Chesterfield pulled the trigger. "Why you and not somebody else?"

Abby placed her head on the arm of the couch. "Because I've been with the department for the shortest amount of time. And it's not like I'd want to see someone else go. I mean, she said she was laying off two people, and I don't know who the other person is, but I don't wish this on any of them. Maggie is a single mom with two kids. Sharlene's oldest is in college and the youngest is headed for UT in the fall." Tucking the bottle against her chest like a teddy bear, she added, "Sweet Delbert is only two years from retirement. He'd be completely screwed if they let him go now."

She made it sound as if she deserved to go before the others. "I'm sure those are all nice people, but you aren't disposable because you don't have kids to put through college."

"Doesn't matter," she said, opening her eyes and rolling to face him. "It's done and I'm screwed. Just not the kind of *screwed* my friends think I need."

A crude transition, but Justin went with it, if only to distract her. "I thought Haleigh did the bidding. Why do you keep saying *friends*?"

Abby sat up and took a long swig from the bottle before wiping her mouth on her sleeve. "They took up a collection. A bunch of people who claim to care about me got together behind my back and plotted to buy me a date. A date I'd already told Haleigh I absolutely did *not* want to go on."

That didn't hurt his ego at all. "Since it worked out in my favor," Justin said, "I'm not sorry they did it, but I don't see the point. You could have any guy in this town. You sure as hell don't need to buy one."

She leaned her chin on the top of the bottle. "I haven't been on a date since Kyle died. Haven't even been asked. So while I appreciate your faith in my feminine wiles, no 'guy in this town,' as you put it, sees things your way."

If she hadn't dated, then she hadn't . . .

"Two years?" he said. "For real?"

She frowned. "For real. So if you don't mind, I'm going to drink this wine, take a long nap, and then have the other bottle for lunch."

Justin couldn't get past the two years thing. He'd never gone without for two months, let alone two years. In fact, the two-month mark would hit in a couple of weeks. No wonder he'd been feeling antsy.

And what kind of idiots lived in this town? Talk about losing faith in his fellow man. Abigail Williams should be fending men off with a shovel, not setting celibacy records. Unless she talked about clogged catheter lines with all her dates.

Plastic crunched as Abby tried to get comfortable.

"Do you want me to find you a blanket?"

"Go away," she said, tucking her legs beneath her. "Let me drown my sorrows in peace."

The last thing she needed was to be alone, especially with a full bottle of wine, but at least he wouldn't be far away. "I'll be outside if you need me."

She waved him off as her eyes drifted shut.

Chapter 7

Abby woke from a deep sleep with a crick in her neck, plastic stuck to her face, and a mouth that felt like the inside of a sock.

For one nauseating moment, she couldn't figure out where she was. Wiping the grit from her eyes, she gently rose onto an elbow and heard a thud. With one eye open, she leaned forward to see what it was, felt her stomach roll, and quickly leaned back. "That's not good," she mumbled, taking several deep breaths.

Once the threat of vomiting subsided, Abby slowly glanced over the edge again to find an empty wine bottle on the floor. All at once, the morning came back to her. With a groan, she threw an arm over her face.

"I put a couple pain pills on the coffee table," said a baritone from behind her. "And a bottle of water."

"Bless you." Taking her time, she gingerly turned, sliding her feet down to the floor as she sat up. Tossing both pills into her mouth, she tried the cap on the bottle but couldn't get it to turn. Holding it in the air, she said, "I need hep." The pills made her sound like a toddler.

Justin unscrewed the cap without comment. Once the pills were washed down, reality began to creep in.

"What time is it?"

"Twelve thirty," he answered.

"Wow." She scooted forward on the couch. "I can't believe I slept that long."

"Does the world look any better now?"

Abby closed her eyes. "Not one bit."

"Didn't think it would." Taking the chair at the end of the coffee table, Justin set a pair of gloves over his thigh. "Not sure if you intend to stay with your meal plan, but I highly suggest you have something for lunch other than that second bottle of wine."

He could shove his suggestion up his fire hose. "I'm not in the mood for a lecture, thank you."

"No lecture coming," he assured her, palms up. "But if you feel as bad as you look, that second bottle might send you back to the hospital as a patient."

A hand shot into her hair to find her ponytail dangling loosely on the right side of her head. After dragging out the hair tie, she shook the strands free, paying a hefty price for the thoughtless movement.

"If I wasn't a medical professional, I'd swear my brain just broke in half."

He chuckled. "Do you do this often?"

"Do what? Get drunk and pass out on my couch? Not since last fall when I drank way too much at Lorelei Pratchett's—now Boyd's—bachelorette party."

"The name sounds familiar."

Abby slid the hair tie onto her wrist. "Lorelei told the whole town to go to hell at a Main Street Festival about fifteen years ago."

"Oh, yeah," Justin said. "I definitely remember that. But didn't she leave town right after?"

Desperate to rid her mouth of the invisible cotton, she took a long swig from the water bottle before answering. "Yep. Came back nearly two years ago, and last fall she married her high school sweetheart, Spencer Boyd. Now they're living happily ever after."

"You don't sound all that thrilled for them."

Abby didn't begrudge Lorelei her happy ending. She and Spencer had always been meant for each other. But they'd been the ones to set off a steady pattern of people Abby knew who followed their lead, finding love and ending up passionately content. Even her mother had gotten in on the act.

"Did you know that my mom is getting married?" she asked.

Justin took the tangent in stride. "Yeah, my mom told me. How do you feel about gaining a stepfather?"

How did Abby feel about her mother's beau? Her parents' marriage had been rocky at best, with Dad choosing the bottle over his family on more occasions than Abby cared to count. Until the day he drank himself to death at what most would consider a young age. Still in her fifties, Mom deserved to be happy, and Bruce Clemens seemed like the guy to make that happen.

"I like him," she said. "Mom practically glows when he's around. It's kind of cute, really."

"I sense a *but* in there somewhere."

"Not a *but*," Abby replied. "Not really. It's just that in the last two years, I've watched five different couples get together. Ten people obnoxiously happy while I've experienced the complete opposite. So while I'm tickled pink for all of them, I can't help but covet a little of what they have."

Leaning forward, Justin balanced his elbows on his knees. "That's pretty deep for a woman as hungover as you are."

To her surprise, Abby laughed. "How's the saying go? I've got layers like an onion."

"Is that what I smell?"

Abby tried to throw a pillow at him but they were all out being cleaned. "I should probably take a shower."

Justin rose to his feet. "Good idea. When you're done, come out and see the work in progress. I want to make sure you're happy with the placements before I get too far."

He stepped around the couch, heading for the front door.

"Hey," she said. "Thanks for listening."

"Any time, Abby." Justin placed a soft kiss on her forehead. "Any time."

⌇

Standing back to assess his work, Justin debated whether to put the blanket flowers on the left and the delphiniums on the right or vice versa. Or better yet, the hydrangeas on each end, the blanket in the middle, and the delphiniums between them on each side. That was probably the better way to go. Decision made, he reached for the shovel as his phone went off in his pocket. Sliding off a glove, he checked the screen. The name Quintin Culpepper flashed across the top.

"I don't think so," Justin said, ignoring the call. Twenty seconds later, the notification came for a text message. He hadn't heard from Q since they'd both been fired six weeks before. At the time, Justin had cleaned out his office, turned in his company badge, and then informed his former college buddy that they'd speak again once hell froze over. Though April had been chilly so far, he doubted that Hades had hit an ice age.

All of which meant he ignored the message as well. But three angry shovelfuls later, curiosity got the better of him.

I need to talk to you, bro. Potential deal in your neck of the woods. Could put us back in the game.

Justin stared at the cell in his hand. "You've got balls, Q. I'll give you that."

"An interesting statement." Abby strolled toward him in sweats, a hoodie, and a pile of wet hair atop her head. She'd never looked sexier. "Do I want to know what you're looking at on that little screen?"

He slid the phone back into his pocket. "A message from a former coworker. Nothing important."

"Does he have a job lead for you?"

"He seems to think so, but this isn't a reliable source. I doubt I'd be interested."

"I see." Taking in the long flower bed to her left, she shaded her eyes as she said, "Where are all my little monkey plants?"

Justin pointed to the bags in the back of the truck. "Most of them are in there. I put a few around the side of the house for the snails and slugs."

Dropping her hand, Abby flashed him a broad smile. "You relocated my snails?"

"The ones I came across, sure."

"That was very considerate of you." Green eyes went soft as her mouth tilted higher at one end, making Justin long to run his thumb across her bottom lip. "Now what's the new plan?"

Dragging his brain back to the conversation, Justin cleared his throat. "I've decided to anchor the ends with the hydrangeas, center the blanket flowers, and then place the delphiniums between them on each side. The holly will fill the empty spaces so you'll get dark green throughout, with pastels on the ends and the brighter blooms in the middle."

As if attempting to picture his vision, Abby chewed her bottom lip as she stared at the blank canvas of dirt, redirecting Justin's focus once again. His body reacted to the erotic gesture, forcing him to use the shovel to hide the evidence. If this kept up, he'd need something more substantial than a skinny wooden handle.

"I like this idea," she said, taking his arm to pull him away from the house with her. "But maybe we need to add one more type of flower. It feels like there's going to be too much green." Abby leaned close enough to brush her breast against his elbow. Which made thinking damn near impossible.

"I don't . . ." he started, unable to form a coherent thought. "You could . . . maybe . . ."

"Am I screwing up your idea?" she said, contrition in her tone. "You're the expert. I should let you decide."

"No," Justin said. "It's your flower bed. The customer makes the final call." Putting space between them, he forced his upper brain to once again take over. "We have white on the outside, then the light blue coming into the bright red with yellow tips. Adding one more option to smooth the transition is actually pretty smart."

"Great. But what should we add?"

He pondered the color scheme, running various choices through his mind, dismissing them all until he landed on the perfect solution.

"Ice plant."

"What the heck is an ice plant?"

Justin pulled out his phone and did a quick search. "They look fragile but they're really hardy. The name comes from the white flecks around the center. Looks like the frost that builds up in your freezer." Finding his target, he touched a picture to make it larger. "See? The yellow with orange tips would be the perfect bridge from the pastels to the stronger hue of the blanket flowers."

Abby leaned close to see the phone, wrapping herself around his arm. Justin's body tensed with desire.

"You're right," she said. "Those are perfect. But I didn't see them at the nursery yesterday. Can we find them around here?"

"I'll find them," he assured her, knowing in that moment he'd travel to the moon if that's what it took to give Abby Williams what she wanted.

"Then I say go for it. Justin, this is going to be beautiful." Glancing up, she added, "Can I stay out here and help or do you need to go shopping right away?"

Not the question he expected. "Sure. Help all you want."

With cautious enthusiasm, Abby worked by his side for the next hour, asking about everything from the mineral content in the soil to whether they could bring some of the snails back to the front when they were finished. Apparently she liked the fairy dust trails they made across her front porch during the night. She'd never struck him as the fairy dust type, but he'd promised to bring them back at the end of the project.

As they measured the location for the delphiniums, an idea struck.

"Have you thought about what you're going to do for a job?" he asked, easing into the subject.

She brushed a loose lock from her forehead, leaving a dirt streak behind. "I'll check with the nursing home over on Hillsboro. And Doc Mason's office. Last I heard they weren't hiring, but it's worth a try. Unless I want to drive a hundred miles a day round-trip, there aren't many choices."

Justin lowered a stake into the proper spot. "What about jobs outside of nursing? Like we talked about yesterday."

Abby shook her head. "That was nothing but silly dreaming, Justin. I'm a nurse. That's all I'm trained to do."

Undaunted, he pressed on. "You said you'd like something creative that would change every day, right? A job that offered tangible results and didn't involve working with people."

With a roll of her eyes, she propped her hands on her hips. "That's what I said, but nothing fits that description. I can't do anything creative, remember?"

Holding his tongue, Justin cast his eyes to the freshly planted flowers before meeting her gaze again, waiting for Abby to catch the hint.

"What?" she said. "This?" A gloved hand pointed at the dirt. "Are you suggesting I become a landscaper?"

He counted the requirements off on his fingers. "Creative. Check. Variety. Check. Tangible results. Check. No people. Check."

Another lock came loose as she shook her head. "You have got bats in your belfry, my friend. This is your line of work, not mine."

"My line of work is developing shopping malls, sports stadiums, and high-rise office buildings," Justin said, insulted by her tone. "But there's nothing wrong with getting your hands dirty until another opportunity comes along."

"Don't get all defensive," she muttered. "I'm not suggesting that this isn't respectable work, but what do I know about flowers and bushes and . . . irrigation?"

"You know more now than you did an hour ago," he pointed out. "You can learn the rest on the job."

The lip chewing returned in earnest as Abby stared at the hydrangea bush she'd meticulously placed. When her eyes shot to the heavens, he thought he had her.

"Nope," she snapped, ripping off the gloves. "This is insanity. I have a résumé to put together. You'll have to finish this by yourself."

"But Abby," Justin called as she marched into the house and slammed the door behind her. Shaking his head, he mumbled, "Couldn't have gone better," before driving the shovel into the dirt.

◦⌒◦

Landscaping, Abby thought, storming into the living room. What a ridiculous idea. She'd be completely out of her depth. As clueless as if he'd suggested she take up flying or race car driving. The license in her wallet did not mean she should strap in at Talladega and have at it. *Learn on the job*, he says. *Ha.*

So what if the last hour had been fun? Interesting, even. That didn't mean she needed to jump off the practicality train into dreamland and hope for the best. Heck, he didn't even have the business up and running yet. Did he expect her to be a partner? Because she sure as heck would not be his employee. Working *with* Justin was one thing. Working *for* him was another.

Determined to make that point clear, Abby marched toward the door. They would be equal partners or nothing at all. But inches from the threshold, common sense returned. They weren't going to be partners. They weren't going to be anything. Because Abby was not taking up landscaping, no matter how much she wanted to get her hands back in that dirt.

In a full dilemma, she paced the foyer, warring with herself. Going back out there would give Justin the victory. She'd have to admit that she *liked* playing in the dirt. That in no way meant she wanted to do so for a living. Right now, he was working in *her* flower bed, and if Abby wanted to be involved, he couldn't stop her.

Once again on the precipice of stepping outside, Abby startled when her cell phone rang from the living room. On her way to answer, she caught her reflection in the foyer mirror. Several strands of hair hung around her face while a dark streak lined her forehead. Leaning closer, she noticed specks of black on the tip of her nose.

"I look awful," she said aloud, brushing off her nose. She did have to admit that fresh soil smelled a lot better than the muck she regularly encountered at the hospital. The phone continued to ring, and Abby shuffled to the coffee table before the call could land in voice mail.

"Hello?" she answered.

"Where have you been?" Haleigh demanded from the other end. "I've been trying to reach you for an hour. One more unanswered call and I was ready to send Cooper out on a rescue mission."

Heaven forbid Abby be out of touch. "I'm at home. Where else would I be?"

A relieved sigh echoed down the line. "I have no idea. Considering the mood you were in this morning? Either in a ditch somewhere or belly up to a bottle."

Between her father and her best friend both being alcoholics, Abby didn't touch the stuff very often. She'd made a rare exception this morning, but that didn't give Haleigh the right to make such an assumption.

"I'm fine. What do you want?"

"What do you mean, what do I want? I want to make sure you're okay."

"I am. Anything else?"

"Come on, Abbs," Haleigh pleaded. "I know you're pissed and I don't blame you. I shouldn't have told you about the collection thing."

Talk about missing the point. "That's what you're sorry about? That you *told* me? How about, 'I'm sorry that we all went behind your back and plotted to embarrass the hell out of you because we think you're desperately lonely'? Let's start there."

Silence loomed.

"Last fall you admitted that you're lonely," Haleigh snarled. "You walk around like you're haunting the world instead of living in it, you rarely laugh, and yes, your friends and family decided to try something a little different to cheer you up. We gave to a good cause in the process, which we all would have done anyway, and you got a nice afternoon with a man who could easily grace the cover of a firefighter calendar. Excuse the hell out of us for caring."

The call ended, leaving Abby staring at her phone. Deflated, she dropped onto the couch behind her. Every word that Haleigh said was true. She *was* lonely. And a little depressed. Grief could no longer serve as a viable excuse for her lack of energy and reluctance to socialize. Kyle was gone, but Abby wasn't. God willing, she had fifty or sixty years left on this planet, and spending those decades wallowing in something she couldn't change didn't sound all that pleasant.

Slouching into the plastic, she closed her eyes and contemplated her future. What did she really want? Not in an occupation, but in life? Letting her mind wander, she landed on the same answer over and over.

"I want to be happy," she whispered, opening her eyes. "I just have no idea how to do that."

Chapter 8

"Justin Charles Donovan, you stop right there."

Obeying the order, Justin froze, one foot off the curb at Fourth and Main. A sigh of frustration accompanied the quick check of his watch. Thea Levine expected him at city hall in ten minutes, and arriving late could jeopardize his chances of winning her favor. From what he'd heard, the leader of the Ardent Springs Garden Society maintained high standards, for both her Damask roses and anyone who dared touch a petal anywhere in her domain.

But his mother's use of his full name did not bode well. Justin had never charmed his way out of a talking-to in less than ten minutes. Doing so now would be more difficult since he had no idea what he'd done.

"I'm expected at an important meeting, Mom. Can this wait until noon?" Since returning to town, they'd had a standing lunch date every Thursday at Tilley's Diner. A date that Justin had canceled the past two weeks in a row. The first time to help Abby with the insurance rep and the next to work on her flower bed, which had to be completed in order to present Mrs. Levine with an example of his work.

"You mean you intend to join me today?" Karen Donovan asked, hands planted firmly on her hips. "You sure you don't have another girl who needs your attention on the one day you've set aside for your mother?"

Justin managed not to roll his eyes. No sense in adding fuel to an already combustible situation. "Mom, you know why I had to cancel our last two lunches. If I wasn't going to be there today, I'd have called you."

Smacking him in the chest with a piece of paper, she said, "Calling people doesn't seem to be your strong suit these days. Poor Quintin Culpepper had to call *me*. He says he's been trying to get in touch with you. In case you've lost it, here's his phone number. I told him you'd call him back."

Nearly five hundred miles away and the douche was still screwing with Justin's life.

"Mom, if I wanted to talk to Q, I would. I'm sorry he bothered you, but I really need to go."

"Are you telling me that you're refusing to speak to one of your best friends?" Mom asked, ignoring his plea to leave. "What could he possibly have done to destroy a ten-year friendship? First you break off your engagement, giving us no reason or explanation, and now you're ignoring your friends. I don't understand what's going on with you, Justin."

Justin had neither the time nor the inclination to answer his mother's questions, since doing so would mean revealing humiliating details he wasn't ready to share.

"There won't be anything going on with me if I don't get to this meeting." He placed a quick kiss on his mother's cheek. "I love you, and I'll see you at noon. I promise. Now I really have to go."

"You better have a darn good reason for running away," she called after him. "And I don't mean from this conversation."

Picking up his pace, Justin ignored the implication and kept moving.

No matter how many times she shifted in her seat, Abby could not get comfortable. Her stomach had been in knots from the moment the alarm went off, and now that she'd arrived for the interview, it was as if her skin no longer fit.

"Ms. Williams," called the secretary who'd greeted her ten minutes earlier, "Mr. Ludlow will see you now."

Abby nodded, wishing she'd been offered a drink of water. Her mouth had gone traitorously dry. The woman led her down a narrow, gray hall that smelled of antiseptic. Even the doors they passed were a muted pewter, making Abby feel as if she'd stepped into a black-and-white movie.

At the last door on the left, the brunette stepped aside and smiled. "Here you go."

Sweat beaded on the back of her neck and Abby prayed her deodorant wouldn't let her down. A quick breath and she stepped into an assault of color.

In a completely unexpected twist, Mr. Ludlow possessed a clear and powerful obsession with a certain candy-coated chocolate treat. And he was not shy about showing it. They were everywhere. Stacked against the walls, on a shelf that hovered a foot below the ceiling, and circling the entire room. Model cars, toys, dispensers, signs, ads, and even what appeared to be a race car driver's candy-themed jacket. There must have been thousands of items in the cramped space, made more so by the overzealous collection.

And in the middle of the gaudy chaos stood a round, smiling man with tiny glasses perched at the tip of his button nose. In contrast to the world he'd created, Mr. Ludlow sported black pants and a gray shirt. Even his tie was black. An outfit more suitable to the staid halls she'd traversed on the way than the intense kaleidoscope surrounding them.

"Welcome to Serenity Rest Nursing Facility, Ms. Williams. Come in and have a seat."

Forcing herself to act normal, Abby shuffled to the chair in front of his desk and accepted the offered handshake. "Thank you, Mr. Ludlow. I appreciate this opportunity."

"We're happy to have you," he said, lowering into his chair without waiting for Abby to do the same. "Let me look over your paperwork here a second."

Dropping slowly onto unremarkable gray vinyl, she caught sight of the phone at the corner of the desk. An animated red candy held a large yellow receiver over his head, while a circle of colorful numbered buttons rested at his feet. Curiosity over whether the contraption actually worked made her nearly miss the fact that he'd waited until now to review her résumé.

"I see you have your degree from Austin Peay. Excellent school," he said, keeping his eyes on the paper.

Uncertain how to respond, she said, "Yes. I enjoyed my time there."

A clock chimed, and Abby looked up to find a multicolored cuckoo clock with a yellow candy dangling by his foot to form a pendulum, while the same red candy from the clock popped from a set of doors at the top.

For half a second she wondered if this wasn't an elaborate setup with hidden cameras watching her every reaction. Either someone would leap out and admit this was all a gag and her real interview was down the hall, or Mr. Ludlow would spin in his chair, spewing bright chocolate candy from his ears. Neither scenario would have surprised her.

"So you're an RN?" he asked. An odd question from a person looking to fill a nursing position.

"Yes, sir."

He grumbled, the frown creating thick lines across his broad forehead. Not an encouraging sign.

"Is there a problem, sir?"

Mr. Ludlow slid the résumé forward. "We aren't hiring RNs right now, Ms. Williams. My secretary seems to have wasted your time."

The secretary? Had he not lined this interview up himself? She'd only communicated via email until today, each correspondence bearing his signature.

"But you have openings, correct? Your email said that I was a great candidate and offered this interview."

"Miss Willoughby vets the résumés and sets interview appointments. She doesn't usually make mistakes like this. We're hiring LPNs, I'm afraid. You're overqualified for the position we're filling."

"I understand that the pay would be less, but—"

"Ms. Williams, it's about more than the pay. Our staff needs to feel comfortable with each other. Putting an RN into an LPN position, especially a nurse with your experience and credentials, would create an imbalance. You'd be answering to people that might have fewer qualifications, and those working beside you might feel inferior or become concerned that they'll be replaced by someone with a more advanced degree or license. I can't create that sort of tension in my team."

In the ten days she'd been job hunting, Abby had already been denied two other interviews with this same excuse. Serenity Rest had been her last resort.

"Sir, I assure you that I can blend with your team. I'm happy to report to whomever I'm assigned, and you'll know that you're getting a dependable, skilled employee willing to work her way up."

He rose from his chair. "I can't chance it, Ms. Williams. I do apologize for taking up your time. If any RN positions come open, I'll have Miss Willoughby give you a call."

How could a man with a childish obsession for candy-themed toys possibly be dismissing her out of some ridiculous notion of creating an imbalance in his team? This office was the very definition of *imbalance*.

Frustration and anger trumped common sense, and Abby let her tongue fly.

"Do us both a favor, Mr. Ludlow, and toss that résumé into your candy-coated garbage can down there. I'd rather swing a shovel than work for a child-man with a candy fetish who thinks so little of his staff that he assumes they'd let something as stupid as petty jealousy get in the way of doing their jobs."

Swinging her purse onto her shoulder, Abby showed herself out.

❧

"I have to be honest, Mr. Donovan. One flower bed is not much to go on," said Mrs. Levine after reviewing several images of Abby's newly redesigned flower bed. "The landscaper from Gallatin has a much broader portfolio."

"As a new business, it's true that I have fewer pictures, but what I've shown you is only a minor display of what I can do. With your taste and expertise, along with my skill and experience, we can have Main Street—especially the town square—bursting with blooms in time for the start of festival season at the first of June."

A hefty promise on his part, considering he'd have to measure, design, consult, *and* buy the supplies before he could even think about breaking ground, but Justin knew his competition could hit that deadline without an issue. To compete, he would have to do the same. With luck, hinting that Mrs. Levine should be an integral part of the project would sweeten the deal, since few landscapers would play that card.

Toying with her pearls, the older woman perused his pictures again. *That's it, Thea. Keep looking.*

After finding the additional plants to fill Abby's flower bed, Justin had worked ten days straight, adding the final mulch layer late Tuesday afternoon. He'd then returned Wednesday to take pictures in the best light.

"Did you choose these particular flowers or did your client?" Mrs. Levine asked.

"This project was a collaboration. We shopped together and I made suggestions, while she had the final say. When it came down to layout and design, again, we both had input."

And they'd worked well together, too, until she'd taken offense at his suggestion she take up landscaping. He'd seen her car pull in or out of her garage several times while working the project, but Abby hadn't spoken to him for more than a week.

Sliding the images back into their envelope, the society matron folded her hands on the conference room table. "I've seen and heard enough. As this is a community project, I prefer to hire a native over an outsider. You have the job, Mr. Donovan."

Justin bolted to his feet. "Thank you very much, Mrs. Levine. You won't regret this."

"I certainly hope not." Allowing him to open the door for her, she added, "A quick trip to Magnolia Bank and Trust and we'll get you a check. Half now. The other half when the project is complete. To my satisfaction, of course."

"Of course," he repeated, happy to follow his new benefactor to the bank next door.

⁓

As far as burning bridges went, Abby may have just earned a prize for dumbest match toss ever. Which put her firmly out of options. Unless she wanted a hefty commute or to physically move to another town. Her wanderlust may have been renewed by her chat with Justin, but she'd never actually wanted to live anywhere else. Visit, sure. But not live.

A few minutes early for a ten-thirty meeting with her mom, Abby walked into Bound to Please bookstore barely aware of her surroundings. The last two weeks had been one giant lesson in humility. She couldn't bake. She couldn't hold her liquor. She'd turned out to be an expendable employee, and ironically, was now overqualified for every nursing position open in the area. All three of them.

With no job and no prospects, Abby felt like a kite cut loose from its string. One stiff wind and she was lost with no way to get back on solid ground.

"Whoa there," cried a male voice as two strong hands gripped Abby's upper arms. "Watch yourself."

Abby looked up to find Justin's hazel eyes staring down with concern. "Sorry," she said, feeling small. And stupid. "I wasn't looking."

"I got that," he said. "Are you okay?"

The question seemed so absurd she almost laughed. "No. No, I'm not."

Taking her hand, Justin pulled her toward a couch along the side of the store. "Let's sit down."

Following without argument, she took a seat, hugging her purse in her lap.

"I'm going to get you a coffee," he said. "How do you like it?"

"Cream and sugar, please." Maybe caffeine would make this nightmare more tolerable.

Abby had convinced herself that a change of scenery would revive her love of nursing. New patients. New coworkers. And maybe even more regular hours. Finding a nursing position had been the first step in the plan to getting her life back. To finding joy again.

"Here you go." Justin set a steaming mug on the coffee table in front of her.

Abby's future stepfather, Bruce Clemens, owned the store, and he'd given it a homey feel, creating a warm and inviting space—a direct reflection of his personality. Seating areas dotted the stacks, and locals were welcome to settle in, use the free Wi-Fi, and hopefully leave with a book.

"Do you want to tell me what's going on?" he asked.

She didn't want to tell anyone of her most recent failure, so instead of answering, she asked a question of her own. "Why are you here?"

"I live in the apartment upstairs," he answered. "Now back to you. What's wrong?"

How had her mother not mentioned that Bruce rented his old apartment to Justin Donovan? Once they'd set a wedding date, the happy couple had bought a new house, which Bruce had moved into right away. Under the guise of some old-fashioned notion, the bride would move in after the wedding.

Retrieving her drink, Abby pondered how much to tell. Studying Justin's clear, unwavering gaze, she felt an odd need to tell him everything.

"I had an interview today," she started, eyes locked on the hot coffee. "He said I'm overqualified for the position."

"Being too good for a position is better than not being good enough," Justin pointed out.

"No," Abby said, shaking her head. "No, it isn't. If I can do the job, then let me do the job. How could it possibly be a bad thing to hire a person with more skills than they need?" She clenched the mug in a white-knuckle grip. "Why should I be punished for being smart and capable and experienced? How is that fair?"

Justin slowly reached for her drink. "Let's put this back down for a minute." He pried the cup from her fingers and set it on the table before turning to face her. "This is where I'm probably supposed to remind you that life isn't fair, but since I know what it's like to be unfairly out of work, I say screw that. Getting passed over for a job sucks. And whoever interviewed you today is a moron for turning away the best candidate he's likely to ever get."

"Yes, he is," she agreed, validated by his support. "A total moron. And I told him so on my way out."

Honey-gold eyes went wide. "What did you say?"

Abby teetered on the edge of the couch. "I told him that I'd rather swing a shovel than work for him. And I would, too."

"Really?" Justin asked. "Does that mean you're open to my idea?"

Confused, Abby said, "What idea?"

"That you work with me. I landed the downtown beautification project this morning. I have less than two months to turn Main Street and the square into a flower show, and that would be a more doable task with another set of hands. What do you say?"

In her current predicament, Abby couldn't afford to turn down anything. Before this morning's interview, taking up landscaping would have meant walking away from the only occupation she'd ever known. But she couldn't walk away from something that didn't exist. The fact was, Abby didn't have a job. Justin had one to offer. A creative job that didn't involve bedpans or overnight shifts.

"One question," she said, heart racing as she considered such a drastic change.

"What's that?" he said, flashing a smile that launched a thousand butterflies in her chest.

"Am I working *for* you or *with* you?"

Justin tapped his knee. "Well, I have the truck and the experience, but you have the tools you bought this weekend and a fresh perspective on design. How about we work together?"

Nervous excitement sent Abby to her feet. "Are you serious? Like, partners?"

"I haven't picked a name yet, but AJ Landscaping sounds good to me." He stood and extended a hand. "What do you say? Partners?"

Abby slid her palm against his as a smile split her face. "I'm willing if you are." She'd never done anything this crazy in her life. Then again, maybe Justin was the crazy one in this scenario. "Are you positive about this?"

"Absolutely," he assured her.

Feeling truly hopeful for the first time in days, Abby let her hand linger in Justin's, too distracted to notice they had company.

"Did I miss something?" asked Abby's mom, breaking the spell.

"Hello, Mrs. Ridgeway," Justin said. "Your daughter and I just agreed to—"

"Have lunch," Abby interrupted, grabbing her discarded purse from the leather couch. "Sometime soon." Turning to Justin, she shot him an *I'll explain later* look. "I'll be in touch."

Mama did not look happy as Abby dragged her to the back of the store. The last thing she needed was for Justin to share their news before she'd had the chance to explain the situation. When they reached the back office and the table filled with wedding-themed magazines, Linda Ridgeway turned on her daughter.

"What in tarnation is going on between you and that boy?"

Struck dumb by the question, Abby stuttered, "What? I . . . he . . ."

"You're embarrassing yourself, Abigail."

"But we . . ." she tried again, pointing toward the front of the store.

"That child is much too young for you," her mother declared, pulling a chair away from the table. "Thank goodness I was the one to find you instead of someone else. Talk would be all over town within the hour that the widow Williams was taking up with a younger man. Now let's get this guest list whittled down before we have the whole town tearing up your brother's backyard."

Abby stood paralyzed near the door, stunned by her mother's words. *The widow Williams?* Was that what people called her? The descriptor made her sound like a sad old woman, counting the days until her own time came. That was not the life that Abby wanted, nor did she appreciate being cast in the role.

Not that she'd altered her original stance regarding a more personal relationship with Justin, but if she did, it would be nobody else's business. Taking a seat at the ancient Formica table, Abby realized that, for better or worse, the universe was clearly pushing her toward change, and stirring up a small-town scandal would go a long way toward making her life more interesting. But did she dare?

"Don't forget about your fitting next week," Linda Ridgeway reminded her daughter. "I've told Maureen to make sure the hem hits below the knee."

Her mother found the exact words to tip Abby over the edge. She was neither too old nor too widowed to show a little thigh at a wedding. And just maybe she wasn't too old for Justin Donovan, either.

Chapter 9

His luck looking up, Justin whistled his way down Main Street with a tape measure in one hand and a notepad in the other. Thankfully, downtown Ardent Springs already offered a fair share of green, which would save him and Abby a wheelbarrowful of work.

Justin paused on that thought. Him and Abby. Working together. Not the kind of together he wanted, but definitely a step in the right direction.

Trees dappled Main at fifteen- to twenty-foot intervals, their bases surrounded by large grates. This didn't leave many options for installing flower beds down the block, but what he couldn't put in the ground, he could put in planters. They'd need to be heavy, sturdy, and fit the aesthetic they were going for—simple and welcoming with a hint of small-town charm.

Reaching the square, which, ironically, was a well-used roundabout, Justin stared up at the nearly forty-foot monument holding court over the grassy knoll. The Confederate soldier, having occupied his perch for more than a century, appeared almost bored yet unwavering despite the chip in his hat brim—an injury obtained the day he was erected. Legend had it that the Daughters of the Confederacy had worked too hard to raise the funds for their beloved monument to let something as insignificant as a chip halt their forward progress.

Crossing to the center, Justin roamed the flattened mound, imagining the possibilities. The expanse of grass exposed to full sun for most of the day provided the perfect blank canvas. Upkeep would be a pain, as keeping whatever they did plant alive and vibrant past the end of June would require lots of water, but his short meeting with Miss Thea left him with the impression that she'd devise a solution for any foreseeable problems.

Not sure what to expect, he'd gone in imagining the garden society chair to be much like his paternal grandmother. At first glance, Clara Donovan had appeared friendly and frail—from a distance. But there'd been times Justin would have chosen a lion's den over walking into Granny Clara's house on a day he'd disappointed her. She could take out a rattler from fifty paces and quell a window-breaking nine-year-old with one squinty glare. She'd passed away Justin's senior year of college, and he'd always wanted to make her proud.

Turning the town she loved into a middle Tennessee showpiece would go a long way toward that goal. With a grin on his face, Justin glanced up once again, past the stalwart soldier to the clouds above them both.

"I'll make it pretty, Granny C."

Thea Levine had not been nearly as intimidating as Justin's grandmother, but she'd shown a fearless determination to make her vision for downtown Ardent Springs a reality. He'd liked her from the first handshake, and considering how quickly she'd hired him, Justin assumed the feeling was mutual.

As he drew his focus back to the task at hand, the cell in his pocket went off. Justin failed to check the screen before answering, assuming Abby would be on the other end.

"Donovan here."

"About time you picked up," returned a voice nothing like Abby's. "How's it hanging, bro?"

Ignoring the question, Justin said, "What do you want, Q?"

"Come on, buddy. You aren't still mad, are you?"

"Mad about what? That you slept with my fiancée? That you got me fired?"

"I didn't get you fired," Q corrected, refuting one accusation but not the other. "And I saved you from marrying the wrong chick, which you should be thanking me for."

A simple *This girl is wrong for you* would have sufficed. Instead, Q, in his own estimation, had taken one for the team by screwing Victoria in Justin's bed. An act witnessed with his own eyes, thanks to Justin's last business trip ending unexpectedly early. A trip that was supposed to include his good buddy Q.

"Your card is in the mail. Now lose my number." Before he could end the call, Q yelled, "Get your head out of your ass and listen to me, dammit. I've got a killer lead that could put us both back in the game."

Remembering the text from earlier, including the mention of said lead being in Justin's neck of the woods, he gave his former friend thirty more seconds.

"Talk."

As expected, Q went straight to the point. "There's a tract for sale just off the interstate in your area. It's perfect for commercial development, and the proximity to Nashville is enough to bring in some big investors. Small beans compared to what we were doing up north, but it's a solid deal with the potential to reestablish our reps."

If it weren't for Q, Justin's rep wouldn't need reestablishing. And yet. Having the details couldn't hurt. "Email me what you have."

"You've got it, bro." After a moment's hesitation, he asked, "Have you heard from Vicki?"

Victoria Bettencourt had detested when Q referred to her as Vicki. But then again, she'd also gone to bed with him.

"That's over," Justin replied.

Another heavy silence.

"She called me."

Justin rolled his eyes. "Good for you."

"She asked if I thought you'd forgiven her yet." Priceless. Ask the guy you screwed if the one you cheated on might be ready to forgive and forget. That makes perfect sense. "What should I tell her?"

"That I'm not the forgiving type," he replied and ended the call.

Slipping the phone into his pocket, Justin glanced once more to the soldier high above. "Women, huh, buddy?" he said, shaking his head.

Victoria had been everything he thought he'd wanted. Beautiful. Sophisticated. Connected. She'd also been bratty, shallow, and conniving. The temper tantrums and constant demands had begun wearing thin long before she and Q had betrayed him. Justin liked to think he'd have come to his senses before walking down the aisle, but he couldn't be sure. Ambition had been his driving force for so long that not until losing his fiancée and his job in the same week had the blinders come off.

Though ambition still stirred his blood, Justin vowed to take his time and be more thorough going forward. He *would* get back in the game, but not with Quintin Culpepper along for the ride. The cell phone chimed, indicating the arrival of a new email. Justin resisted the urge to check the message. All in due time. Right now, he had a town square to design.

Abby endured two hours with her mother, locking in the final guest list for the wedding and then searching various websites for country-themed details to add charm to the festivities.

Back in the eighties, Linda Ridgeway had taken her vows standing before a justice of the peace, stone-faced and wishing for the lavish wedding she'd always imagined. But throwing a party hadn't been Malcolm Ridgeway's style. Quiet and serious, he'd preferred to keep things simple and then get on with living. Only he never truly lived the life he wanted, settling for a small-town insurance job while drowning his failures in liquor. Kind and generous when sober, Abby's dad had been a mean drunk who tormented his family as if determined to make them as miserable as he was.

Sometimes Abby feared she might be too much like him. Too serious. Too practical. Too ready to give up on her dreams. If she accomplished only one thing in life, it would be *not* following her father's path. Whatever happened, however her life turned out, Abby never wanted to be a bitter, angry person. And yet, since Kyle's death, she'd drifted uneasily close to that ledge. Become snappish with friends and family. Even downright mean at times.

Shaking off the fears, she pulled her car to the side of the narrow gravel path and cut the engine. Staring over row upon row of weathered stones, Abby breathed in, let the air fill her lungs, and then exhaled until her shoulders slumped. The time had come to let go of something bigger than a cup or a football jersey.

Thanks to Kyle being scheduled to ship out, he and Abby had also done the quickie wedding, except in her case she'd almost immediately waved her new husband good-bye. There had been so few moments during her marriage when she could relax and not stress over where he might be or if he might be hurt. Within the first year, she understood why so many military marriages ended in divorce. The life was not for the faint of heart.

As she stepped through the stones, careful not to be disrespectful with her footing, a warmth surrounded her, as if the tenants of this quiet place were helping her along. That they knew this walk and the strength it took to tread it. Reaching her destination, Abby stopped before the small ivory stone with the tiny flag perched atop it.

"Hi," she said, dropping to her knees, as she always did during these visits. "I didn't bring any flowers today, but I doubt you mind that. You were never big on flowers."

Rationally, Abby knew that Kyle didn't reside in this covered hole in the ground, but she still came here to talk to him. To feel close to him.

"Speaking of flowers, I'm trying something new and I wanted to tell you about it." She'd always longed to pick up the phone and tell her husband anything remotely exciting that happened in her life. Most of the time, that hadn't been possible. At least now she could talk to him whenever she wanted. "I'm taking up landscaping," she said, and could almost hear Kyle's deep chuckle in her ear. "I know, right? Not what you'd expect from me."

But plants and flowers weren't why she'd paid this visit.

"I've also met someone," Abby said. "Though I've met him before. I mean, I knew him when I was younger. Much younger," she murmured, picking a clover from the grass. "He's all grown up now. We both are. And I think he likes me."

Despite sounding like her fifteen-year-old self, she pressed on.

"I've been really lonely since you left. Since before you left, really. We had so many plans, and I didn't know what to do with myself once those went away. Once you went away."

A tear dropped onto the clover.

"It's time for a new plan now," she said, wiping the damp from her cheek. "But I want you to know that no matter what happens in the rest of my life, I'll never stop thinking about you. Or loving you. Not that you'd ever let me forget you." His devilish smirk danced before her eyes. "I know you send me signs to let me know that you're around. They were hard at first, but I've gotten used to them."

A butterfly landed delicately on the top of his stone, flapping soft wings of muted greens. Just like Kyle's army fatigues.

Abby laughed. "Now you're just showing off." Sobering, she took another deep breath. "Anyway, I don't know if anything will happen between me and Justin, but if not him, then I hope that someday I'll meet another man. Someone strong and caring, who will remind me not to be so serious all the time." Tilting her head, she touched his name etched deep in the stone. "Someone like you."

Feeling lighter, she brushed the leaves from in front of the marker before rising to her feet.

"One more thing," she said, crossing her arms. "Mom's marrying Bruce the first weekend of June, and she's getting a little Bridezilla on me. I'm probably going to tick her off a bit between now and then, and since she always liked you, I was hoping you might send some good thoughts her way. A little calming effect to help her through this." Watching another butterfly pass by, Abby smiled. "Maybe send her one of these pretty things now and then. She's always liked butterflies."

Confession over, Abby lingered a few minutes more before retreating back to the car. "Now," she sighed, "it's time to move on."

◦⌒◦

"I wish you'd put that away," Karen Donovan said, casting her eyes toward Justin's phone.

He closed his email and shut off the screen. "It goes back in the pocket right now."

Unable to resist, Justin had given Q's email a quick perusal. The lot up for sale screamed retail potential. Directly off the Ardent Springs exit. Prime, level land that had been a pasture for at least a century, which likely meant less rock to break through. Most of middle Tennessee required blasting for any level of development, but every once in a while an exception arrived. And this one had landed in Justin's lap. Or rather, his email.

"Something good must have come out of your morning meeting," Mom observed. "Are you going to tell me about it?"

"You, dear mother, are looking at the newly hired landscaper for the Ardent Springs downtown beautification project." Justin stabbed a crouton in his salad. "I'm teaming up with Abigail Williams to create AJ Landscaping, and together we're going to turn Main Street and the square into a botanical showpiece."

Though Thea didn't know about Abby's role yet, Justin had no reason to believe she'd object to adding another female perspective to the team. Even a wholly inexperienced one.

Mom's fork halted halfway to her mouth. "Did you say Abigail Williams? Your old babysitter, who bought you during that embarrassing auction? Edna and Maggie are still talking about your little performance."

Justin shuddered to think what the older women had to say about his amateur striptease and ignored the topic for his own mental health.

"Yep, that's her."

Fork still lingering, she said, "But Abby's a nurse. Why would she go into landscaping?"

"She wants a change," he explained before stuffing an oversize piece of lettuce into his mouth. If he was lucky, his mother would do the same.

Instead, she dropped the utensil and leaned back. "I'm confused. How did this come about? Is she quitting her job at the hospital?"

Despite his reluctance to share too much of Abby's personal business, Justin saw no way around it.

"The hospital let her go. She's looked for other positions in her field but hasn't found the right fit." He shared a casual half shrug. "So she's trying something new."

"That just doesn't sound like something Abby would do. She's so sensible. A woman doesn't dedicate a decade to one career only to walk away for something completely different."

"Why not?" Justin asked. Karen Donovan had never worked outside the home, at least not since adopting him. The realization dawned that he'd never asked her if she ever wanted to do something else. "Why can't a person change course whenever they feel like it?"

The question seemed to leave her speechless. A rare occurrence in Justin's experience.

"Haven't you ever wanted to do something new?" he asked. "Take on a new adventure?"

Recovering with style, she said, "I doubt anything could top the adventure of raising you." Fiddling with her salad, she admitted, "There were times over the years when I thought about the possibilities. What it would have been like to be a flight attendant, jetting all over the world. Or a journalist, reporting from a foreign country. But those are silly imaginings. Nothing serious."

"They could have been serious," he pointed out. "You could have done either of those things."

"I couldn't have done them and still raised you," she replied. "Justin, being a mom is the only real job I ever wanted. When you came to us, my dream came true. I wouldn't change a thing."

Appeased but still curious, he couldn't help but wonder what she did all day. "What about now?"

"What *about* now?" she asked before popping a cherry tomato between her lips.

"I've been gone for ten years. What keeps you busy now?"

Cheeks reddening, she said, "I do things, Justin. Maybe not the kinds of things your generation thinks are exciting or worthwhile, but I do have reasons to get out of bed in the morning."

Great. Now he'd insulted her. "I didn't mean—"

"I know what you meant, pal. Eat your salad and stop worrying about your dear old mom."

The waitress arrived with their entrees, bringing the conversation to a temporary halt.

"Thank you, Jeanne," his mother said. And then as if to prove a point, added, "Will you be at the book club meeting tomorrow night? Bruce has agreed to let us have the store for as long as we want."

Jeanne nodded. "I'll be there. Two chapters to go and I'll hit The End. But next month I'm picking the book. I've cried through half a box of tissues reading this one you chose."

The founder of the Sylvester Family Public Library book club beamed. "It's good, isn't it? This is my third time through and I cried at the same parts all over again."

Why did women enjoy crying? Justin would never understand that.

As the waitress left them to their meal, he bit into a hot fry. "I see what you did there."

"What?" she asked, feigning innocence.

"Like you don't know." He loaded his burger with ketchup. "What's Dad up to today?"

"It's air conditioner tune-up season," she replied. "All the calls are keeping him busy."

Ken Donovan had been running his own HVAC business for thirty years now. During Justin's teen years, there had been mention of him joining the family business, but once he made his college plans known, his parents had accepted the inevitable fact that their son would not spend his life fixing air conditioners in Ardent Springs.

"I hope he isn't too busy to take his best girl on a date." Justin's parents had maintained Friday night date night since his childhood, which had been the reason he'd needed a regular babysitter all those years ago.

She waved a bite of fried cod in the air. "That man hasn't stood me up yet, and he knows he'd never hear the end of it if he did. But speaking of dating, are you going to tell me what happened between you and Victoria?"

Having danced around this question for the last six weeks, he decided to offer a diluted version of the truth.

"All right, I'll tell you." Justin kept his eyes on his salad. "Victoria found someone else. When I discovered the affair, I ended the engagement." Even the watered-down version left him feeling like a fool. "It's fine. I'm over it."

"Do me a favor," his mother said, one dark brow riding high. "Don't ever take up lying for a living. You're terrible at it. Now give me that hussy's number so I can give her a piece of my mind. How dare she cheat on my boy?"

One more reason he'd kept the facts to himself until now.

"There will be no calling anyone. I told you. I'm over it." And though the humiliation still stung, Justin took solace in the fact that his initial anger had never spiraled into abject heartache. "It's better to see her true colors now than after the I-dos, right?"

Mom continued to scowl. "I have half a notion to fly up there and shove one of those fancy high heels down her throat."

As much as he would pay to see that, Justin chose the higher road. "There will be no assault with a Louboutin. Victoria isn't worth the jail time."

Jeanne returned to fill their drinks, cutting off whatever his mother intended to say next. Gratitude for her perfect timing would be reflected in her tip.

So his ego had taken a hit. Justin wasn't the first person to be cheated on, and he wouldn't be the last. What mattered now was the future, and he already had another girl in his sights. Correction. A woman. A smart, beautiful, caring woman with eyes like polished emeralds and a smile that hit like a sledgehammer.

All he had to do now was convince said woman that they were perfect for each other. And what better way to do that than over a fresh bed of flowers?

Chapter 10

Abby had never visited Firehouse Number Seven before, let alone met a man for dinner there. After leaving the cemetery, she'd made a stop by the library to check out every book she could find on landscaping and gardening. If they were going to be partners, Abby didn't want Justin to feel as if he were dragging around a dead weight. They couldn't be equals on the subject overnight, but she'd study for this test as she had every other in her life—with determination and endless pots of coffee.

When she and her stack of books were back in the car, she sent Justin a text about meeting up to discuss the project. Due to having duty at the firehouse, he'd suggested she meet him there, where he'd make her dinner and they could plot their future flowerpots. Abby couldn't bring herself to turn down such an inventive invitation.

Abby hadn't mustered the courage to tell her mother about the sudden career change. In a moment of convenient rationalization, she'd come to the conclusion that sharing her new endeavor before a full launch would be pointless. What if Justin changed his mind? What if they couldn't get along? What if *she* changed *her* mind? Better to keep her mother in the dark than deal with a full-on argument over what Linda Ridgeway would no doubt consider utterly irresponsible behavior from her only daughter.

The daughter who never did anything crazy. Or impractical. Until now.

Due to the fire station facing east, the setting sun cast long shadows along the front of the building. Two identical doors, each bright red with a row of windows across the middle, stood tall before her, split by a solid brick wall. Abby hovered for several seconds, uncertain how to get in. Another historic redbrick building adjoined the firehouse on the right, so she stepped around the left side into a small parking lot in search of an entrance.

Beneath a dim, flickering bulb she spotted a door near the back corner of the building, and despite feeling like the first victim in the opening scene of a horror flick, she navigated the pothole-ridden asphalt to knock on the door. No response came, and as the shadows grew longer, the hair on the back of Abby's neck rose.

She pulled out her phone and fired off a quick text to let him know she was there, and waited several more seconds until the door flew open without warning, causing Abby to scream like a howler monkey.

The giant silhouette didn't flinch. Based on size alone, he was likely greeted with fearful cries on a regular basis.

"I never took you for the screaming type," Frankie Beckham mumbled, stepping aside for Abby to enter the building. Frankie worked for Cooper at the garage, and though he'd trimmed the beard a bit, the light from the stairwell still made him look menacing. Well, as menacing as any man wearing incredibly thick spectacles could be.

"I wasn't expecting the door to fly open like that," she defended, gathering the remnants of her dignity and stepping past him. "Do I go straight up?" Abby asked from the base of the stairs.

"Unless you want to hang out with the trucks, yeah."

Lips pursed, she took the first step. "You'd suck as a butler, Frankie."

"Damn," he said behind her. "I had that on my bucket list."

Abby couldn't help but laugh. The bearded giant didn't make jokes very often. Or maybe she hadn't been around him enough to catch them. Spending time at Cooper's garage had not been part of her daily routine since he'd first bought the place and the whole family had worked hard to make it shine. That had been four years ago, and the business had become a steady success, due mostly to the fact that Cooper was the best mechanic in town and everyone knew it.

When she reached the top landing, the room that opened before her felt more like someone's well-used living room—albeit one from 1987—than anything she expected in a firehouse. A long table surrounded by ten spindle-back chairs occupied the kitchen side of the room, while large, fluffy furniture engulfed the small living area. An ancient tube-model television took up the center of a large built-in that, as far as Abby could tell, held every DVD ever made. She could only assume there were more behind the four closed doors along the bottom.

"Hey there," Justin said from the stove. "Spaghetti is almost ready."

Frankie stomped to the couch without another word and sank into its cream tweed depths. As Abby stepped into the kitchen, the scent of garlic and oregano filled her senses.

"That smells amazing."

Justin scooped a taste of sauce onto his wooden spoon. "Granny Clara Donovan's secret recipe. I could tell you, but then I'd have to marry you."

Normally Abby would shoot back a safe response, but having a man cook for her was such a novel experience, she took the flirtatious route.

"Is that a threat or a promise?" Swiping some with her finger, she quickly licked it off, sending flavor explosions across her tongue. "Holy spices, this sauce would totally be worth the sacrifice."

Looking offended, Justin frowned. "Are you saying that marrying me would be a sacrifice?"

"We'd better see if we can work together before discussing a lifetime commitment." Abby breathed in again and her mouth watered. "Donovan isn't a very Italian name. Where did your grandmother learn to make sauce like this?"

Setting the spoon on the table, Justin moved to the fridge and bent to retrieve something inside, offering Abby a prime shot of his prime rump. "Granny Clara started life as a Giovanni," he explained, offering her a bottle of water. "To her parents' eternal shame, she ran off with an Irishman who took their feisty signorina to America. Thankfully, not before she learned all the family cooking secrets, which she refused to share with my mom but gleefully passed to me."

Abby shook her head. "He cooks. He gardens. He puts out fires. Talk about a most eligible bachelor." Letting curiosity lead the way, she asked, "How have you not been snapped up before now?"

Justin's charming grin faltered. "I came close to getting shackled," he said, dragging a strainer from an upper cabinet, "but the bride-to-be revealed her true colors in time for me to save myself."

Now she was really curious, but his tone revealed more than his words. This was a touchy subject.

"Is there anything I can do to help?" she asked.

"Is that an offer to help me forget my conniving ex-fiancée?" He grinned.

"It's an offer to set the table." Abby laughed, not yet willing to pry into his personal life. "Where are the plates?"

One hand flattened over his heart. "It isn't nice to get a man's hopes up like that."

Feeling sassy, Abby flipped the hair off her shoulder. "Keep making me dinners like this and you never know what might happen." While Justin stared slack-jawed, she located dinnerware in the second cabinet over and strolled to the table with the plates.

"How come you haven't made this before now?" Frankie asked, loading another serpentine bite of spaghetti onto his fork.

Justin swallowed his drink of soda. "I save the good stuff for when pretty girls are around." Which was true. Normally he'd have poured a cheap jar of sauce over a pot of noodles and called it a meal. Tonight he had a woman to impress.

"Then Abby needs to come around more often." As Frankie leaned close to shovel in the food, his glasses steamed up. Justin had no idea how the man ever saw through the things, since the lenses, which could easily start a wildfire if held to the sun just right, were always smudged.

"I'd have no problem with that." Justin winked at Abby.

"What would I be?" she asked. "The station mascot? Or is that limited to dalmatians?"

Eating around his garlic bread, which Justin had no intention of touching—just in case—he let Frankie field the question.

"We have a cat for that," the brooding member of the squad offered. "Perkins is around here somewhere."

"Perkins?" Abby asked, failing to hide her smile. "You have a cat named Perkins?"

Frankie nodded but kept his eyes on his food. "Named after Thaddeus Perkins. We lost him in a factory fire five years ago."

The reminder sobered all three of them, and Justin considered kicking the other man under the table. Green eyes turned hollow a second before disappearing behind dark lashes. She'd lost her husband to war, and though danger came with the territory in the firefighting business, he saw no reason to remind her of that reality.

"Weren't you watching a baseball game, Frank?"

Still chewing, the other man said, "I'm eating."

"You eat in front of the TV all the time. Come on. Abby and I have work to discuss."

Bushy brows met as one. "Since when did you take up nursing?"

Justin stared him down. "I haven't."

"Then—"

"I'm trying out a new hobby," Abby cut in. "A little gardening. Justin has experience and offered to teach me what he knows."

"You play with flowers?" Frankie asked Justin, face incredulous.

"Landscaping," he corrected. "Now if you don't mind . . ."

Magnified eyes glared suspiciously before their third wheel pushed back his chair. "I'll leave you alone, but I'm coming back for seconds when this is gone."

Nodding in agreement, Justin said, "Have at it. There's plenty more on the stove." Once Frankie was out of earshot, he turned to Abby. "That's twice today you've cut me off from revealing our new partnership. You want to tell me why this has to be a secret?"

"It doesn't *have* to be," she hedged, failing to meet his eyes. "Not forever, anyway." When she finally looked up, Justin raised a brow. "I don't know how to tell them," she whispered, perching her elbows on the table.

"Tell who what?"

"My family," she hissed. "How do I tell them that I'm not going to be a nurse anymore?"

Going with logic, he replied, "You're still a nurse. You just aren't working as one for a while."

"Right," she snapped. "Instead I'm helping start a business in a field I know absolutely nothing about. That's totally sensible."

"Sensible is overrated."

"My family won't see it that way."

"They'll come around."

"Eventually," Abby admitted. "I guess I should just tell them and get it over with."

Her reluctance planted doubts. As much as Justin wanted an excuse to spend time with her, he also intended to make a full effort at this business, at least for the summer. "If you don't want to do this, you need to tell me now, Abby. I'm giving you an opportunity, not a mandatory sentence. No hard feelings if you've changed your mind."

"No," she said, eyes sincere. "I want to do this. I checked nine books out of the library this afternoon and I've already started studying. I promise, I *want* to do this."

"Good to know," he said, relieved. "But this means we'll be spending a lot of time along Main Street, visible to pretty much the whole town. If you don't tell them soon, you're going to have a harder time explaining why you didn't later."

Abby twirled her fork in circles. "That's a practical thing to say for a guy who thinks sensible is overrated."

"I can be practical when the situation calls for it," he assured her. "Does this mean we're ready to get to work?"

Pushing the plate away, she pulled a notebook and pen from the purse beside her chair. "I'm ready," she said, opening to a clean page. "Where do we start?"

Charmed by her enthusiasm, he said, "Why don't you tell me what you learned from that book today?"

Her face fell. "I only read a few chapters. I haven't learned anything."

"Then you picked up the wrong book." Justin had transitioned his manual labor experience into two design classes in college, so he could have easily taken the teacher role. But if this was going to work, Abby needed to feel confident enough to collaborate, not just follow his orders. "You had to learn something."

"Well," she started, tapping the end of the pen on the notebook, "the author said that the biggest mistake most landscapers make is not focusing on the big-picture design first. If that's right, then we need to focus on a whole design for the entire project, rather than the different parts individually."

As he suspected, she'd already absorbed more than she realized. "That's exactly right." Justin crossed to the side counter and returned with a long sheet of graph paper. Earlier in the day, he'd sketched out the square with Main Street darting off east and west. "This is the canvas we have to work with. I took a few measurements this morning, but we'll need to complete a more precise survey tomorrow."

"That's a huge canvas," she muttered, staring at his basic pencil drawing.

In a perfect world, a job this size would require a month for planning alone. They didn't have that kind of time.

"But not a blank canvas, which is good. Trees are in place, which will save us an incredible amount of time and money."

Abby tapped the paper next to the corner of Fourth and Main. "Have you thought about using planters along the sidewalks? Maybe we could find a style that would complement the older architecture of the buildings."

When he didn't immediately respond, she brought her eyes up to his face, and Justin didn't bother hiding the grin. "That's exactly what I was about to suggest."

"No," she said, sitting back in her chair. "Really?"

"We're going to make an excellent team," he stated, sliding a stray lock off her forehead. A subtle blush dappled her cheeks, making him long to touch her again.

"This does seem like the start of something good," she breathed, sinking a tooth into her bottom lip.

Justin sat mesmerized by the glimmer in her eyes and the way her slender neck curved just right, offering the perfect spot for a kiss.

"Hot damn!" yelled Frankie from the living room, breaking the spell that had fallen over the new partners. "Did you see that home run?"

As Justin took a deep, frustrated breath, Abby giggled. Neither of them answered Frankie's question.

"We should work on our design," she suggested. "Four weeks isn't a lot of time."

"You're right," Justin reluctantly agreed, putting a few extra inches between them. "Let's get to work."

Chapter 11

Abby never knew landscaping could be so sexy. She also never imagined her first creative meeting would include playing footsie with one of the hottest men she'd ever met. Poor Frankie had no idea what was going on at the other end of the room, but if he had, she was certain a scandalized blush would have been visible through the woolly beard.

Practical Abby would never have approved of mixing business with pleasure. Good thing that uptight biddy hadn't come to this meeting.

Somehow, through the flirting and occasional innuendo, they'd managed to conceive of a rather impressive plan. They'd even searched the Internet for the necessary planters, locating several possibilities that wouldn't break the budget. There were three items on the immediate to-do list.

In the morning Justin would stop by the local nursery for a full price list and to see what plants would be readily available in the next month while Abby paid a visit to the local newspaper, the *Ardent Advocate*, to discuss buying ad space. One project was good, but not enough to sustain a business.

When their individual tasks had been completed, the pair would meet at the bookstore and start filling in the measurements that Justin had skipped. Abby planned to arrive early enough to catch her mother and confess her sudden occupational change, since, as Justin had pointed out, once they started working in the square for all to see, news would travel fast. Better that Mama hear the news from Abby than from someone else.

Feeling good about what they'd accomplished, Justin had cleaned up the kitchen while Abby packed her purse and made a quick trip to the powder room. When she returned, Justin cornered her next to the fridge.

"I have a surprise," he whispered against her neck before reaching for the freezer door. If he kept breathing in her ear like that, Abby might have to climb in the freezer just to cool off. "Don't let Frankie see," he added, slipping something hard and cold against her palm before he tugged her toward the stairs by her free hand.

"Where are we going?" she asked.

Justin didn't answer until they reached the parking lot. "Come on," he said, leading her to a small bench she hadn't noticed earlier. An ancient arbor, which appeared less than stable, kept the little seat hidden in the shadows.

When he motioned for her to sit, Abby said, "Are you serious? The whole thing looks ready to fall over at any second."

"Live a little," he urged, taking a seat and pulling her down beside him. "Now eat your ice cream bar before it melts."

"Is that what this is?" She tore through the plain white wrapper to find a chocolate-covered treat on a stick. "I can't remember the last time I had one of these."

He ripped his open. "Frankie doesn't know I put them in there. It's our little secret."

"That isn't very nice," Abby scolded, nibbling on her chocolate. "Didn't your mother teach you to share?"

"She did," he answered, tapping his treat against hers. "But he's already invaded our date. He doesn't get to share in dessert."

"I thought this was a business meeting," she reminded him before taking a full bite.

"I'm a multitasker." His thigh pressed against hers. "I'm good like that."

Voice husky, she said, "I bet you are."

They ate their desserts in companionable silence until Abby thought she might burst from anticipation. Though of what, she wasn't sure. They certainly weren't going to have sex on this old, rickety bench, but she could think of worse locations for a first kiss.

"At the risk of pushing my luck," Justin said, stretching an arm across the back of the bench, "I don't suppose we could do this again tomorrow night? The date part, that is."

"I'm free," she replied, "but you should probably let Frankie check his calendar."

"Your interest in a threesome is duly noted, but I was thinking just the two of us this time?"

Abby tucked her head against his shoulder. "I'm willing to try that."

"Good." His chin settled against her hair. "Abby?"

"Yes?" she said, casting her face toward his.

"Would you mind if I kissed you right now?"

Suddenly shy, she looked away. "I wouldn't mind that at all. I was kind of hoping you would."

"Thank God," he muttered, placing a hand beneath her chin. "I've been wanting to do this for a long time."

Though she couldn't see his eyes in the dark, Abby imagined them glowing like polished gold. "It's only been a couple weeks since the night of the fire."

He lifted her into his lap. "This fire started long before that one."

Tender lips brushed hers. Light. Gentle. Testing. A lick at the corner. A quick nibble along the bow at the top. All the while, his hands caressed her body, one along her hip while the other slid up her spine.

Abby's blood went hot as her muscles tensed with need. She hadn't been touched, let alone kissed, in what felt like forever.

Her hands slid around his neck, pulling. Conveying what she didn't have the words to say. And finally he deepened the kiss, the taste of cold chocolate mingling in their shared breath. Abby's head swirled as she pressed against him, his mouth hot and giving, and she greedily took all that he offered. Heat pooled between her thighs and a moan slipped free, a sound foreign and yet distantly familiar. Sweet, delicious desire coiled through her body as the kiss intensified, leaving her tethered to reality by nothing more than the muscles flexing beneath her palms.

Justin broke the connection first, leaning his forehead against hers. "Abby girl, you're going to kill me."

"There are worse ways to go," she murmured, panting against him. "But I didn't mean to lose control like that."

"Don't ever apologize for passion, darling." He leaned back far enough to brush the hair from her eyes. "The last thing I want to do is send you home, but I'm on duty until morning and I'd rather not spend our first night together in a bunk under a snoring Frankie Beckham."

The idea didn't appeal to Abby, either. "We should probably slow down anyway," she said, toying with a wisp of hair at the collar of his shirt. "There must be some rule against starting a relationship while trying to start a business, but I don't feel much like following rules these days."

"I like this rebellious side of you," Justin whispered before tasting her earlobe. His teeth toyed with her bottom lip. "Now you're giving me all sorts of ideas. And if we don't get off this bench, I might say to hell with duty and take you right here."

Abby shivered, her body fully aroused. "I've never had a fireman fantasy before, but maybe I've been missing out."

"I'll fulfill any fantasy you want, baby. Just say the word."

The bench creaked as she rocked against him, reminding her of their precarious perch. Gathering all her strength, Abby pushed against his chest and slid to her feet.

"I'd better let you get back upstairs," she said, feeling something soft beneath her foot. "What was that?" she squealed, nearly jumping into his arms again.

Justin laughed. "That *was* my ice cream bar." He surveyed the area around the bench. "And I'm guessing that one is yours."

"Dang it," she pouted. "I wanted that."

"The sacrifice was worth the prize," he uttered, lifting off the bench and pulling her in for another scorching kiss. By the time this one ended, Abby was trembling and could barely feel her feet. "This is going to be the longest night of my life," he breathed against her ear.

Unable to speak, she nodded.

"You'd better get going before Frankie comes looking for us," Justin said.

"My purse is still upstairs."

"Shit." The expletive echoed her feelings exactly.

"I don't think I can face Frankie right now," she said, rubbing her swollen lips. "Could you bring it down for me?"

"Like I said, anything for you." They walked back to the door, but instead of opening it, Justin tugged her close. "I don't want to let you go," he groaned, burying his nose in her hair.

Knowing what she had to do, Abby let her practical side slip back into place. "You have a job to do, and I have books to read." A gentle pat on his chest and he let her step away. "We'll see each other in the morning, right? And then our date tomorrow night. I'd volunteer to cook for you, but I still don't have a stove."

"There's always pizza," he said, a wicked grin teasing his talented lips. "I could pick it up on the way."

Abby nodded. "Okay. Now hurry and get my purse. The longer we're down here, the more Frankie is going to wonder what we're doing."

"What does it matter if Frankie knows what we're doing?"

"He works with my brother," she reminded him. "The big, over-protective brother who's well skilled with a tire iron."

"Right." Justin opened the heavy metal door. "I'll be back in a second."

More aroused than she'd been in a long time, Abby paced the small lighted area, keeping an eye out for anything that might pop out of the dark. When a raccoon scurried past the bench, she nearly leapt out of her skin.

"What's the matter?" Justin queried, charging out the door seconds after she screamed. "Are you okay?"

Working to catch her breath, she pointed toward the arbor. "Raccoon," she panted. "Scared me."

"Come on," Justin chuckled, handing over her purse. "I'll walk you to your car."

When they reached her Corolla on the street, he opened her door. "Are you sure that you're okay?"

Mostly recovered, she smiled. "That raccoon is not the reason I'll be losing sleep tonight." Seeing her words as an invitation, Justin leaned down for another kiss, but Abby's self-preservation kicked in. She held him off with one finger pressed firmly against his sternum. "Save it for tomorrow or I'll never get out of here."

Strolling backward, he gave her enough space to climb inside and close the door. After tossing the purse on her passenger seat, Abby started the engine and gave Justin one last wave before driving off, but at the red light a block away, she fought the urge to turn around.

"Patience is a virtue, Abigail," she said aloud, driving on when the light turned green, confident that tomorrow night her two-year drought would finally come to an end.

⌒

After tossing and turning for several hours, Justin finally drifted off, only to be awakened an hour later by the firehouse alarms. By the time he'd suited up, four more squad members had arrived to leap on the truck at the same time he did. By five a.m., an hour before his shift ended, they'd extinguished the brush fire and headed back to town. Justin dropped his gear and went straight home, which meant walking two blocks down Main Street to his little apartment above the bookstore. Eyes burning, he'd grabbed a quick shower and sprawled across the small hand-me-down sofa for a brief nap.

The nursery opened at eight, but he had another stop to make first. Using the info in Q's email, Justin located the available real estate and pulled off the road to have a look around. The mostly level lot featured a thin cropping of trees that would require minor clearing. Due mostly to the direct access straight off the exit, he had to agree with Q. This was a prime spot begging for development. And as the sun crested behind him, Justin leaned against his Infiniti, imagining the possibilities.

A large gas station was a given. Maybe two if they could get the parcels on both sides of the road. Retail shops of some kind, and maybe a small hotel or two. There were no fast-food chains in Ardent Springs proper, but based on his research, this location rested outside the city limits, which would make any protests from the natives irrelevant. They could raise a fuss, but they couldn't stop progress.

The finished project took shape in his mind, as clear as the gravel at his feet. Absorbed in his thoughts and smiling at the gift Q had handed him, Justin failed to notice the truck pull onto the shoulder behind him.

"Need some help?" called a deep voice from his left. Justin rose off the car as Cooper Ridgeway approached. "A jump or a tow?"

"Neither," Justin replied, offering a neighborly smile. "Just checking out the area."

Cooper glanced off to the trees across the way. "You get up early to gander at an empty lot?"

"You see an empty lot," he explained. "I see potential."

As if intrigued by the vague response, the bigger man mimicked his lean against the fender. Justin swallowed the command not to scratch the sports car. Ridgeway had a good twenty pounds on him, after all. And there was the tire iron thing.

With a shake of his head, the mechanic queried, "What are you seeing?"

Reluctant to show his hand, Justin said, "Nothing specific, but the location is good. Close to the interstate. Good-sized lot. I have ideas."

"You going to buy this?"

This deal would be more complicated than a simple purchase. "More like help someone else buy it."

A beat of silence danced between them, and Justin could almost feel the next question coming.

"Are you back here for good, Donovan?"

"I haven't bought a ticket for anywhere else, but you never know." He shrugged. "I'm here for the next few months, anyway. I'll see where life takes me after that."

"Hal says you like my sister."

Justin struggled to figure out who this Hal person might be. "I do. I like her a lot."

"Hal seems to think Abbs likes you, too."

This was starting to feel like passing notes in homeroom. "Who is Hal?" he asked. "I don't think I've met him."

Cooper snorted. "Sorry. I mean Haleigh Rae."

Now that made more sense. Since Haleigh had done the bidding at the auction, Justin ventured a guess that she supported whatever might happen between him and her friend. The giant leaning next to him was proving harder to read.

"Here's what I know," Justin said, preferring to clear the air and keep things simple. "I like your sister, and, based on, well . . ." Describing to her brother what they'd done the night before didn't seem like a smart move. "Let's just say that I have good reason to believe she feels the same way about me. Does that answer your question?"

"She'd be pissed as a wet hen if she knew I was saying this," Cooper drawled, shifting off the car to stare Justin in the eye, "but I'll tell you what I know. Abby doesn't do casual. She never has. She's all in or all out, so if you don't see this as an all in for you, I suggest you keep your eyes on those trees over there and off my sister."

Ridgeway had no idea how reassuring his speech was.

"At eighteen years old, I had my eye on a pretty girl," Justin shared, relaxing against the car. "She was perfect and smart and barely noticed me. You know what that's like?"

Green eyes exactly like Abby's narrowed. "Yeah. I know what that's like."

"Good." Justin rose to his full height and squared his stance. "Then you get it. I'm all in, Cooper. Always have been. Always will be. The rest is up to Abby."

As if a truce had been reached, Cooper relaxed, sliding his hands into his pockets. "Nice car you've got here."

Justin didn't miss a beat. "She's my pride and joy."

"2014?"

"2015. Customized her to exactly what I wanted, down to the three-point-five-liter hybrid engine."

"That doesn't slow her down?"

Brushing a speck of dust off the roof, he replied, "Not one bit."

"Damn," Cooper whispered. "I prefer a classic, but still appreciate your taste."

They may not be friends—yet—but Justin had earned a little respect.

"Let me know if you ever want to take her for a spin," he said, shocking himself with the offer. No one drove Justin's car. Ever. But if anyone could handle her, Cooper was the man.

"Got some time right now," the older man replied, a challenging twinkle in his eye. Good thing Justin hadn't been bluffing.

Stepping away, he nodded toward the door. "Keys are in it."

Ten minutes later, heart beating like a dad waiting for his daughter to return from her first date, Justin watched his Hagane blue Q50 appear on the horizon as pristine as when she'd faded out of sight. Once again able to breathe, he lingered by Ridgeway's old gray Ford until the car enthusiast parked and climbed from the vehicle.

Hiding his true feelings, Justin met him halfway. "What do you think?"

"I think I'm in love." Cooper beamed, tossing him the keys. "You were right about the power. I kicked her in over the hill and the response was killer."

Justin didn't like the words *kicked her in* but kept the smile in place. "That's my baby."

Cooper chuckled. "I'd better get the shop open. Thanks for the test-drive." Before climbing into the cab, he said, "How about we keep this conversation between us?"

A fan of discretion, Justin said, "What conversation?"

A crooked grin flashed seconds before the truck pulled away. Happy to have a new ally, Justin lowered into his car, patting the wheel as if to make sure she was okay. As the engine hummed to life, Justin cast one last glance across the weed-covered field. "This is my ticket back in," he murmured, shifting the sedan into gear as a new plan rolled out before him.

With three simple steps, he would have everything he wanted.

First, he'd win the girl. Second, he'd close the deal. And third, when Chesterfield Developers begged him to come back, Justin would merrily tell them to go to hell.

Chapter 12

Placing the ad with the *Ardent Advocate* had been simple enough until Piper Griffin had caught Abby on her way out and commenced a fact-finding expedition. A well-known member of the newspaper sales team, Piper had the fashion sense of a woman half her age and the curiosity of a caffeinated five-year-old.

Why are you here? Since when do you do landscaping? Didn't you just set your house on fire?

Dodging as much as she could, Abby had failed to defer the employment query. Not only was she now late for her next stop, but she'd unavoidably informed the most fervent member of the Ardent Springs gossip lines about her change of career *before* telling her own mother. The moment Abby made her escape, the race was on.

Since Linda Ridgeway began every day helping her fiancé open the bookstore, Abby's next challenge turned out to be locating a parking space in the store's vicinity. She circled the block twice before stealing a spot from Mrs. Abernathy, who waved a gnarled fist out her window. Abby would receive a proper scolding at church on Sunday, but desperate times called for desperate measures.

Charging through the front door, she found the main section empty. A quick search through the stacks and still nothing. Finally she found Bruce in the back office.

"Where's Mama?"

Bruce looked up from a box of old magazines. "It's Friday. She's at her hair appointment."

Resisting the urge to smack herself in the forehead, Abby zipped out through the front door as quickly as she'd zipped in. Gertie Carlyle had been doing Mama's hair every Friday for the last seven years. How could she have forgotten this regular occurrence? And, of course, Gertie's shop rested four blocks away. Jogging through pedestrians, Abby felt her lungs burning by the middle of the second block. Though nursing had kept her on her feet, she was obviously more out of shape than she realized. As she rounded the corner at Fifth, headed toward Bridge Street, Abby decided that a gym membership might be in order.

When the salon came into view, she staggered to a halt, bent at the waist to catch her breath. "I can do this," she mumbled, holding her side. "This is what I get for using that treadmill as a towel rack." Stutter jogging the last one hundred feet, Abby saw the car parked before the salon entrance and her heart sank. The license plate on the little pink Jetta bore one word.

PIPER.

Dammit.

Maybe she hadn't told her yet. Maybe Mama was eyebrow deep in a rinse and Piper hadn't even spotted her. Bells jingled overhead as Abby hurried through the glass door to hear the words, "I can't believe a woman would throw away decades of a career to plant flowers."

One decade. Abby had been a nurse for *one* decade.

"You've clearly got your story wrong, Piper," Abby's mother assured from under the towel draped atop her head. "Abby had an interview for a nursing position just this week."

"I'm telling you—" Piper started, her back to Abby.

Mama cut her off. "I'm her mother, for heaven's sake. Don't you think I'd know if my daughter lost her mind enough to pick up a pair of trimming shears?"

The rest of the staff, of course, had spotted Abby right away. Three sets of wide, heavily lined eyes stared her way, all filled with excitement over having a front-row seat for the scene about to unravel.

Piper opened her coral-tinted lips, but Abby cleared her throat before another word could be uttered.

"Gertie, how long are you going to leave me under this towel? Did you wander off or something?" Mama lifted the terry cloth and spotted her daughter lingering like a lightning-struck hummingbird near the front door. "Abigail. What are you doing here?" Dragging the towel into her lap, she waved her own question away. "Never mind. Will you tell Ms. Griffin here that you have not given up nursing?"

Heart beating like a kick drum, she said, "Mama, I need to talk to you."

"Why? What happened? Is Cooper okay?"

"He's fine, Mama." Abby looked to Gertie. "Can we use your office for a minute?"

"Sure, sugar," Gertie replied, sliding the towel off Mama's lap. "Take all the time you need."

Remaining seated, her mother said, "It's true, isn't it? Piper is right."

"I *told* you—" the gossip started.

"You've said enough," Abby snapped, hushing the busybody. "Mama, please just come back to Gertie's office with me."

"It's that boy, isn't it?"

"If you'll give me two minutes, I'll explain everything."

"I know Thea Levine gave him the beautification project. Abigail Louise, what are you thinking?"

Patience thin, she let the words fly. "I'm a grown woman who can make my own decisions, that's what I'm thinking. I'm trying something new. Something that I might actually enjoy." Turning her attention to the audience, Abby added, "Would you all please excuse us for one minute? I would like to finish this conversation in private."

Gertie burst into action. "Of course, darling." She took the broom from the younger stylist's hands, saying, "Let's step outside and get a bit of sun, ladies. We don't do that near often enough." As the staff shuffled toward the exit, Piper held her ground. "You, too, Piper. We can talk about my Memorial Day ads outside."

For a second, Abby thought Gertie would use the broom on Piper's heels, but the gossip queen joined the exodus, and within seconds the room had cleared.

"I can't believe you spoke to me that way in front of my friends," Mama pouted.

"I asked you to step into the office."

"Why bother? The butter was out of the biscuit by that point." Arms crossed beneath the brown vinyl cape, she said, "Explain to me why you would walk away from an established career to play garden games with Justin Donovan."

Abby fought to control her temper. "I was fired, Mama. The hospital let me go, and the only nursing positions I can find around here consider me overqualified. Two wouldn't even talk to me, and the other ended the interview as soon as he saw my résumé. I'm not walking away from nursing—it walked away from me."

Slightly mollified, her mother's tone shifted. "What did you mean, trying something you might actually enjoy? I thought you loved being a nurse."

"I did, but I haven't for a long time," Abby confessed. "I'm not sure when things changed. Maybe after Kyle died. Maybe before. All I know is that nursing doesn't make me happy anymore."

"I want you to be happy, honey. That's all I've ever wanted. But landscaping? That just isn't you. You don't even have houseplants."

"That's beside the point. And this could be me," she said. "I helped Justin with my flower beds and I really enjoyed the work. I don't even know if I'll be good at it, but I deserve the right to try."

"You want to spend your days playing in dirt?"

"Dirt smells a lot better than ninety percent of the muck I've handled in the last ten years."

Mama's face twisted in disgust. "I hadn't thought of that. So yesterday . . ."

"You saw us agreeing to work together, yes. I should have told you right then what was going on, but I chickened out."

"Because you thought I'd do what? Throw a fit?" she asked.

Abby smiled for the first time since leaving the newspaper office. "I'd say the last few minutes proved me right on that assumption."

The older woman chuckled. "Like I said, I want my children to be happy, but I want them to be sensible. None of this sounds very sensible."

"I'm not buying an RV and going off the grid," Abby pointed out. "I'm changing paths, that's all. Maybe we aren't meant to do the same thing for our whole lives."

Mama sighed. "Maybe we aren't. But honey, I saw the way you looked at that boy yesterday. Are you sure this is all business?"

"He's twenty-eight years old, for heaven's sake. Stop calling him a boy." Abby plopped down in the chair next to Mama's. "And no, what's going on with me and Justin isn't strictly business."

"Baby, he's five years younger than you are."

"And Kyle was seven years older than I was. No one made a peep when we got together."

A sensible shoe tapped the footrest. "I would have if you hadn't come home from college so *in love*. Kyle was much too old for you."

Amazed that her mother had never aired this opinion before, Abby leaned forward. "Age is just a number, Mama," she said, ignoring the fact that she'd had the same misgivings a mere week ago. "When you're in love, you don't see someone's age. You just see them."

Thin gray brows arched. "Are you saying that you're in love with Justin Donovan?"

Abby took a moment to consider her feelings. She was in like, maybe. And a whole lotta lust. But not love. Not yet.

"We're enjoying each other's company," she offered. "That's good for now."

Mama rolled her eyes. "That's code for having sex and even I know it."

To her dying day Abby would never forget hearing those words cross her mother's lips. "Mama! We are not having sex." Not yet, anyway. "I need to go. I'm meeting Justin at the bookstore for my first official day of work." She shuffled off the chair and placed a quick kiss on her mother's cheek. "By the time your wedding rolls around, we'll have all of Main Street blooming."

"Good luck, baby," the older woman offered, reaching for a dry towel on the station in front of her. "And keep it strictly business with that boy."

Gertie and her crew chose that moment to rejoin them, in time to catch Mama's parting words. Avoiding eye contact, Abby made her second escape of the day.

"Hey there, good-looking."

Justin spun to find Haleigh Mitchner strolling up behind him. He'd been waiting for Abby in front of the bookstore for ten minutes and had assumed she'd be the only person offering such a greeting. But the slick blonde sporting jeans and a denim jacket proved him wrong.

"Good morning," he tossed back, not sure what to expect after his earlier visit with Cooper. This could either be a friendly chat about the weather or another interrogation.

"I heard you talked to Cooper this morning." So much for keeping the conversation between themselves. "Don't worry," Haleigh added. "Cooper won't tell Abby, but he tells me everything. Is that stuff you told him true?"

As usual, honesty had not been the best policy this morning. "Maybe I was buying sympathy from her brother or maybe I wasn't. Either way, I have work to do."

He spun away only to find a hand on his arm. "Wait," she said. "I realize we keep poking our noses into your business, but Abby means a lot to us. I guess we're both a little protective of her."

No harm in caring for your friends and family, but they had a funny way of showing it. "Did you know that she didn't like being a nurse anymore?"

Brown eyes narrowed. "Not until they let her go."

"And do you know how hard it is for her to watch you and her brother be blissfully happy while she feels totally alone?"

"Abby is happy for us."

"She can be happy for you and still be miserable," he purported. "If you really want to protect her, maybe you need to pay attention to her instead of being caught up in your own little world."

Haleigh's mouth opened and then closed again. The set of her jaw said she wanted to argue, but the thoughts flitting across her face revealed the truth. He was right and she knew it.

"I do pay attention to her," she finally said. "That's why I bid on you in the auction. That night of the fire, I saw her face when she looked at you. There was a light in her eyes I haven't seen in a long time. An interest of a *carnal nature*."

"That's an interesting way of saying Abby has the hots for me." Leaning against the antique streetlight beside him, Justin sobered, bent on getting his point across. "She was hurt that you all went behind her back to do that."

"And you?" she asked. "Did you mind that we did it?"

"Not one bit," he admitted. "But I'd rather she come to me on her own than be pushed by her friends."

The blonde flashed a crooked smile. "As much as Abby might appear weak and manipulated, I can promise you that she doesn't do anything unless she wants to. I knew that going in at the auction. In fact, I was afraid that even after I won the bidding, she might refuse to go with you."

Ego slightly appeased, Justin returned the grin. "Is that your way of saying our first date was Abby's choosing and not yours?"

"That's what I'm saying." Gesturing with her chin, brown eyes cut to the sidewalk behind him. "Here she comes now. Based on the smile she's sending your way, I'm guessing things have progressed since that first date."

Justin uncurled off the light post. "Your boyfriend might tell you everything, but I don't." He turned to catch the smile Haleigh mentioned and fought the urge to kiss her into an even sexier one. The one he'd coaxed from her lips the night before. "Good morning, partner," he said, waving his trusty notepad. "You're late. We have work to do, you know."

"You have what to do?" Haleigh asked.

"Work," Abby answered. "Justin and I are now AJ Landscaping, and we've been tasked with prettying up the square."

A little shocked himself, Justin enjoyed watching Haleigh's jaw drop open.

"What about nursing?" she asked.

Abby shook her head as the sun whipped a lock of hair into her eyes. "I couldn't find another position," she said, clearing her vision, "so I'm trying something new. Justin is going to teach me what he knows, and together, we're going to bring this street to life."

With a nervous laugh, her friend found her voice. "Who are you and what have you done with Abby Lou? You don't even have houseplants."

"Why does everyone keep bringing that up?"

"Because you killed three ficus trees in three years, remember? Now you're going to landscape an entire street?"

"Not by herself," Justin cut in, unwilling to let anyone dim Abby's light. "She has a good eye and isn't afraid of hard work. That's all I need in a partner."

Contrite, Haleigh backed off. "Then I'm happy for you. For you both," she added, the smile not reaching her eyes. "I can't wait to see the place when you're finished."

"Take a drive down Main and you're sure to see it," Abby replied, appearing unfazed by her friend's reaction.

An awkward silence landed like a boulder on the dusty sidewalk before Haleigh made her excuses. "Snow is expecting me, so I should probably get going and let you kids get to work."

"Tell her I said hi," his new partner said with a wave, but before her friend traveled ten feet, she added, "I'll call you tomorrow, Hal. We can talk more then."

The slender woman turned, a genuine smile back in place. "I'd like that," she said, and then moved on.

"Ficus killer, huh?" Justin whispered as they watched the other woman walk away.

"They were half-dead before I got them," she claimed.

"I'm sure they were." He'd have to watch her when planting time came. "Do we have an ad?"

"We do. And Mama now knows about us."

"Us?" he asked, curious if she meant professionally or personally.

"Yes," she replied. "Us. The business. The other stuff. No more secrets."

Throwing an arm over her shoulder, Justin turned her toward the west end of Main. "You've been a busy girl this morning, Abby Lou."

A pointy elbow cracked his ribs. "Only Haleigh calls me that, mister. And yes, I've been busy. How about you? Do we have the price list?"

"Yes, ma'am."

"Good." She wrapped an arm around his waist. "Then let's start measuring."

Chapter 13

"That's the last one," Justin sighed, leaning left and right to stretch out his back. They'd been bending over every fifteen feet for four blocks. "I'll get these added to the layout sheet, and then Monday we'll compile a few design options for Thea to review."

"We aren't working over the weekend?" Abby asked, assuming they'd need every available hour to hit the short deadline.

He tucked a pencil behind his ear. "If necessary, we'll go seven days a week when we get closer to the deadline, but weekends off is the plan for now."

"Oh." She hadn't had a full weekend off in years. What would she do with the time? There were always the design books. Or maybe Abby would get really wild and read a novel. Something else she hadn't done in far too long.

"We're off to a good start, Abby girl. What time should I show up with the pizza?"

Holy cheese and pepperoni, she'd almost forgotten about their date. How was that even possible? She'd twisted her sheets into a knot the night before, thanks to her brain balancing on a wire of anticipation. The construction crew, who'd finally finished repairing the kitchen wall, had turned her house into a dusty mess. Regardless of the fact Justin had seen the place at its worst, this was a date—though some might call it a premeditated booty call—and her house would be clean.

"Is six thirty too late?" Abby asked, uncertain what time he'd been thinking. A quick check of her watch showed it was nearly three. Between cleaning and getting herself ready, that still didn't leave her a lot of time. Speaking of getting ready, a man was coming to call and Abby didn't have a thing to wear. Two-thirds of her wardrobe were scrubs, and the other third didn't come anywhere near date material. "Or seven?" she squeaked. "Maybe seven would be better."

"The sooner the better," he replied, tugging her into motion until they were strolling along the sidewalk side by side. "But if I have to wait until seven, I can do that."

Accommodating of him, but she'd feel better if he were as nervous as she was.

"About tonight . . ." she started, determined to give him fair warning. "I mean, just so you know . . ."

Justin squeezed her hand. "Know what?"

Closing her eyes, she blurted, "I might not be very good."

He stopped walking, and Abby opened her eyes to see the spring-themed flag hanging near the entrance to Virgil's Boutique.

"Good at what?" he asked, clearly confused.

She glanced up and down the street before looking him in the eye. "You know. It's been two years. I might be . . . a little rusty."

"Wow," he breathed, hazel eyes locking with hers. "First off, I don't think you ever want to use the word *rusty* in that context. And second, after last night, I have no doubts about your skills in this area, Abby. But we probably shouldn't leave anything to chance." Justin paused, and she feared what might come next.

Did he want to wait? Or call the whole thing off? As panic loomed, he leaned in close to whisper in her ear. "I'd better perform a full inspection to make sure every inch of you is humming like a well-oiled machine. Maybe even run through the process two or three times. We wouldn't want to overlook anything."

Abby nearly swallowed her tongue as a fire lit up her spine. Any dormant areas were certainly engaged now.

"Right." She nodded, struggling to form a coherent sentence. "Two or three times." Did she really need to clean the house? Maybe they should skip the pizza and head home now.

His wicked grin nearly melted her panties right there on the sidewalk. "Feeling better now?" he purred.

Feeling everything now, she nearly moaned. Instead, she stuttered, "Uh-huh. Yeah. All better."

Planting a hot, brain-numbing kiss on her lips, Justin pulled her hard against him, revealing that Abby wasn't the only one affected by their conversation. A faint hint of sense squeaked through, reminding her where they were.

She broke the kiss but didn't pull away. "We're putting on a show for the natives," she panted, oxygen a thin commodity in that moment. "I'm all for no secrets, but I'd rather not be front-page news, either."

Placing a chaste kiss on her forehead, he loosened his grip to put a breath of air between them. "Seven o'clock can't come soon enough," he growled.

Abby couldn't agree more, but in light of his erotic promise, presenting him with a woman worth worshiping took on greater urgency.

"I'll walk you to your car," Justin offered, setting them in motion once again, hands firmly clasped.

Virgil's flag whipped in the wind as if sending Abby a signal. A signal she picked up on right away.

"Why don't you go ahead. I have a quick stop to make before heading home."

"All right then." A few steps away, he spun to walk backward. "Should I bring something to drink?"

She shook her head. "I still have that second bottle of wine."

Justin gave a thumbs-up, turning back around in time to dodge Mrs. Abernathy, who ordered him to watch where he was going. Preferring not to answer for her parking sins quite yet, Abby bolted into the boutique, nearly plowing into the front rack.

"Hey there, Miss Abigail," greeted the proprietor from three racks away. "I wondered when you were going to grace us with a visit. How can I help you?"

Virgil Lexington had lived in Ardent Springs his whole life, except for the two years he spent in Vegas, where he'd allegedly lived with a famous singer of an earlier generation, one who preferred that people like Virgil stay firmly in the closet. Once the love of his life had made his grand exit, presumably through the pearly gates, Virgil returned to his hometown, more determined than ever to be his authentic self.

Personally, Abby loved him for it, and after twenty years of dressing nearly every female in town, so did pretty much everyone else. There would always be dissenting voices regarding Virgil's lifestyle. He shaved his legs, snapped his fingers (though who didn't?), and knew how to flatter any figure that walked through his door. Thankfully, the supporters far outnumbered the nonsupporters, and so their little town lumbered its way toward progress.

"You can start by telling me this dress comes in my size," she said, running a hand along the wine-colored number she'd nearly taken down with her entrance. Other than the rich burgundy color, Abby couldn't say why the dress spoke to her, but it practically screamed her name.

Abandoning his task, Virgil joined her. "Ah, good choice. What's the occasion?"

Abby toyed with the slender collar. "Prepare yourself for a shock, Virgil, but I have a date."

"About damn time," he muttered. "Where is this intelligent man taking you? We might need to find you something a little fancier."

Time to confess her hussy ways. "Actually, he's bringing pizza to my house," she confided, catching the store owner's knowing smirk.

Unlike some people in this town, Virgil could keep a confidence. "I'm looking for sexy but casual. Something that'll make him lose his breath, but nothing too slinky."

"Then this is your winner, honey. Shirt dresses never go out of style, and this length will show off those gorgeous legs of yours." Virgil whipped through the five garments available. "Here it is. A size eight. Let's get you into a fitting room."

Normally Abby picked out her clothes with little thought and never tried anything on. Which was probably why she returned more pieces than she kept. Tonight she needed to step up her game, and she obediently followed the well-dressed man to the curtained stalls along the left side wall.

"How do you know I have gorgeous legs?" she asked. Other than a simple number for Lorelei's wedding the previous fall, which had draped to her ankles, Abby hadn't worn a dress in ages.

"You've spent how many years as a nurse?" he asked, opening the curtain of the largest dressing room.

"Ten years," she answered, not sure what her occupation had to do with anything.

"And how often do nurses get to sit down?"

Abby snorted. "They don't."

Virgil shuffled her into the elegantly decorated stall. "Exactly. Now shimmy into this beauty and call me when you're ready."

The curtain whizzed shut and Abby found herself staring at her reflection in a three-way mirror. Remembering the time crunch, she did as Virgil ordered, slipping off her shoes first, and then the jeans and sweatshirt. Seconds later she looked up to find a stranger staring back.

"Are you decent, honey?"

"I'm something," Abby replied, floating in an out-of-body experience. The tiny cap sleeves accentuated her toned arms, while the hem, which stopped mid-thigh, proved the fashion expert correct. She did have gorgeous legs.

"I'm dying out here," Virgil whined. "Let me see."

Abby whisked the curtain open and chewed her lip, waiting for the professional's approval.

"My word," he said, holding his palms against the perfect five o'clock shadow that was his trademark. "Forget about losing his breath. Your man is going to hit his knees."

A husky laugh burst from her chest. "I wouldn't mind that reaction, either," she said, spinning to see herself from all sides.

"And there's an obvious bonus with this one," Virgil whispered, peering over her shoulder. Without warning, he reached around and unfastened the top three buttons to reveal a rather provocative amount of cleavage. "Buttons mean easy on, and easy off."

Modesty tested, Abby assessed Virgil's alterations. Though she wouldn't be caught dead looking like this in public, for this very private evening, she heartily approved. "You are officially my fairy godfather, Mr. Lexington. I'll take it."

Justin exited Main Street Pizzeria with a pizza in one hand, his cell in the other. He'd spent the last two hours primping, as his former fiancée often called it. Victoria had complained regularly that he was too high maintenance, but Justin preferred the term methodical. Nothing wrong with looking good, and when preparing for a night with the one woman he thought he'd never have, a man needed to look and feel his best.

In reality, her reminder of the two-year hiatus elicited a nervous reaction Justin hadn't anticipated. Sex had always been a mutual pleasure shared with a willing partner. Something to enjoy but nothing that altered his life in any way. Tonight would be different. Abby deserved perfection, and he would settle for nothing less. The promise of two or three times had not been an empty bluff, the proof of which resided on his passenger seat in a Puckett's Pharmacy bag—one brand-new box of condoms.

He'd timed the drive down to the minute, pulling into Abby's drive at exactly six fifty-nine. Justin liked to be precise. Ironic considering he'd lost his job in Chicago due to a lack of due diligence. Upon reaching her front door, he gave his breath a quick smell check—because this night had apparently set him back a good decade in maturity—before ringing the doorbell.

The moment Abby opened the door, wrapped in a thin sheath the color of mulberry wine, Justin forgot how to breathe. The pizza nearly slipped from his fingertips as the instinct to reach out and touch nearly overruled all other thoughts. Several buttons at the top had been left undone, revealing enough skin to make his knees weak, while the one left open at the bottom exposed enough of her milky thighs to shut down his nervous system.

"Hi there," she said, a shy smile accentuating her full lower lip.

Since talking required breathing, he filled his struggling lungs to mutter, "You look gorgeous."

Pink peppered her cheeks. "Thank you. You look pretty good yourself."

Glancing down as if he'd forgotten what he'd worn, he met her eye again with a shaky stutter. "Not as good as you, but I did my best."

Abby shook her head as a husky laugh escaped her glossy lips. "Do you want to come in or should we stand here arguing over who's better looking?"

"In," he answered. "Definitely in." By the time she closed the door behind him, Justin had unloaded the pizza onto the foyer table to free up his hands. "Let me try that greeting again," he growled, hauling her against him and taking her mouth in one swift movement.

With a startled yip, she molded to his body with every curve as her arms slid up to clinch around his neck. Her mouth was hot and tasted of mint and something sweet. Something heady and intoxicating. Justin wanted more. He wanted to give her more. Taking one step forward, he gripped her bottom and pressed her back to the wall. She arched into him, as frantic as he was to taste and touch and please.

Running on instinct, he broke the kiss and lifted her higher until he could lick the alabaster skin between her breasts. "You taste even better than I imagined," he mumbled, breathing in her scent. "And you smell damn good, too."

"Sweet peas," she breathed. "I hoped you'd like it."

"I like everything about you, Abby." Letting her feet slide to the floor, he forced himself to slow down. She deserved better than a quick toss against a wall. "Are you hungry?" he asked, still holding her hips.

Flattening her palms against his chest, she held his gaze, her eyes darkening to the color of damp moss. "Not for pizza," she whispered. "I've waited two years, Justin. I don't want to wait anymore." Without another word, she led him through the living room and down the hall. As she pulled him into her bedroom, his body tensed, his erection almost painful against his zipper. "Have a seat," she said, pressing him down onto the teal comforter.

Obeying her command, he lowered onto the bed, his eyes never straying from the breathtaking image hovering before him. She looked so perfect he feared this might all be a dream. And then she began unbuttoning the dress, and it was as if every fantasy he'd ever had melded into the perfect reality.

Pleasure and pain fused as Justin gripped the blanket beneath him, determined to let Abby set the pace. For now. When she reached the button at her navel, his chest caught fire. As the last button, just below the juncture of her thighs, gave way, the flames spread, singeing every cell in his body. She stood before him, dress open from neck to knee, a goddess testing the limits of his control. No undergarments lingered beneath the delicate material, turning the already erotic performance into something he'd never forget for the rest of his days.

"You're exquisite," he whispered.

The pink that had dappled her cheeks moments before rolled into a full-body blush. "Thank you, but I'm starting to lose my nerve a bit. Maybe you could take over from here."

He thought she'd never ask.

Chapter 14

Justin hit his knees, just as Virgil had predicted, and gently, as if her skin were an open flame, trailed his fingertips up her legs. When her knees wobbled, he said, "I've got you, baby. Hold on a little longer."

Abby closed her eyes as his hands slid beneath the hem of her dress. Seconds later, his breath teased the flesh several inches below her navel. "Oh, God," she murmured, shoving her hands into his hair. He kissed her then, teeth and tongue stealing her ability to breathe or think or stand. "Justin, please," she said, desperate for more but uncertain she could endure what came next without something to hold her up.

In one swift motion, he rose to his feet, sweeping Abby off of hers in the process. By the time the startled cry crossed her lips, he'd placed her onto the mattress and was already gliding down her body, the bed dipping beneath his weight somewhere around her weakened knees. The dress fell open like a curtain falling away, exposing every inch of her to the man already driving her mad.

Hot air danced across her belly, and then lower still, until a moan of ecstasy ripped from her throat.

"Pace yourself, baby," he said, every word like a match to her skin. "This is only the beginning."

If this was the beginning, Abby might not survive until the end. When his teeth locked on her most sensitive spot, she growled his name as waves of sensation flooded her system. Firm hands spread her thighs, and her core lifted in anticipation, desperate for the torture about to commence. Seconds that felt like days passed before he finally slid his tongue along her folds. She gritted her teeth as the waves grew stronger, creating a buzz in her ears and tingles in various other locations.

When his oh-so-talented tongue plunged deep, her body rocked against him as inaudible moans and whimpers filled the air. Abby dug her toes into the bed, lifting her hips higher, demanding more while her head rolled from side to side, unable to bear the intensity of her arousal.

He licked and teased, sucked and kissed, until her body snapped, the orgasm rocketing from her core to flare out in every direction, leaving her trembling and shaken, as weak as a rag doll caught in a hurricane.

Slowly her grip on the comforter loosened as her lungs recovered. There would be no need to join a gym if they continued this kind of activity. Sex with Justin Donovan felt a hell of a lot better than any Zumba class ever would. And then she remembered they hadn't actually had sex yet.

"Heaven help me," she muttered, still panting as the last ripples of satisfaction ricocheted through her limbs.

"Is that a prayer or a plea?" he asked, prowling up her body like a panther stalking his prey. His lips grazed hers, the sensual taste of his achievement salty and sweet.

Abby ran her hands along his rib cage. "How about a request for mercy?" she asked, wanting nothing of the sort.

Flaxen eyes, barely visible by the light from the hall, softened to liquid gold. "Uh-uh," he rumbled, shaking his head slowly from side to side. "Tonight isn't about mercy, darling. It's about making sure that you are thoroughly"—he paused to take her mouth in a hungry, sensual kiss before continuing—"sexually satisfied."

Her body responded instantly to the images his words evoked and, as if an earth-shattering orgasm hadn't flung her to the stars mere seconds ago, Abby grew wet and restless, grinding up against him, desperate for more.

"Is that a surrender?" Justin murmured, driving hard against her core.

Abby didn't answer. Instead she pushed up hard, flipping them both until she hovered above the man wearing far too many clothes for her liking. "I need skin," she breathed, opening the buttons of his shirt as quickly as her anxious fingers could manage.

Justin caressed her breasts, distracting her from the task. "You're so perfect," he whispered, hands sliding around her rib cage and down to her hips. She arched into him as if his touch controlled her every move. "You're like a drug I'll never get enough of."

"And you're still wearing too many clothes," she argued, desperate to taste and touch. To feel him sliding into her over and over. When the last button gave way, Justin leaned up enough for her to pull the shirt down his arms. The linen landed on the floor as she scooted down to undo his pants, which quickly followed suit. Black boxer briefs were now the only things standing in her way.

Determined to slow down, Abby cupped him through the strained cotton, testing the length and girth of him. What she found pressed against her palm put an eager smile on her face.

"I want to ride this," she purred, bending to drop a hot kiss on his broad chest. The thin sheen of hair tickled her nose before she sat up and let the dress fall off her shoulders.

"Yes," he growled, releasing his erection. "I want you, Abby." Reversing the roles once again, Justin spun her onto her back, bracing above her while reaching for something on the nightstand. Abby didn't know when he'd put the silver box there but was grateful he'd come prepared. Trailing her fingers over taut, defined abs, she watched him open the package with his teeth before she took over, sliding the condom into place.

Instead of taking her right away, he lingered, watching her with a reverence she'd never seen in a man's eyes. This was about more than scratching an itch. Or breaking a dry spell. She could see it on his face, feel it in his touch.

For one brief, beautiful moment, time stopped, the world fell away, and nothing else mattered. "I know," she said, running her knuckles along his jaw. "I know, baby."

As if these were the words he needed to hear, Justin lowered his hips until he was seated against her. Dragging him down, Abby kissed him with every inexplicable emotion surging through her. And as she did, he drove home, slow and steady, until their bodies became one. When he withdrew, aching pleasure suffused her. The kiss deepened as he picked up the pace, their movements shifting from reverent to primal, and at a certain point Abby could do little more than hang on. She clenched around him, lifting to his powerful rhythm.

He abandoned her lips to worship her breasts, suckling one nipple before biting hard enough to make her moan with ecstasy. Passion raged and Abby teetered on the edge. The pressure was almost unbearable until his thumb circled her clit and his name ripped from her lungs, guttural and pleading. She gripped his forearms as her teeth clenched and her ankles locked behind his back. Justin plunged on, roaring through his own orgasm seconds later.

Abby held him tight, reveling in every shake and tremor, knowing exactly how he felt. Their labored breathing cut through the sacred silence, and he finally relaxed against her, careful to shift his weight onto an elbow.

"I thought I knew how good sex could be," he panted, head tucked beneath her chin. "I was wrong."

The smile of a sated woman curled Abby's swollen lips. "And to think," she murmured. "This is only the beginning."

His laughter shook them both. "Me and my big promises."

She edged his face up to look in his eyes. "You aren't crying uncle already, are you?"

Justin brushed a damp lock off her forehead. "Never," he said, reaching down to slide a thumb over her nipple. "I'll make love to you for as long as you'll let me, Abby girl."

An emotion she hadn't experienced in far too long settled deep in her chest. And just like that, her heart drifted into dangerous territory.

"You do make big promises," she said, hoping he couldn't see the tear sliding down her temple.

He kissed the tear away. "Only for you, angel. Only for you."

Justin soaked in the sensation of holding Abby in his arms for several more minutes before sliding off the bed to find a trash can in the bathroom. On his way back to the bed, he lingered in the doorway, savoring every curve sprawled out before him. Though he'd been determined to make this night one that Abby would never forget, the past half hour would be seared in his memory for years to come.

Not only was she beautiful and smart, but one look from her could turn him inside out. Justin would do anything for this woman. He knew it to the center of his soul. And damn if the knowing didn't scare the shit out of him. He'd wanted to please her. Had been determined to have her. And in getting what he wanted, Justin had handed Abby a power he'd never given any woman before her.

The power to break him.

While he lamented the situation, well aware that there would be no undoing what was done, Abby leaned up on her elbows, perfect breasts bare and begging to be licked.

"Are you coming back to bed?" she asked, the vixen demanding a ride replaced by a blushing brunette. "Or do you want something to drink?"

Resigned to his fate, Justin strolled toward the sex-tossed blankets and the woman who now owned his soul. "The only thing I want is you," he said, lying down beside her. Abby rolled onto her side, using his arm as a pillow and wedging her bottom against his growing arousal. When he kissed the tender skin beneath her ear, she sighed, wiggling in tighter.

Body fully recovered, Justin trailed kisses up her shoulder as his hand slid over her abdomen. He squeezed her breast and went rock hard when she moaned from deep in her throat. They ground together, a sensual rock forward and back. When she twisted for him, he took her mouth as his hand dipped lower, past her navel, to find the tiny patch of dark hair between her thighs.

Abby sighed into his mouth as she shivered against him. He hitched his leg over hers, pulling her open to his touch. Her breathing labored, her breasts rose and fell, swelling against his shoulder. After a quick nip of her bottom lip, he stroked his tongue over her taut nipple and found her slick and wet against his searching fingers. Justin entered her, first one finger, and then two, keeping his thumb against her clit, bringing her higher with every stroke.

"Oh, baby," she murmured, eyes closed and body writhing. One adept shift and he lifted her off the mattress to straddle his hips, her hot ass curved against his stomach.

She leaned forward, bracing her hands against his knees, and Justin made quick work sliding the condom into place. As soon as his hands gripped her hips, Abby lowered onto him, his name like a prayer on her lips as he drove into the hilt. Scorched and senseless, he gritted his teeth as she rose up to take him again. Her cries devolved into incomprehensible begging until he pushed her forward, rising onto his knees as her hands locked on to the oak footboard.

A tight grip on her hips, he entered her again, and Abby thrust back as her head dropped with a moan. Seconds before his control snapped, Justin reached around to bring her to climax, and with a final lunge, her head shot up, sending dark hair trailing over his shoulder as they touched the sky together. Dragging her up until they were both on their knees, he clasped her against his chest and whispered in her ear.

"You're mine, Abigail." His arms tightened with the power surging through his veins. "You're mine."

❧

The moment Abby sensed Justin had drifted off, she slithered from the bed an inch at a time, careful not to wake him. Plucking his shirt off the floor, she slipped into it and hurriedly fastened several buttons before shuffling into the hall.

As if she'd escaped from a terrifying situation, she pressed her back to the wall, holding her breath in the silence. Soft snores carried from the bed and Abby relaxed. Unsteady legs carried her to the couch, where she plopped down and hugged a newly purchased pillow in her lap. Staring at the bare coffee table, she struggled to process the last hour.

For one, sex with Justin would undoubtedly be the highlight of the year. Possibly the decade. She could still feel his hands touching her, smell his scent on her skin. Hear his words in her ears.

You're mine, Abigail. You're mine.

She couldn't argue that after what they'd just done; she'd belong to him as long as he'd have her. But did that mean *he* belonged to *her?*

Thinking rationally was almost impossible with the sex fog muddying her brain. Her teeth were still tingling, for heaven's sake. Curling her toes against the couch cushion, Abby rested her chin on the pillow and forced herself to focus. She hadn't been with a man in a long time. No one but Kyle in nearly a decade, and with him deployed so often during their marriage, she'd never really been intimate with anyone on a regular basis. All of which explained the mixed emotions spinning in her stomach. Doubt, hope, panic, wonder.

But most of all, fear.

Like a tsunami, the what-ifs rolled in. What if they'd gone too fast? What if they couldn't stand each other in the morning? Or worse, what if she never wanted him to leave? Abby panicked at the idea of Justin becoming a permanent part of her life. Saying that she wanted what her friends and family had and actually staring it in the face were two drastically different things.

You're mine, Abigail.

Abby flung the pillow to the side as she bolted from the couch. The orgasms must have knocked something loose in her brain, she thought, tiptoeing to the kitchen. Wine wouldn't clear her mind, but it might calm her nerves, and right now Abby was willing to try anything.

Justin woke in a strange bed, staring at an empty pillow and picking up faint music in the distance. Within seconds he knew he was naked, and then he remembered why.

"Abby," he whispered, rolling onto his back. A quick search of the room revealed no other inhabitants. The clock on the nightstand said eight thirty, and the darkness visible through the curtains assured him he hadn't slept through to morning. Thank God.

Brushing the sheet off his hips, Justin dropped his feet to the floor and found his boxer briefs. If Abby was skittish enough to put distance between them, he probably didn't need to creep up on her buck naked. Leaning through the doorway, he paused to locate the source of the music. Not a voice he recognized, but he liked the sound.

Stepping into the hall, he could see the empty living room and headed for the kitchen, where he found Abby engulfed in his shirt with a glass of wine in her hand. A female voice, bluesy and filled with longing, debated whether or not to fall in love through a tiny speaker next to the stove.

Justin didn't know what the singer would ultimately decide, but he knew without a doubt how he'd like things to go in real life. Some men ran from commitment, but Justin had never been that type. With Victoria he'd let ambition and money cloud his vision and nearly made a hefty mistake. One he *could* have undone, but not before she took him for everything he was worth.

A near miss with the wrong woman made it damn clear when the right one came along.

"Hey there," he said, keeping his voice soft so as not to startle her. "I missed you."

Abby didn't flinch. Or turn his way. "I decided to have a drink."

Justin spotted the half-empty bottle on the counter and the empty glass next to it. "Mind if I have some?"

"Help yourself."

Stepping around the island, he poured half a glass before leaning a hip against the edge of the new countertop. He could see her face clearly now, at least the half not covered by dark, tousled hair. Green eyes stared forward, unfocused, as if whatever she was looking at didn't exist in the room with them.

"Nice music," he said, and her eyes cut to his.

"You like this?"

He listened for a few more lines, until the singer voiced her fear of ending up alone. "I do," Justin said. "Not exactly a happy tune, but she's hopeful."

Her attention returned to the little speaker next to the hole left by the missing stove. "You think?"

"Yeah," he said, closing the distance between them. "I think." Trailing a knuckle along her jawline, he took a chance. "Why did you leave the bed, Abby?"

She shook her head. "I couldn't think in there."

"Maybe we don't need to think tonight."

"Maybe we don't, but my brain has a mind of its own." Justin chuckled, but Abby didn't seem to catch the humor in her statement. "What's so funny?"

He sobered. "Nothing, honey." Setting his glass on the island behind her, he brushed the hair from her eyes and tipped her chin up. "Do you regret anything we've done tonight?"

"No," she whispered, allowing Justin to breathe again.

"Good. Now, based on your song choice, I'm guessing that you're trying to figure out where we go from here. Am I close?"

"It's a lot," she said, trailing a fingernail down his breastbone. "I haven't felt this much in a long time. Maybe ever."

He'd celebrate that little triumph later. "That's a good thing, right?" he asked.

Abby sighed. "That's a scary thing."

Lifting her off the floor, he propped her on the island and nestled between her legs. "There's nothing scary about this," he soothed, sliding his hands beneath the hem of the shirt. "Just let go, Abby. I'll catch you."

Slipping her arms around his neck, she twirled one hand into his hair. "I like the sound of that."

"And I like the sound you make when you come apart against me." Skating his palms up her rib cage, he leaned in closer. "Let me love you, baby. Come back to bed."

Silky legs locked around his hips as she murmured "Yes" against his cheek.

Justin carried her down the hall, one hand tucked beneath her ass while the other worked open the buttons of his shirt. Before they reached the bed, the shirt hit the floor, followed by an empty wineglass that they were too distracted to see roll out of sight. The mattress dipped as he lowered her gently into the center, but Abby didn't seem interested in gentle this time. With impressive speed, she dragged the boxer briefs to the floor and kissed the tip of his erection. A groan ripped from his lungs as she took him deep, and it was Justin's turn to feel weak in the knees.

Her tongue slicked down the side of him and then back up until he filled her mouth again. Jaw locked tight, Justin closed his eyes and shoved his hands into her hair, using every ounce of focus to hold back. To make it last. God, she was so good. Scalding heat threatened to fry his brain as every muscle tightened with unleashed desire. When she cupped his balls, he roared with release as the orgasm splintered through him, leaving him breathless and shaky.

Unable to support his own weight, he leaned forward until his hands pressed to the bed and his forehead rested on her shoulder. "You're amazing," he panted, dropping a quick kiss along her collarbone.

"I've been wanting to do that all night," she drawled, leaning back and pulling him down with her. "That seemed like the right time."

Nuzzling into her neck, Justin licked behind her earlobe. "Whenever you get the urge to do that again, I'll happily oblige."

Suddenly playful, she trailed her nails up his rib cage. "What if I get the urge in the middle of the day?"

"Anywhere. Anytime. I'm all yours."

Abby tipped up his face until their eyes met. "That's what I needed to hear."

Dazed by the weight of her words, he brushed his thumb over her damp lips. "I was always yours, Abby. And I always will be."

As if sealing a vow, Justin spent the rest of the night fulfilling the promise he'd made in the kitchen—loving her until they drifted off to sleep together.

Chapter 15

"Earth to Abby," Haleigh said, snapping her fingers an inch from her friend's nose. "Are you in there?"

Shaking her head, Abby dragged her thoughts back to the present, blinking at the bright walls and eclectic decor surrounding her. "I'm here," she said, rising off the leather bench inside the entrance of Mamacita's Mexican Restaurant. "I'm ready."

Though she wasn't really here at all. She was still in last night, punch-drunk on sex, floating on an emotional high both raw and addictive. Justin had kissed, suckled, and deliciously tortured every inch of her body until she'd screamed his name loud enough to wake the neighbors. Once he'd talked her off the cliff in her kitchen and then stroked her body to heights she hadn't even known existed, she'd slept like a woman spent and satisfied until he'd woken her—in the best way possible—just before eight.

Mowing his parents' yard had been on the agenda for first thing that morning, though Karen Donovan would never know that her yard was technically the second thing her son had *done* that day.

"I said your name three times," Haleigh whispered as the hostess showed them to their table.

"I was thinking about something else," Abby admitted, working to keep the smile off her face and failing miserably.

Her friend chuckled. "That was obvious."

The voluptuous brunette stopped at a corner booth and spread five menus around the table. "Here you go," she said with a lovely Spanish accent.

"We don't need—" Abby started, but Haleigh cut her off.

"This will be fine, thanks." She edged onto the red vinyl seat and scooted around to the back of the large, round table. Looking up at Abby, she said, "What are you waiting for?"

Unless her friend had three little mice in her pocket, their lunch for two had been upgraded. "Who else is coming?"

"Just Lorelei, Snow, and Carrie," the blonde said, tapping the seat beside her. "But not for another fifteen minutes, so get in here and start talking."

Great. Abby's quiet lunch with her best friend would now be a gathering of four crazy-in-love women—and her. Lorelei had become the baking queen since returning to town two years ago, Snow owned a charming flea-market-type store downtown, and Carrie ran a women's shelter on the outskirts of town. Including Haleigh, all four women had significant others who treated them like the desirable, deserving women that they were.

And then there was Abby.

"You could have told me they were coming," she mentioned, taking the spot Haleigh had tapped.

Haleigh opened her menu. "And you could have told me that you were going into business with Justin Donovan instead of blindsiding me with the news yesterday."

Not telling her mother had been intentional, but she hadn't kept the news from her best friend on purpose.

"The business idea only came to fruition Thursday morning. By the time I finished helping Mama with wedding stuff and ran another errand that afternoon, you were on duty at the hospital."

"You could have come by and told me. Though I suppose the hospital is the last place you want to be these days. Still, a call would have been nice."

Recalling what she'd done instead of calling, Abby hid a blush behind her menu. "I was busy."

One slender finger lowered the laminated flyer. "Busy with your new partner?" Haleigh asked.

Once upon a time she and Haleigh had shared every single secret, from the first time either of them went to second base with a boy—Abby had rounded first three months before her friend—to the difficult times when Haleigh had fallen off the wagon. But since Kyle's death, which for a while had planted a wedge between them, their friendship hadn't been the same. To the point that Abby had, in her anger and grief, nearly ruined her friend's romance with her brother.

The fact was, she missed how things used to be. And maybe moving on meant going back, in this one way.

Closing her menu, Abby clasped her hands on the table. "Justin made me dinner at the firehouse on Thursday, and then he brought a pizza to my place last night." Tossing a wicked grin Haleigh's way, she added, "We had sex all night and I couldn't even tell you how many orgasms I had."

Haleigh jerked back as if she'd been smacked. "Are. You. Serious?" she loud-whispered. "All night? Is that why you're freaking glowing?"

Abby nodded. "I don't know if not having it for two years made it that much better, but holy cheese and crackers, that man is *good*. I mean, he's *really good*."

"He must be," she laughed. "I haven't seen you lit up like this in years. But what happened to all that 'I'm too old for him' crap?"

That really had been crap. "It's only five years. Kyle was seven years older than me and no one batted an eye." Recalling the scene in the beauty salon, she corrected, "Except my mother, apparently, but she never said anything until yesterday."

"Linda didn't approve of you and Kyle?"

"Not at first, I guess. When I told her about me and Justin, she got all bent out of shape and kept referring to him as 'that boy.' As if he's still ten years old."

A waiter appeared with two glasses of water and a bowl of chips and salsa.

"We have some friends coming, so we're going to wait to order," Haleigh said.

"No problem. I'll come back when the table is full." Dark brown eyes lingered on Abby longer than necessary before he smiled and walked away.

"I think our waiter likes you," Haleigh mumbled. "They say men can tell when a woman's been getting busy. I bet he can smell it."

"That's gross," Abby declared. "Besides, I showered this morning." Not alone, but she'd showered.

"I'm just sayin'," Haleigh defended. "It's simple science. Pheromones, I tell you."

"You can shove your pheromones up your—"

"Be nice, young lady. Getting yourself a boy toy is supposed to make you nicer."

Abby reached for a corn chip. "I don't like that term."

Once again flipping through the menu, Haleigh said, "He's the younger man with whom you're having a fling. What else would you call him?"

"This isn't a fling," she corrected, snapping the chip in half. "I don't do flings and you know it."

Awarding Abby her full attention, her tablemate grew serious. "If it isn't a fling, then what is it? Because you can't really see Justin Donovan as long-term material."

Abby reached for the salsa. "I can see Justin Donovan in whatever way I want. He's a good man, and he cares about me."

"You've known him for a week."

"I've known him for nearly twenty years. I know his parents," she pointed out. "I know where he grew up and we went to the same school. And his senior year he used to deliver flowers to the hospital and would stop to see me all the time."

"You make it sound like we ran in the same circles when in reality we graduated a year *before* he stepped foot in the hallowed halls of Ardent Springs High. I couldn't even tell you what he looked like back then. And he hasn't been a senior for a decade, which means you have no idea what he's been doing for the last ten years." As if sharing some ominous secret, she added, "Mom says he's back in Ardent Springs because he got fired from his job in Chicago for some shady business dealings."

Losing her appetite, Abby dropped the chip onto her napkin. "I'm not interested in town gossip. I know he lost his job."

"Not lost," Haleigh corrected. "Was fired. There's a difference. A man used to closing million-dollar deals doesn't settle for seasonal landscaping in Ardent Springs."

Amazed by the sudden disapproval, she shook her head in wonder. "A few minutes ago he was an acceptable candidate to sleep with, but now he's a money-hungry, possibly corrupt businessman who's going to what? Embezzle my life savings and leave me heartbroken? The classic tale of a young con artist and the unwitting, love-starved widow who believes he really loves her?"

"You've never been a drama queen before," Haleigh muttered, pinning her with an angry glare. "Did you know that he accused me of not paying attention to you? He says that I flaunt my relationship with Cooper in your face and that it makes you miserable to see us happy."

Staring at the cluster of hubcaps attached to the ceiling, Abby said, "He shouldn't have told you that."

"Then it's true?"

Gnawing the inside of her lip, Abby didn't answer right away.

"Be honest with me, Abbs. Is that how you feel?"

"It's just hard," she confessed. "I'm happy for you guys. Really, I am. And I'm happy for everyone else. But I've spent two years mourning and watching you all pair off. Even Mama." She ripped her straw paper into tiny pieces. "I'm like the last woman standing. I must have mentioned my feelings to Justin, but I didn't mean for him to repeat them."

Haleigh lowered her voice. "Abby Lou, I want you to be happy. I want you to find love. But don't mistake the first guy to come along for the right guy."

Abby hadn't labeled Justin as Mr. Right. At least not yet.

"I'm not saying I hear wedding bells or picture us growing old together. I get it. It's fast—probably too fast—and crazy, and a month ago I'd have run in the opposite direction, but I'm through running from things that scare me or don't fit in my practical little box. I'm going to see where this leads, and I don't want to feel like my best friend is sitting around waiting for me to be wrong."

"But what if you are?"

"What if I'm not?" Abby took a deep breath. "The truth is, Haleigh, I don't have anything to lose. This is a win or break-even situation for me, and I'm ready to take the risk."

Softening, the woman who knew her better than anyone in the world shook her head. "I knew you were attracted to him, but I didn't see this coming at all. You've never even gone out with a younger man."

Voicing what seemed to be her motto these days, Abby said, "There's a first time for everything."

"I guess so," Haleigh laughed, diffusing the tension. "He seems to really like you, so I'll give him the benefit of the doubt for now, but do me one favor."

Relieved to have her friend's support, she said, "What's that?"

"Ask the important questions. Find out what happened in Chicago and if he's back for good." When Abby bristled, she added, "You don't have to share what you learn. Let the gossips think what they want. I'm simply saying that you're less likely to regret this if there are no surprises down the road."

She had a point. Not that Abby doubted him, but she *was* curious about those complications he'd mentioned before.

"That's fair," she agreed, "but I won't interrogate him. If there's anything he doesn't want to share, I won't force him."

Haleigh didn't appear to like the compromise, but the rest of their party finally arrived, leaving her no option to argue.

Justin stank. Why couldn't his parents have one of those cozy quarter-acre lots? No, they had to have five acres. Because two people with no young kids or animals or even a freaking garden needed five acres. Dropping onto the glider inside the screened-in porch where he'd spent many a night growing up, Justin gave his aching muscles a break. To be fair, some of the soreness likely stemmed from last night's rigorous activity, but Justin regretted nothing.

They had eventually gotten to the pizza, Abby once again clad in his shirt and him in his underwear. He couldn't remember ever having that comfortable a meal with a woman. Justin had regaled her with stories from his days at Northwestern, many fueled by liquor and bravado, while she shared tales of her most bizarre patients over the years. His favorite had been the elderly gentleman who kept ringing for a nurse and then stripping himself bare before they arrived and demanding a sponge bath.

When it came down to it, you couldn't blame a guy for trying.

"I see you're sitting down on the job," his father said, stepping onto the porch and letting the screen door slam behind him. "Am I paying you to lounge around my glider?"

"You aren't paying me at all," Justin reminded him, accepting the chilled glass of tea. He'd missed sweet tea while living in Chicago. The one time he'd ordered it, the young waitress had brought him a tiny pot of hot water, a mug, a tea bag, and twelve packs of sugar. Needless to say, he hadn't made that mistake again.

Father and son rested in companionable silence, watching a determined fly bounce off the screen. Over the years, they'd learned to appreciate these quiet moments, mostly because they were few and far between. The word *silence* did not reside in Karen Donovan's vocabulary. She believed in conversing *all the time*, and lucky for them, required little to no participation on their part. They loved her. They'd do anything for her. But that didn't mean they couldn't enjoy her absence from time to time.

"Pulled in a little later than planned this morning, didn't you?" Pop asked.

Justin's target start time had been seven thirty in order to beat the heat, since the cool April temps had given way to hot May days. But showering with a wet, purring Abby had delayed his departure. Again, Justin regretted nothing.

"I got hung up," he replied, keeping the details to himself. Details that had been replaying in his mind all morning, doing more to raise his body temperature than the sun or heightened humidity. Lost in the memories, he'd smiled wide enough at one point to nearly swallow an unsuspecting bug. Hard to tell which one of them had been more surprised.

After swallowing a sip of his own drink, Ken Donovan switched topics. "Your mother says you got the job of prettying up our downtown."

Justin nodded, rolling the cold glass across his forehead. "We did, indeed. The turnaround will be tight, but I think we'll hit the deadline."

"We?" his father asked, always more astute than one would guess from his slow drawl and even keel.

"I got myself a partner," he explained. "Abigail Williams. Do you remember her?"

"Your babysitter?"

"That's the one."

A weighted pause preceded his next question. "She's a widow now, isn't she?"

Though his wife would swear the man never listened, her husband proved her wrong on a regular basis. "Yes, she is." Justin saw the next question coming as clear as the weeping willow bowing in the distance, but he let the older man ask it anyway.

"Is that where you got hung up?"

Gripping his pop's knee, Justin grinned. "You taught me never to kiss and tell, remember?"

"Well," he said, rubbing the gray stubble along his chin. "I wasn't asking for any details. She's a good girl. A lot better than that bit of fluff you were going to marry up in the big city."

Pop had only met Victoria twice, and the Donovan patriarch had never voiced an opinion about her one way or the other. Interesting to know that his father saw the fluff before he did.

"I can't argue with that." Eager to finish the trimming, he chugged the rest of the tea and set the empty glass on the table beside him. "You have a full schedule today?" Justin asked, rising to his feet. His father had been working six days a week for as long as he could remember, always making time to come home for lunch.

The older man rose beside him, a little slower than he used to be. "Not too bad. Does this new business mean you plan to stick around for a while?"

Justin's long-range plan still included moving back to the city. He just didn't know which one yet. Or when. "For the time being, sure," he answered. "But I'm keeping my options open."

Stepping out of character, Pop said, "I've never been one to give advice, but I have a suggestion, if you're interested."

Curious, Justin kept an open mind. "I'm interested."

"If the option to stay for the long haul comes around, think about taking it."

His mother had always been vocal about wanting Justin to come home for visits, yet neither of his parents had ever pressured him to return for good. Which made this *suggestion* all the more unexpected.

"My line of work doesn't really fit in a small-town setting."

Ice clanged as Pop tapped his glass against his leg. "Mom misses you when you're gone. And she's been right happy to have you home. As have I." A strong hand patted Justin's shoulder. "Might be nice to make it permanent. But it's just an idea." He shuffled toward the door to the kitchen. "Finish up out there before it gets any hotter. Seems like summer comes earlier every year now. Good for business, but tough on an old body."

As he reached for the screen, Justin said, "You're barely pushing sixty, Pop. That isn't so old."

The laugh lines around deep blue eyes lengthened. "Old isn't always a number, son. Just think about what I said."

The slam of the screen door echoed like a punctuation mark on his father's parting words. Sure, his parents were getting up there, but sixty was the new forty, right? And as far as Justin knew, Ken Donovan was the model of good health. Mom made sure he ate right, and just last year he'd charged ahead of the pack, dragging poor Aunt Dodie along, to win the annual sack race at the church picnic. Justin knew because he'd received a slew of pictures from his mom. Enough to fill two emails.

Maybe it would have been nice to cheer his dad and Dodie on in person, but his career had kept him somewhere else. And would likely take him away again. Trudging out to the edge of the fence, where he'd left the trimmer, Justin shoved his earbuds into place and cranked the music. If the lot Q had found worked out, there might be a chance he could work the development angle from Nashville, which would put him close enough to visit as often as he wanted.

Letting the idea simmer, he jerked the trimmer to life and made quick work of the growing weeds.

Chapter 16

"Let me get this straight," Lorelei chimed. "The bearded giant with a Harley, a killer leather jacket, and muscles that go on for days is making cookies?"

Carrie beamed with pride. "That's right. He says it calms his nerves, and he likes the precision of it."

Abby didn't know much about Noah Winchester. A bit older than all of them, he'd spent years in the military, mostly serving in the Middle East, and had fallen hard for Carrie Farmer over the winter. There'd been rumors that he'd nearly killed a man to protect Carrie, but nothing was ever confirmed, and every time Abby saw him, he was either toting Carrie's little girl, Molly, around on his shoulders or flying her through the air, eliciting an endless supply of giggles and hand claps.

Neither of which seemed like something a man with a murderous streak would do.

"He did a fabulous job on our deck," Snow cut in. "We expected the work to take a week, but he knocked the whole thing out in four days. Caleb says he's never seen anyone with that kind of focus."

Caleb McGraw was another mystery to Abby. He and Snow were the only non-natives in their circle of friends. The media conglomerate heir hailed from an old-money family in Baton Rouge, Louisiana, and had chosen Snow, an ordinary girl from Birmingham, who happened to be biracial, over his parents' less-than-tactful protestations. Movie-star gorgeous, Caleb had ingratiated himself with the locals from the moment he crossed the city limits sign, and by all accounts, no one seemed to remember that he hadn't been born on Tennessee soil.

"Spencer would have helped with that deck," Lorelei offered. "Though the custom cabinet orders have kept him busy lately, he'd have made time."

The Spencer and Lorelei story beat the others for both duration and complication. The pair had been high school sweethearts before Lorelei gave the town the big *F you* and headed for the lights of Hollywood. After which Spencer recovered and married Carrie. By the time Lorelei returned two years ago, her ex was once again a free man, Carrie was married to someone else, and before long they were all close friends, sending more than one tongue wagging with speculation.

That same summer, Carrie's husband, Patch, managed to get himself killed in a bar fight, leaving her pregnant and alone. Thanks to Lorelei, by the time Molly was born Carrie had a job and a place to live, which just happened to be on Noah's grandparents' old property.

When Abby really thought about her friends and their happy endings, all earned and much deserved, she couldn't help but wonder what they'd done right and what she'd done wrong. When the day started she'd felt like maybe Justin could be her second chance, but Haleigh's misgivings delivered a hefty dose of reality. Abby didn't really know him, not yet anyway, and until they reached a few more milestones, she'd do well to keep her heart protected.

"Stop arguing with me," Snow said, jerking the bill from Haleigh's grasp. "I said I'm paying for everyone."

"Wait. What?" Abby said. She'd zoned out and missed something.

When Lorelei and Carrie began to protest, Snow held up two hands to shush them all.

"I'm paying for this as a celebration," she said, pressing a tight curl out of her eyes. "Because nine months from now I won't be able to fit in this booth anymore, and not because I will have eaten too much queso dip."

Four women blinked in unison as Snow's announcement sank in. And then, all at once, they burst half out of their seats, hindered by the large table holding them in.

"Scoot!" Haleigh shouted, shoving Carrie, who was already shuffling over, out of the booth. "Wait. Why am I just now hearing about this?" she asked. "Tell me you aren't using another doctor. I'll be crushed if you do."

As an OB/GYN, Haleigh had delivered Carrie's daughter as well as Jessi's little girl, Emma.

"I took a home test and have an appointment with you this week," Snow informed her, laughing happy tears. "And I can't stop doing this." She pointed at her cheeks. "I'm a freaking waterspout."

"Ah, hormones," Carrie said. "You gotta love 'em."

By the time Abby broke free of the table, Lorelei had engulfed Snow in a hug and was jumping up and down.

"Oh my gosh," she said. "Am I shaking the baby?" Lorelei patted Snow's flat stomach. "I'm sorry, little one. I'm just so happy to meet you."

"What did Caleb say?" Carrie asked as Abby finally took her turn at the hug.

"I thought he was going to faint when I first told him." Snow laughed, glowing as only an expectant mother could. "And then he started talking about bed rest and swing sets, and I haven't had to load the dishwasher in four days."

"You've known about this for four days?" Lorelei bellowed.

Snow nodded like a bobblehead. "It's killed me to wait to tell you all." The tears picked up steam now, and soon all of them were crying.

Abby grabbed a handful of napkins off the table and passed them around. "I'm so happy for you, Snow," she said, and meant it. Right before Kyle had been killed, they'd decided to start a family on his next trip home, which was supposed to be an extended one. Losing him had also meant losing that chance, and for a long time she'd felt a twinge of remorse whenever the subject of babies came up.

Just one more thing she needed to let go of.

Dabbing at her lashes, Snow sniffled. "We've actually been trying for six months. I was starting to think it wasn't going to happen."

Crying as one now, they came in for a group hug, immune to the curious stares from surrounding diners.

"I have lots of clothes for you if it's a girl," Carrie said.

"And I'll buy more," Lorelei assured her.

"We all know what I'm offering," Haleigh added, leaving Abby as the lone bystander.

With a shrug, she said, "I'm an excellent babysitter."

Laughter mixed with tears as purses were gathered and leftovers packed up. By the time they stepped into the midday sun, predictions had been made, a shower had been discussed, and Lorelei and Carrie had all but designed the future nursery. Abby watched and laughed, pretending that she fit somewhere in the picture but still feeling like a spare wheel. These women had husbands and fiancés, and before long they'd all have growing families.

While she'd be Auntie Abby, the fun old lady who never had kids of her own. Rolling her eyes at her own wayward thoughts, she reminded herself that thirty-three was *not* that old, and there was plenty of time to have a family. After all, Mama was in her fifties and planning a wedding. Not that Abby wanted to wait that long, but twenty years was better than never.

Once good-byes were shared, Snow, Lorelei, and Carrie crossed the parking lot toward Lorelei's fancy new Nissan Rogue while Haleigh walked Abby to her car.

"You okay?" she said, locking arms.

"I am," Abby assured her.

"Really?" Haleigh pressed, nudging her shoulder. "Because you're walking a little funny."

She pushed the evil woman away, laughing as she did. "See if I tell you anything ever again, Haleigh Rae."

Sauntering toward her own car, Haleigh called, "Love your guts, Abby Lou!"

"Yeah, yeah, yeah," she replied, smiling at the endearment they'd been exchanging since they were kids. "Love you, too."

∽

By the time he'd locked the yard equipment in the shed, Justin was thankful he'd driven the old Chevy instead of his Infiniti. There was no way he'd crawl into his baby covered in this much sweat, leather seats or not.

Desperate for a shower, he found a parking space half a block from the bookstore and tried not to offend those he passed on the sidewalk. To avoid stinking out Bruce's patrons, he turned at the corner to take the back entrance up to his apartment, but before reaching the back corner of the building, a voice called from behind him.

"Heya, buddy," said Q, his suit loose and wrinkled, as if he'd slept in it. "'Bout time you showed up."

Hackles up, Justin cut the distance between them. "What are you doing here?"

The cause of all his problems waved a hand in front of his face. "What did you roll in, man? You smell worse than our frat house bathroom."

"Answer the question," Justin ordered.

As Culpepper slid his hands into his pockets, a smug grin curled his thin lips. "You didn't think I'd let you cut me out of this, did you?"

"There's nothing to cut you out of," he pointed out. "That lot you found isn't worth the time." A bald-faced lie Justin uttered with no remorse. If, once he'd done his research, the interstate lot showed potential, he'd move forward. Alone.

"Give me a break." Q's grin didn't falter. "I know you, buddy. And I know a deal when I see one. That land is our redeeming grace, and I'm not going to let you screw me out of my half."

Justin didn't like surprises. He'd counted on the die-hard city slicker's repugnance for small towns. That he'd shown up on the streets of Ardent Springs meant Q was desperate, and desperate men made mistakes.

"There are plenty of other deals out there, Q. Go back to Chicago and find one."

"My name is mud in Chicago, thanks to you."

Dangerous and delusional. "We both know how that went down. You screwed up, not me."

"You gave the go-ahead," Q reminded him. "You cut the same corners I did."

"No," Justin bit out. "The only mistake I made was trusting you to do your job."

"As the leader, checking the reports was *your* responsibility."

"Reports that you put together. You knew that Rockwood was on the verge of going under, yet you guaranteed that the numbers looked good."

"Howie told me they could pull it off. Our job was going to save his dad's business."

Howie Rockwood had been another college buddy that Justin had mistakenly put his faith in.

"Rule number one of real estate development," he growled. "Make sure the money is there. You don't trust someone's word, no matter who they are."

"I trusted Howie, and you trusted me," Quintin snapped. "But I'm the fuckup and you're the one who got screwed? How do you figure?"

Justin had run through the facts countless times, always arriving at the same conclusion. He'd been as much to blame as Q was, only more so because he'd known better. A realization that never failed to piss him off.

"The fall came down on all of us," he consented. "Lesson learned. You want to redeem your name? Do it somewhere else."

He turned away, but Q didn't give up. "Nashville is one of, if not *the* fastest-growing cities in the country. That means expansion, and your little burb is plenty close enough to benefit from that growth. The interstate lot could be just the beginning. Within five years we could turn Ardent Springs into a Music City suburb. Housing developments are small beans compared to skyscrapers, but they're steady money. Money that can be invested elsewhere for a bigger profit."

Meaning he'd fill their town with cookie-cutter houses, putting quantity over quality, and then, instead of investing the profits back into the local economy, he'd gamble them away on bigger, riskier deals. Justin might be ambitious, but he still had a conscience.

"Go back to Chicago," he snarled. "Your kind of deals aren't wanted here."

"Dammit, Donovan, I have nothing to go back to."

Before he could answer, Justin spotted Abby coming their way. "I can't talk right now," he said, eyes focused over the other man's shoulder. "Call me later."

Too bad Q didn't take the hint. Instead he spun to see what or who had captured his friend's attention. Pretty in a light blue skirt and white T beneath a denim jacket, she strolled up to them, curiosity in her emerald eyes.

"Hey there," she said, glancing from Justin to Q and back again. "What's going on?"

"Nothing important," he snapped, sending his friend a warning glare.

"I'm Quintin Culpepper," the bastard said, knowing full well the friendly greeting would piss Justin off. "Donovan and I went to college together."

"Oh." She seemed surprised, likely because Q was a stranger, and those didn't pass through Ardent Springs very often. Especially not while wearing disheveled gray suits. "Nice to meet you, Quintin."

"You can call me Q. All my friends do." Dull blue eyes assessed Abby from head to toe, tempting Justin to rip his head off. "Are all the girls in this town as pretty as you are?"

That did it. "Time to go, Q." Justin gripped his buddy's arm, dragging him toward Main Street. "If you want me to help save your ass," he whispered, "stay away from the locals. Call me tomorrow."

Twisting to catch another glimpse of Abby, he said, "Does Vicki know you've already replaced her?"

Slamming the piece of shit against the wall, Justin leaned in until their noses nearly touched. "I will not hesitate to show you exactly what we do to worthless weasels down here in the South. And if you think small town means there aren't plenty of places to lose a body, you're wrong."

Breathing heavy, Q no longer smiled. "Careful, bro. Your redneck is showing."

"Suck it, Culpepper."

Ticked off at himself as much as Q, Justin returned to Abby without looking back.

As he blew by her, Justin snagged Abby's hand and pulled her along with him. Struggling to keep up, she said, "Call me crazy, but that seemed like an odd way to talk to a college buddy."

"It's a long story," he said, rounding the corner into the alley behind the bookstore.

"I'd like to hear it," she huffed. Her legs weren't long enough to maintain his pace.

Pinning her against the rear entrance to the store, he kissed her senseless, igniting her body and dragging a ragged moan from deep in her chest. She clung to strong shoulders, the gray cotton damp to the touch.

Justin broke the kiss. "Don't ask me about Q, okay?"

Dazed and distracted, she murmured, "Why not?"

"He has nothing to do with us."

The instinct not to push warred with the promise she'd made Haleigh. "You can tell me anything, Justin. I want to know about your life."

"That part of my life is over." A green-stained hand trailed down her neck before he jerked away. "I'm filthy," he said. "I'm going to get you dirty."

Abby didn't mind a little dirt and sweat if it meant being kissed like that. Unable to let the previous scene go, she said, "For a minute there I thought you were going to hurt him."

Hazel eyes darkened like the sky before a spring storm. "I didn't like the way he looked at you."

"I didn't like the way he looked at me, either," she confessed. "But whatever happened out there involved more than a harmless leer. Why did you react like that?"

He shook his head, sending a wilted clover cascading to the ground. "I told you. He crossed a line."

All kinds of lines were being crossed today. Accepting defeat, for now, Abby said, "You should probably go take a shower. I'm actually here to help Mama with something for the wedding."

Humor returning, he teased, "You mean you aren't here to see me?"

"Sadly, no. But my schedule *is* clear for this evening."

"Are you propositioning me, Ms. Williams?" he asked, the storm clouds fading.

"Maybe," she teased. "Would you like to see a movie with me?"

After two years of endless fundraising and hard work, the Ruby Theater had finally reopened for business. For weeks, she'd been dying to watch a film from the old-fashioned balcony.

"*The African Queen* is playing at the Ruby," Abby added. "I'll even buy you a bag of popcorn."

Justin tugged on the edge of her jacket. "No way I'd pass up an offer like that."

Not many men jumped at the chance to watch a classic from the fifties, even with stars like Hepburn and Bogart. "Really?" she asked. "You'll go?"

Strong hands drew her to him. "Abby girl, I'd go anywhere with you. Just say the word and I'm there."

Their lips barely touched, and she pressed up on her toes to get closer. "You always know just what to say," she breathed.

"And you always smell like heaven."

Feeling flirty, she asked, "How do you know I smell like heaven?"

"Because whenever I'm with you, it's like holding an angel."

A husky laugh bubbled out. "That might be your best line yet."

"I might have read that one in a book," he confided.

"Well, at least you're honest." Abby caved to the urge and dragged him down for a searing kiss, longing to show him how much he meant to her. The moment he once again crushed her against the door, the cell phone in her pocket chirped to life. Breaking contact, she sighed. "That's probably Mama wondering where I am."

"Do you want to text back and tell her we're testing the strength of her boyfriend's alley door?"

Abby pushed him away. "Cute *and* funny. Look at you." Checking the phone, she accepted her fate. "I need to go. She's got mason jars and rope, and I have no idea what we're going to do with them, but when there's a glue gun involved, it's always painful."

When she stepped aside, Justin opened the steel door. "I'll kiss any burnt fingertips tonight. What time should I pick you up?"

"I'll meet you here." Since the Ruby was only blocks away, making him drive to her place and back seemed pointless. "Movie starts at seven fifteen, so I'll be here by six forty-five. Sound good?"

"Works for me."

"There you are!" exclaimed her mother as they stepped into the darkness of the back offices. "What were you two doing out there?"

Being the smart man that he was, Justin gave the older woman a silent salute before disappearing up the black metal stairs to his apartment.

"Are we ready to decorate mason jars?" Abby asked, ignoring the question.

One cherry-blonde brow arched. "The glue gun is hot and ready to go. And don't think I don't know what was going on out there."

Abby lowered her voice. "Like I don't know what goes on when Bruce's car stays parked in your driveway all night long? Why don't you just move into the new house already? It isn't as if you're remaining chaste until your wedding night."

Dimpled cheeks turned the same shade as her thin curls. "I don't know what you're talking about, Abigail."

"Sure you don't, Mama," she chimed, coaxing the woman toward the office on the left. "And Justin and I were discussing knitting out in the alley."

Chapter 17

"This is going to be too easy," Q bragged, clueless as usual.

"We need to go walk it again." Justin curled into the Infiniti, waiting for his shortsighted friend to settle into the passenger seat.

He hadn't liked the idea of taking a morning away from the downtown project to research the interstate tract, but if he wanted his former coworker gone, they needed to determine if the property was even worth pursuing. Abby had needed the time off for a dress fitting for the wedding, so he'd moved forward with a meeting, tired of Q's endless text messages on the subject.

In order to prepare, Justin had insisted they walk the property to see for themselves what they'd be getting. The sign near the highway read plus or minus six acres, which, depending on the investors, could be an adequate amount or not enough.

Building a couple of gas stations alone wasn't worth the effort. Hotels were a must, and if they really wanted to entice folks off the interstate, they'd include an outlet mall featuring all the top brands. The jobs created, plus the tax revenues for the county, should silence any naysayers who saw progress as a four-letter word.

"Come on, Justin. It rained yesterday. That field is going to be a mess, and these are my best shoes."

"Then you can sit in the car."

The broker's office had been in Madison, a mostly commercial area of Nashville east of I-65. During the hour drive—normally forty-five minutes but extended thanks to Friday morning traffic and an accident at the Goodlettsville exit—Justin had endured Q's nonstop chatter.

In Q's world, which was seemingly filled with rainbows and unicorn parades, no one held a grudge, everything was simple, and the past never happened. He was the human equivalent of a goldfish.

In most situations, boundless optimism combined with unlimited generosity were admirable traits. In the real estate development world they were seen as faults, especially when the person in question leaned more toward gullibility than altruism. When Justin had convinced Rupert Chesterfield to bring his old college buddy, Quintin Culpepper, onto the team, he'd felt comfortable putting his credibility on the line, because despite his less-aggressive nature, Q had an incredible head for numbers. In college he'd tutored the entire fraternity through every math class offered and had actually taken engineering classes for fun.

And then Howie Rockwood had come along with false promises about what his family's construction business could do, taking advantage of Q's trusting nature, and ended up putting them all out of a job. Howie's dad's construction business went under—something that would have happened no matter what Q and Justin had done—the development deal came to a screeching halt, and Justin's credibility had gone up in smoke. No other firms would touch him. Chesterfield made sure of that.

As they merged onto I-65 north, Q said, "Vicki really wants to talk to you."

Justin's jaw tightened. "I'm not interested."

Why he didn't hit the gas and then shove Q out of the car for even mentioning Victoria, Justin didn't know. He wasn't the type to see all women as evil manipulators and men their hapless dupes, but in this case he had to recognize the specific parties involved. Quintin

Culpepper could be exploited by a Girl Scout. He never stood a chance against Victoria Bettencourt.

But that didn't mean all was forgiven, either.

"Did you know she went to Chesterfield on your behalf?"

And Justin believed she could no longer surprise him. "I had no idea."

Q played with the button along the side of his seat, sliding himself forward and back. "I was always jealous of this car."

"You have a Mercedes," he pointed out.

The passenger seat zoomed forward again. "That was Dad's car. He took it back after I got fired. Said he was tired of me screwing up and that he should have thrown me out a long time ago."

The man *was* pushing thirty, so Justin could see his father's point. But what the elder Culpepper really should have done was stand up to his wife when she coddled their son, insisting he be given everything he ever wanted. Having something to prove—even if to two people who would never know his accomplishments—had lit a fire in Justin that had served him well in his short life.

"Did he kick you out of the house?"

"He tried, but Mom wouldn't let him." Showing more fire than usual, he said, "I'm going to prove him wrong. When this deal scores big, he'll see that I can do something right."

Rolling his eyes, Justin knew immediately that he was going to help make that happen. So much for Q being the sucker of this twosome.

"Once we have a clear layout of the land, we'll send out feelers to local investors." Knowing the interstate would narrow ahead, he shifted lanes. "Thanks to Nashville's economy running far ahead of most other parts of the country, we have a better than average chance of pulling this off, but we need to stay realistic. There are no guarantees."

Like a dog who'd picked up the word *treat*, Q sat up straighter. "That's what I've been saying. We can't miss with this one."

"Let's try this again. *There are no guarantees*," Justin reiterated. "Six acres isn't much when you start adding elements like chain hotels and retail outlets. If the pros don't outweigh the cons here, we're out. End of story. You got that?"

Like a man without a care in the world, Q slid his seat all the way back and crossed his ankles. "You worry too much, bro. We got this."

Amazing. Freaking amazing.

"I say up an inch."

"I'm the bride and I say down an inch."

Abby and her mother had been fighting this battle for nearly five minutes.

"She has great legs," Haleigh said, offering support. "Let her show them off."

Mama held her ground. "A woman over thirty does not wear a dress that short."

"Maybe not in your day," Haleigh quipped, earning a quelling evil eye.

Refusing to surrender, Abby lifted the skirt to exactly where she wanted it, not quite three inches above her knee. "Stick a pin in it, Maureen. This is where it's going."

"Perfect," her best friend cheered, only to be poked by her future mother-in-law.

"Keep that up and I'm wearing black to your wedding."

"Do that and I'll sic my mother on you."

One would never know that these two women actually loved each other.

Maureen snapped her fingers, and a young girl appeared with a large, pin-covered bulb clamped to her wrist. "If this is where you want it, this is where I'll put it."

As if the seamstress were betraying her, the bride pouted. "This is my wedding."

"And this is your daughter's dress," the redhead mumbled, holding three pins pinched between her lips. "Besides, twenty years ago we sure as heck weren't wearing skirts down to our ankles for our girls'-night-out shenanigans."

Haleigh leaned forward. "Do tell."

"Maureen O'Callahan, if you say one more word, I'm taking my business elsewhere."

Undaunted, the seamstress flashed Abby a conspiratorial smile. "Hem high and neckline low described a large portion of your mother's wardrobe back in the day."

"That's it," Mama snapped. "You're all out of the will."

"Damn," Haleigh lamented. "Guess I'll just have to steal that ruby ring before you kick the bucket."

Laughter echoed all around, and even Maureen spit out her straight pins. "This one is ready to go," she said, escorting Abby off the pedestal. "Miss Haleigh's turn now. Come on back and we'll get you into the dress."

As the pair wandered off, Abby twirled before a three-way mirror. The beige heels made her calves look awesome, if she did say so herself.

"People are talking," Mama said, voice low and serious.

"About what?" she asked, lifting her hair off her neck to get the full updo effect.

"About you spending nights above the bookstore."

Abby had spent five of the last six nights at Justin's place, and if it weren't for him having firehouse duty, that number would be higher.

"Where I spend my nights is nobody's business," she replied, annoyed they were even having this conversation. It wasn't as if she were taking walks of shame down Main Street every morning. Between her new stove being back-ordered and the apartment's proximity to their project location, staying above the bookstore had been a practical decision. Spending her nights finding release in Justin's bed had been a strictly personal one.

Mama joined her at the mirror and peered over Abby's shoulder. "You might not care about your reputation, but I do."

Seeing red, she lowered her voice to keep the conversation private. "I have been celibate for two years, Mama. If some prude wants to call me a wanton woman for rejoining the land of the living, so be it. I won't apologize for being happy."

"You were his babysitter, for heaven's sake."

"Eighteen years ago," she argued, throwing her hands in the air. "We're adults now. Both of us. And I won't let you turn this into something dirty or perverted."

Like a dog with a bone, Mama whispered, "Why can't you find a man your own age? Didn't Dale Lambdon ask you out a few months ago?"

Dale Lambdon had asked out every woman with a pulse except the one woman who actually wanted him. A discovery Carrie had shared with her at the time of the asking, which was the reason Abby had turned him down. That and she simply didn't see her former classmate as more than a nice guy to call in an emergency, thanks to his position as a local sheriff's deputy.

"I'm sure that Dale will make some lucky woman very happy someday, but he isn't the man for me." Sensing a double standard, she said, "What if this was about Cooper? What if the ladies social committee at church told you Cooper was shooting above his means by marrying a doctor?"

Mama's face flushed. "I'd tell them that Cooper has loved Haleigh Rae for half his life, and he deserves to be happy, just like anyone else."

Heart falling, Abby fought back tears. "But I don't have a right to be happy, is that it, Mama? Is it because I'm a woman? Because we're expected to keep up appearances and to hell with what we really want?"

"Abigail Louise, are you saying that you love Justin Donovan?"

Dumbfounded, Abby could do little more than stare. The issue was not whether she loved anyone, but that she was entitled to spend her days—and nights—with whomever she chose without being judged for it.

"Answer the question, honey," Mama pushed. "If you love this boy, you need to tell me."

Feeling cornered, she slipped past her mother to pace before the cream satin chairs. "It's only been a week. How can you be in love with someone in a week?"

Taking her by the shoulders, the future bride said, "I loved Bruce by the end of our first date, and then I lost him for more than thirty years because I was too young and stupid to know that the world wouldn't end if I stepped out of my comfort zone. If this thing with Justin is more than a casual romp, I'll support you no matter what. Do you love him or not?"

From the first time they'd kissed, there had been nothing casual about Abby's feelings for Justin. And with every touch he told her he felt the same. Their first night together, when she'd been drowning in doubts, Justin had promised to catch her if she fell. Maybe it was time to test that promise.

Heart in her throat, Abby glanced around at the endless offerings of tulle, pearls, and lace. Ironic that she should have such a revelation in a place where so many happy endings had been celebrated. Hugging herself tight, she met her mother's anxious gaze. "I do," she whispered. "I love him very much."

Without warning, she found herself crushed against Mama's chest. "I'm so sorry, baby. I had no idea."

Laughing, she said, "Neither did I."

Mama released her to ask, "Does he feel the same way?"

Abby's mind slipped back to that first night.

"You're mine, Abigail. You're mine."

"I think he might," she replied, feeling as if her feet were no longer touching the floor.

Shifting into fairy godmother mode, Mama grew serious. "We mustn't rush him. Men don't come around to these things as quickly as we do."

Considering how hard Justin had worked to drag Abby this far, she was almost positive that Mama had things backward. Then again, she saw no sense in creating waves when the current ebb and flow were working so well.

"Here I am," Haleigh called, trudging to the pedestal in a flowing blue garment that beautifully accentuated all her new curves. A year ago she'd been rail thin, surviving on coffee and self-recrimination. Today she looked healthy and happy. As she took her place in front of the mirror, she spotted her future in-laws' teary grins. "I know those tears aren't for me. What did I miss?"

Mama beamed. "Abby is in love."

Eyes wide, the leggy blonde nearly fell from her perch. "You are? Already?"

"I guess so," she replied with an awkward shrug.

Haleigh didn't display the same enthusiasm as Mama had. "You're full of surprises these days, Abbs."

Squeezing her daughter's arm, the bride said, "But she isn't going to push him. It's important that men come to their senses in their own time."

"Right," Haleigh mumbled, holding Abby's gaze. When Maureen called Mama away, she asked, "Did you get some answers?"

"No," Abby admitted. "Not yet."

"Don't go into this blind, Abbs. You need to know what you're getting."

Arms crossed, she defended her man. "Justin cares about me and that's what matters. We'll deal with anything else if it comes."

"Okay," she said, nodding her head. "I hope it works out, then."

"Abby, Maureen needs you in the back, honey," Mama cut in. "She wants to make sure your hem is pinned even all the way around."

"I'm coming." Offering Haleigh a reassuring smile on her way by, she whispered, "I know what I'm doing."

Her friend's silent nod spoke volumes. But Haleigh would come around, she thought, stepping through a burgundy curtain beyond the fitting rooms. Whatever happened in Chicago was in the past, and when Justin wanted to tell her, he would. Until then Abby preferred to focus on the future.

Chapter 18

Surveying their progress so far, Justin stepped back from the center of the square, careful not to put himself into traffic. They'd decided to split the circle into quarters, leaving a path to the statue in each direction. The opposing quarters would match, meaning no matter the observer's viewpoint, they would always see two diverse but complementary flower beds. The cross path would be defined with boxwood, while the beds would feature five different types of flowers.

"I made it," Abby said, jogging across the roundabout to join him.

She'd adopted a shorts-and-T-shirt uniform for days requiring dirty work, pulling her hair into a simple ponytail to keep the dark waves out of her deep green eyes. And though she often called this her grungy look, he still lost his breath every time he saw her. On this warm Friday afternoon, the color was higher on her cheeks than usual.

"Does the dress now fit in all the right places?" he asked, tossing an arm over her shoulder to pull her into his side.

"It does. Are these the plants we're going with?" she asked, approaching the three pots arranged front to back in the closest bed.

Watching her kneel to sniff the centers, he said, "What do you think? Do you like them?"

Through the planning process, he'd made sure to ask her opinion, always making a decision together. As he'd expected, she'd proved to be a fast learner and on at least two occasions offered suggestions that hadn't occurred to him. Like using the same low-growth white roses in the center of each bed to ensure they complemented instead of clashed.

"I think we should bring the pink up so that all the cosmos are in the front." She did exactly that before stepping to the right in order to see the entire back half of the circle in one glance. "These shades of pink and orange pop beautifully, and then subtle tones of the yellow rhododendron and the purple rock cress in the back rows should give a nice, rich feel."

Stepping up behind her, Justin dragged her against his chest. "And the student becomes the teacher," he pronounced, kissing her temple.

She curled into him. "I wouldn't go that far." Tilting her head up, she asked, "What did you do this morning while I was playing dress the bridesmaid?"

Justin hadn't told Abby about the meeting with the broker. He didn't want her to think he planned to abandon their new venture to chase after land deals. If they moved forward, he'd share the details.

"Q is looking at a piece of property on the edge of town," he offered as a half-truth. "I agreed to give him my opinion."

"Is he moving here?" she asked, understandably curious.

"It's more an investment-type deal. Are you ready for some heavy lifting?" he asked, changing the subject. "I've got a truck full of these plants that we need to bring over." The previous four days had been spent installing the boxwoods and readying the beds, meaning they could finally start getting plants in the ground.

Abby rubbed her hands together. "I'm not wearing my grungy clothes for nothing."

Waiting for traffic to clear, they crossed to the old Chevy parked in front of Carter's Barber Shop.

"So you and this Q person went to college together?" she asked.

"Yep," Justin answered, loading her with two pots of rock cress before grabbing four for himself.

"Is he from close to here?"

"No, Q grew up in Chicago."

"Is that how you stayed in touch? Living in the same city?"

They paused again before taking advantage of a lull in traffic. "Something like that," Justin replied, delicately lowering his cargo. He placed Abby's two next to his four and said, "We're going to need five more for this row."

To his relief, Abby didn't ask any more questions on the next trip over and back, but as soon as he lined up the last pots, she resumed her inquiry.

"I'm just curious as to why, if Q lives in Chicago, he's buying property around Ardent Springs."

Running out of evasions, Justin tossed in a little more truth. "Nashville's economy is better than most places. Makes it a smart choice for investing right now."

Abby dropped to the dirt and sat back on her heels. "But he isn't buying in Nashville. You just said he's looking on the edge of Ardent Springs."

"Is there some reason you need to know all this?" he asked, tone clipped with annoyance.

She snapped back with annoyance of her own. "I'm interested because he's a part of your life that you don't ever talk about."

Justin cleared a hole for the first plant. "The past isn't worth talking about."

"The past makes you who you are, Justin. And I've been pretty open about mine." Taking care to remove the first plant from its pot, she handed it over. "I guess sometimes I just feel like I don't know anything about you."

Evading, he said, "You've known me since I was ten, Abby. You know my parents and what the room I grew up in looks like."

"And there's a giant gap between when you left that bedroom and when I brought you back into my life by setting my kitchen on fire. I want to fill in that gap."

At some point Justin would spill all his secrets. Just not today.

"I'm a hardworking guy who aims high and really likes girls who wear stained old T-shirts and high-swinging ponytails. Is that enough for now?"

Abby nodded. "I guess so. For now."

Leaning forward, Justin brushed his lips over hers. "Are we okay?"

"Of course," she said, eyes cast down.

"Abby?" He tipped her chin up. "I need a little time. That's all."

She brushed a bit of dirt off his cheek. "I get that. And I'll be here when you're ready."

"Thanks, baby."

With a deep sigh, she flashed a teasing grin. "We should get back to work now."

Returning to the task at hand, he said, "Yes, ma'am. Back to work."

She could finally cook again. Thanks to a Saturday installation more than three weeks after her epic cake disaster, Abby's kitchen was once again complete. The shiny new stainless steel appliance gleamed like a brand-new penny, and to celebrate she'd promised Justin a candlelit dinner featuring one of the few things she made well—bacon-coated meatloaf.

All week she'd worn frumpy clothes and smelled like a gym bag left out in the mud by the end of the day. Tonight she wanted to look pretty, feel clean, and make a man a home-cooked meal. She had thirty minutes to get ready while the meatloaf cooked, as she'd cut the recipe in half for a dinner for two and timed everything down to the minute.

Justin would arrive at seven o'clock, and dinner would be on the table, hot and ready, at seven oh five.

If all went well, she'd be hot and ready an hour later, maybe sooner.

Their conversation from the day before still lingered in her mind. Until now she'd believed Justin hadn't intentionally been hiding anything. She knew he'd lost his job and had assumed if she ever asked for more details, he'd provide them. Only she *had* asked, and he'd kept her in the dark. Which stirred Haleigh's words in her mind.

Don't go into this blind.

Too late for that, Abby lamented. She would simply have to be patient. Bide her time, take each day as it came, and let things happen. Of course, plenty of things were happening already, which was why she'd gotten off schedule thanks to standing in the middle of her closet, stressing about what to wear.

The little denim number she'd dragged from the back of her closet before her shower no longer fit. At least she had the satisfaction of knowing that in the last three years, she'd gained weight in her boobs as well as her hips. The gym membership was back on.

A ten-minute panic ensued, in which the dark crevices of her closet were searched until Abby found a simple white cotton number with delicate red flowers embroidered around the neckline and the hem. The dress had been a spontaneous online purchase the previous fall, though she'd yet to find a reason to wear it. As she held the hanger high, the fabric swayed, bringing the flowers to life, and her choice became obvious.

A walking garden she would be.

Tossing her towel into the hamper, she shimmied into the dress and checked her reflection. Perfect. A quick sweep of her hair into a clip and she hurried to the kitchen to check the meatloaf. As Abby rounded the corner, the scent of bacon wafted in the air, making her mouth water. A quick stir of the spring veggies before carrying the wineglasses to the table left only one thing to do—light the candles.

As she lit the match, Abby checked the clock on her new microwave. Six fifty-nine. Now all she had to do was wait for her man.

⁓

Guilt had been burning Justin's gut all day. Yesterday he'd justified avoiding Abby's questions by convincing himself that his past had nothing to do with their future. But if he wanted her to trust him, he had to trust her. And that meant talking about his last weeks in Chicago.

She'd worked with him for a few hours that morning but had to hurry home before eleven to meet the appliance folks. Her excitement over cooking him dinner created a disturbing buzz in his chest. All those years ago he'd dreamed of making Abby his. Now that he was wrapped around her finger, anxiety mixed with gratitude. Justin would never know how he'd gotten so lucky, while at the same time, he could hardly breathe for fear of losing her.

The nights he spent at the firehouse were empty and cold without her tucked in beside him. And sometimes his favorite time of day was when he woke with her leg tossed over his, her hair tickling his chin. Justin wanted to start every day for the rest of his life the same way. Which was why tonight would be about coming clean and hoping she wouldn't think less of him when the story was out.

Abby had fallen in love with the small white roses they'd chosen for the square, so he'd taken several home and arranged them into a delicate bouquet, wrapped in a jade-green ribbon that matched her eyes. He'd quickly learned that landscaping skills did not equate to those of a florist, but he'd done his best and knew she'd appreciate the thought more than the artistry, or lack thereof.

As he approached the Infiniti at six forty-five, Justin fished his keys out of his pocket and unlocked the doors, but before he could climb in, the phone in his back pocket went off at the same time an alarm howled down the street.

"Dammit," he said, checking the message.

Three-alarm blaze. Tile factory in Gallatin. All hands on
deck.

Of all freaking nights. Before he could text Abby a heads-up,
Frankie pulled up alongside him in a jacked-up Dodge Ram.

"Get in," he yelled over the siren.

Running on instinct, Justin left the flowers on the car and slid the
phone into his back pocket to climb into the truck. Not until they
reached the firehouse did he realize the phone wasn't where he'd put it.

Controlled chaos swarmed around him as the full team suited up,
jumping onto the lead engine one after another.

"What are you doing?" yelled the chief as Justin retraced his path
in from the parking lot.

"I can't find my phone."

"Forget the damn phone. We've gotta go!"

Jacket half on and helmet under his arm, Justin leapt onto the truck
seconds before it left the station, cursing the fates who'd just royally
screwed up his night.

The candles were still lit, but shorter. At seven fifteen, Abby had moved
from the table to the couch. At seven thirty, she blew out the candles
before checking her cell phone for the eighth time. She held off sending a
text until seven forty, and after ten minutes without a response, she tried
calling. When Justin didn't answer, she left a concern-filled voice mail.

Something must have happened. He would never stand her up like
this. She paced from the kitchen to the living room, imagining the worst.
Going to the front door, she peered through the glass, hoping to see
headlights pull into the drive. Something was wrong. She could feel it.

As she scanned the road left and right, her phone trilled in her hand. But the message came from Haleigh, not Justin.

Turn on the TV Ch. 4.

Abby followed the order without question and found a burning building filling her screen. The scroll across the bottom said a large fire had engulfed a tile factory in White House, and all local fire stations had teamed up to fight the blaze. Scooting to the edge of the couch, she spotted the engine from Firehouse Seven. Four bodies surrounded it, but she couldn't make out their identities.

A reporter appeared, orange flames flaring from the roof of the building in the background.

"As you can see behind me, after an hour with several departments on the scene, they've not been able to contain, let alone subdue, the flames. We've heard speculation that an electrical short could have started the fire but have not been able to confirm that."

Abby watched in horror as shadowed figures ran in and out of the building, any one of whom could be Justin. Her gut tightened and her lungs labored as if she were the one breathing through a mask.

"Residents who live nearby say they smelled smoke shortly before an explosion went off in the back part of the building. It's unknown yet if anyone was in the building at the ti—"

Before the reporter could finish her statement, the roof of the factory lifted up, and then dropped in a burning mass of metal and debris. The woman in front of the camera covered her head and leapt out of the frame, leaving a clear view of the chaos behind her. Abby leaned over the coffee table as she tried to find Justin in the scurry of figures running into danger.

But the scene disappeared as the news station cut back to the studio.

"This is clearly a dangerous situation and we'll bring you updates as we get them. More after this."

Jelly doughnuts danced across her flat screen, jarring Abby backward. What the hell? Didn't they know she *needed* that camera back on? Needed to know if Justin was okay? If he was in there, could he get out? He could be trapped, or worse . . .

Abby bolted to her feet. This was Kyle all over again. The worry. The fear. *Is he alive or dead? Is he hurt and waiting for help?* Only Kyle had been halfway around the world while Justin could be dying one county over, and she still felt completely helpless. Grabbing her purse, she raced toward the garage. She knew where that factory was. She had to go find him.

Only before she slipped the key into the ignition, her nurse's training kicked in. The last thing anyone needed was a crazy woman in a skimpy dress running around a burning building, trying to make sure one man was okay. Not that she didn't care about all the brave souls fighting that fire, but dammit, she needed to find Justin and see that he was whole and breathing.

White-knuckle grip on the steering wheel, one thought played over and over in her mind. She couldn't do this again. Abby wouldn't survive losing another man because he insisted on running into danger.

She dropped her purse and keys on the counter as she reentered and shut off the oven on her way through the kitchen to once again curl up on the couch. Annoyed by the ridiculous jingle, she muted the TV but continued to stare, afraid to take her eyes off the screen lest the news went immediately back to the scene. Three commercials later the news coverage finally continued, and Abby turned up the volume.

"Back to the Gallatin factory fire now," said the anchor behind the desk. "We've received word that several firefighters were injured in the roof collapse witnessed earlier and are being taken to Middle Tennessee Regional Hospital. Their names have not been released, nor do we know the extent of their injuries."

By the time the anchor rolled into the next story, Abby was already in the car.

Chapter 19

Fifty yards, give or take. That's how far the blast had thrown him. Justin's entire body ached, but a thorough check by the EMTs had revealed no broken bones. They'd bandaged the cut on his head, which hurt like hell, and after a pissing match, which he lost, Justin found himself inside an ambulance on his way to have his head examined.

The throbbing in his temples intensified when he moved, so he spent the ride trying his damnedest to hold still. Not easy in a speeding hospital on wheels.

Abby must be furious by now, he thought. Or worried sick. Thanks to the modern technology of having every damn contact at your fingertips, Justin didn't actually know her number. On the way to the fire he'd tried closing his eyes and envisioning the digits on his screen but could only remember the last three, and even then he couldn't be certain they were correct.

"Where are we headed?" he asked the medic with him.

"MTR," the stranger replied. Units from several counties had responded to the factory blaze, and Justin had no idea where this particular crew hailed from but was relieved to know they were taking him home.

Remembering another call he should make, Justin said, "Do you have a cell phone I can use?"

Without hesitating, the medic pulled a phone from his pocket. "No problem, man. Make all the calls you need. This mess was all over the news, so no telling what your loved ones have seen."

"Shit," he muttered, dialing his parents' home number. His mother picked up on the first ring.

"Hello?" she said, anxiety evident in her tone.

"Mom, it's me," Justin said, holding in a wince as the truck swerved beneath him. "I wanted to let you know that I'm okay."

"Thank you, Jesus," she exhaled before her voice grew fainter as she said, "Honey, Justin's on the phone and he's okay." Coming back to him, she asked, "Where are you, baby?"

This was the hard part. He had to be honest, but he didn't want her to freak out, either.

"They're taking me to MTR for a routine check. I bumped my head, but I'm fine. Really."

"Ken, get the keys," she murmured. "We'll meet you there, honey. Are you sure it's just a bump? You don't mess around with a head wound, now. Do you want me to bring you anything?"

Too exhausted to keep up with the rapid-fire questions, Justin mumbled, "Nothing to worry about."

In the background, he heard his father say, "Stop asking the poor boy questions and let's go."

"Hold on, Justin. We're on our way."

He nodded as if they could see him, and his head swayed on his shoulders as the phone dropped into his lap.

"No sleeping, buddy," the EMT said, bracing Justin's face in his hands. After a quick check of his patient's pupils, he yelled to the driver, "Pick it up, Billy. This one is more serious than we thought."

"I'm fine," Justin argued, forcing his lids open. "Just a bump."

"If I had a dime for every time I've heard that," the man said, though the words sounded distant in Justin's ears.

The ambulance jerked left, and Justin lost consciousness.

∽

"Come on, Dottie. I need to know who's come in."

The ER nurse shook her head. "Hon, you know I can't tell you that."

Determined, Abby rose onto her tiptoes to lean over the counter. "Then let me give you one name. Just nod if he's here. Please?"

She'd been sitting in the waiting room, nearly leaping out of her shoes every time the automatic doors flew open. Abby's nerves couldn't take any more waiting.

"All I can tell you is that there are two firefighters on their way here. ETA on the first is two minutes, which means I need to get my butt in gear."

"Dammit, Dottie, give me a name. I'm begging you."

Dropping a hand over Abby's, the nurse said, "I only have a name on the first one, and he isn't your man. Unfortunately I don't know who the other one is, so I can't offer the same reassurance on the second." Dottie didn't bother schooling her expression when she imparted the news. One nurse didn't waste time trying to fool another. Justin could still be the second firefighter.

Abby would have to take the small scrap she'd been given and return to her seat. Two minutes later the doors flew open and a gurney raced in, surrounded by three paramedics, one of whom straddled the patient, administering chest compressions.

Rising from her chair, Abby recognized the patient right away. "Clifton," she whispered, tears filling her eyes as familiar facts were rattled off in a staccato manner. Like a blur, the gurney and the activity around it disappeared behind the heavy brown doors, and she dropped to her seat. Poor Clifton's heart wasn't beating. The sweet old man who'd kept her company not even a month ago might not survive the next hour.

Suddenly angry, Abby burst from her chair, ready to run into the night and rail at the heavens. Why did bad things have to happen to good people? Why did men insist on putting their lives on the line without a thought for those who could be left behind? And by all that was holy, why hadn't Justin called her yet?

As she stormed through the visitors' entrance, Abby nearly barreled over a person coming in. Steadying them both, she recognized the agonized eyes of Mildred Graves.

"Is he here, Abigail?" she asked, clearly assuming that the former nurse was still on duty. "Is my Clifton going to make it?"

Like throwing a switch, Abby put on a brave face. "They just brought him in. I'm sure the doctors are doing everything they can."

Such empty words. She hated herself for saying them.

"They said he had a heart attack after the roof collapsed, but that's all I know." Dazed, she added, "I'm not even sure who called me."

"Come sit down." Abby led her to the waiting area, keeping a tight grip on Mildred's soft hand. "The cardiac team here will do everything they can. Let's think positive, okay? Clifton won't give up without a fight."

Holding her purse in her lap, Mildred watched the double doors behind which her husband's life hung in the balance. "I've always feared this day would come. Forty years of never knowing if the next fire call would be the one." Mildred sighed. "I made him promise that this would be his last year volunteering. I want to sleep in peace in my golden years."

Abby had endured less than ten years losing sleep over Kyle. Forty sounded horrifying.

"How do you do it?" she asked, truly curious. "How did you not lose your mind at some point?"

Taken aback by the question, Mildred shook her head. "You just do, honey. What's the alternative? Should I have given him up?" Voice steadier, she said, "I could never do that."

"But you said yourself, you spent forty years worrying. Losing sleep, all because a man insisted on playing hero." Abby's anger returned. "I did that once and I lost him. I don't think I could survive going through that again."

Turning in her chair, Mildred took on the role of consoler. "Would you give up one second of the love and happiness that you shared with your soldier just to take away the pain that came with losing him?"

Abby searched her heart for an answer. Kyle had been her first love. He'd made her laugh every time her chest ached with another good-bye. Made her feel safe and protected and special, even from the other side of the world. And she wouldn't have missed a moment of their time together. Not for anything.

"No," she replied, tears welling up again. "I wouldn't."

Mildred patted her hand. "I didn't think so."

They each reached for a tissue, dabbing their cheeks as Dottie appeared at the desk.

"Mrs. Graves, you can come back now."

"Is he all right?" she asked, rising wobbly to her feet. Abby rose with her.

Dottie nodded. "He's alive but not out of the woods. The doctor will explain everything."

Watery blue eyes turned to Abby. "Thank God," she murmured. "And thank you for sitting with me."

"No problem," she replied, sniffling into her tissue as the ER nurse escorted the older woman through the doors.

Sending up a prayer of gratitude, Abby returned to her chair, uncertain what to do. She still didn't know if Justin was hurt. The second ambulance should arrive soon, so she decided to stay. If it wasn't Justin,

Abby could at least be there for the next loved ones who needed a shoulder and a reassuring voice.

And then Ken and Karen Donovan stepped through the door, and Abby nearly hit the ground.

Why wouldn't someone stop the damn beeping?

Like rising from a deep hole, Justin returned to consciousness slowly, aware of only the pounding in his head and the security of a warm hand in his. First he needed to figure out where he was. On his back was the obvious part, but what was his back on?

At the risk of angering the little bastards trying to chisel their way through his skull, he struggled to remember what had happened. His first recollection was the heat. Intense, lung-singeing heat. They'd been fighting a fire. The noise came next. The roar of a blaze and a cacophony of steady voices, calling out orders until a deafening boom wiped them all away.

Scenes clicking into place, he remembered feeling weightless as that boom had tried to wipe him away, too. The soreness in his limbs. The blow to his head. The ambulance ride and the call to his mom.

And then the memories stopped. All signs indicated that he'd survived beyond that point, which was encouraging, but he had a feeling he'd scared some people he cared about.

Dragging himself from the darkness, he forced one eye open only to close it again when the light pierced his brain. Good God, how could anything be that bright? The thought made him second-guess the still-alive assumption. Testing his body, he squeezed the hand pressed against his palm.

"Justin?" he heard Abby say, and the subsequent effort to answer got him nowhere.

He needed to calm the fear in her voice. To tell her not to worry and that he was fine. Except he wasn't fine, if the thumping in his head was any indication.

"Is he awake?" his mother asked. "Did he move?"

"He squeezed my hand," Abby said. "Do it again, Justin. Let me know you can hear me."

The gesture took great effort, but he managed another squeeze.

"Oh, thank God. Justin, honey," she said, laying a hand against his cheek. "You need to try to wake up. Can you do that?"

For her, he could do anything.

With Herculean effort, he opened his eyes, blinking with the pain of it.

"Turn off the light," Abby yelled, and a second later someone mercifully followed her order. "Try again, baby. It won't hurt as much this time."

Trusting her, Justin lifted his lids to find the world blurrier than he remembered.

"That's it," she encouraged. "Take your time."

"You can do it, son," echoed his father from the opposite side of the bed.

Justin licked his lips. "Drink," he said, desperate for anything liquid.

"I've got it," Mom exclaimed before Abby slid a hand behind his neck.

"Your head isn't going to like this," she said, holding his gaze. "But bear with me."

She leaned him forward and the angry chiselers switched to jackhammers.

"Motherfu—" he started before reining in the expletive. The pain made him nauseated.

"Take a second," Abby soothed, never letting go of his hand. "Bring it closer, Karen. Let him feel the straw."

As soon as the plastic touched his lips, Justin filled his mouth, driving back the dryness with ice-cold water. Once he'd had enough, he pressed back on Abby's hand.

"Okay," she said, returning him gently to the pillow. "That's a good start."

His mouth finally cooperated. "I'm sorry," he said, angry at himself for putting all of them through this.

Abby hushed him. "There's nothing to be sorry about."

"Speak for yourself," Mom cut in. "He just took ten years off my life, and I already don't have that many to go."

"He's alive," Pop pointed out. "That's all that matters." He squeezed Justin's shoulder before wrapping an arm around his sniffling wife. "Come on, darling. You can relax now. Let's take a walk to the cafeteria. I hear they've got good pastries down there. You know how sugar always makes you feel better."

Justin caught the wink over his mom's shoulder and appreciated the chance to be alone with Abby. As soon as the door closed with a whoosh, he repeated the only words he'd managed since waking.

"I'm sorry."

"Stop that," she said. "You're the one lying in a hospital bed. I should be saying sorry to you."

"You were worried," he mumbled, determined to make her understand. "Remembering what happened before. With your husband."

A delicate finger settled against his lips. "A little worry is just part of life, right? You take the good with the bad." Abby placed a warm kiss on his lips. "For better or worse. That's how love works."

Her words gave him strength. "Are you saying you love me, Abby?" Justin asked, wiping a tear from her cheek.

Abby nodded, and it was as if the light had been turned back on, only this time he wasn't blinded. In fact, his vision cleared completely.

"Say it," he pleaded. "Say you love me."

Something between a hiccup and a laugh danced off her lips. "I love you, Justin Donovan. So, so much."

"I love you, too, Abby girl. More than anything."

❧

"Hey there," Haleigh whispered, finding Abby in the hall outside Justin's room. "How's he doing?"

"Good," she responded, accepting a much-needed hug. "Dr. Benedict is in with him now, but he's already said we can take him home in the morning."

"No swelling then?"

"None, thank goodness." Abby lowered onto the vinyl bench and motioned for Haleigh to join her. "But the concussion is pretty bad. He's on strict orders to rest and won't be fighting fires again for at least six weeks."

Haleigh whistled. "In a way that's good news, but I can't imagine convincing any man to sit still for that long."

"I'll tie him down if I have to." She would not let Justin jeopardize his recovery. "He's already argued that we have to get the beautification project done, but a restriction on bending and lifting means he'll have to settle for supervising. From my couch, if I have my way."

"But can you do it without him?" she asked.

A week ago her answer would have been very different. "I have to. We're partners in this business, and we made a commitment. I won't let Justin down."

Haleigh took Abby's hand. "Are you really okay?"

Confused, she said, "I'm not the one with the head injury. Of course I'm okay."

"I wouldn't have had you turn on the news if I'd known what would happen."

"Why?"

"What do you mean, why?" she said. "Because this could have been Kyle all over again. You can't tell me this didn't bring back memories."

No, she couldn't. But thanks to Mildred, Abby saw things differently now.

"Have you fallen off the wagon since getting together with Cooper?" she asked.

Lips pursed, Haleigh replied, "You know I haven't. Why would you ask that?"

Abby ignored her friend's irritation. "Do you think that might be because loving Cooper makes you stronger?"

Studying the toe of her shoe, Haleigh smiled. "Like loving Justin has made you stronger. I see your point. I guess I should have given you more credit."

"No, you're right, actually. When I saw the roof of that building collapse, my first thought was that I couldn't do this again. But you know what I've forgotten in the last two years?"

"What?"

"There was more to my life with Kyle than tragedy. There was laughter and love, and as a wise woman reminded me, I wouldn't trade those moments for anything. So," she said, "yes, this was a rough night. And I love you for worrying about me. But Justin will recover, and my focus is back where it belongs—on the good times."

Throwing an arm around Abby's shoulders, Haleigh sighed. "It's nice to have you back, buddy."

She relaxed into the embrace. "It's nice to be back, my friend. It's nice to be back."

Chapter 20

"You are going to sit here, and that's final."

The woman was driving him mad. Justin had been out of the hospital for forty-eight hours. In that time he'd been allowed to piss. That's it. And even that had been a negotiation.

"I feel fine," he argued, standing up to prove his point. The world only wavered for a second or two. Nothing he couldn't handle. "We've already lost too much time on this project as it is."

Abby had insisted they take an extra day off to make sure he could handle leaving the house. Thanks to Doc Benedict, Justin couldn't drive for a week, minimum, be on a computer for at least a month, watch more than one hour of television a day, or even read messages on his phone.

Lifting anything heavier than a magazine was out, but then he wasn't allowed to read articles either, so screw that. The bending over was the worst. He couldn't even put his shoes on without Abby insisting he let her tie them. Which was the only argument he'd won today. He would tie his own freaking shoelaces.

"We have two weeks until the deadline. That's plenty of time."

"Not with only one person doing the work." Abby adjusted the fancy bag chair she'd set up on the sidewalk, and pressed one finger against his shoulder until Justin surrendered and sat back down.

"Then it's a good thing I recruited some helpers."

Now she'd crossed a line. "You hired someone without telling me? Abby, I should have been involved in that decision. And we can't afford to pay anyone. We aren't even paying ourselves yet."

Opening a patio umbrella, she secured it to what he'd begun to think of as his time-out chair.

"I didn't say I hired anyone," she replied, adjusting the umbrella until he was fully shaded. "Let's just say some fairy godmothers have offered their services."

Now *she* sounded like the one who'd taken a blow to the head.

"I assume you're going to explain that one?" Justin drawled, fighting back a burgeoning headache.

Like a woman without a care in the world, Abby trilled, "You'll see."

Right on cue the explanation appeared in the distance as a parade of armed garden gnomes, looking remarkably like the Ardent Springs Garden Society, marched down Main Street, led by none other than the head gnome herself, Thea Levine.

"You can't be serious," Justin murmured, marveling at the colorful display before him.

Bright, wide-brimmed hats covered silver-topped heads, and like a surging rainbow of Bermuda shorts and disturbingly pale calves, the botany brigade descended on the square as if reporting for duty.

Struggling to keep his jaw off the ground, he took in the silent soldiers before planting his gaze on Abby. "What is going on here?"

Gesturing toward her minions, she said, "These ladies know more about gardening than you or I will ever know, which made them the perfect solution. It was Ms. Thea's idea, actually." Abby curtsied in the society matron's direction and received a royal nod in return.

"Once she put the word out, all of these lovely ladies volunteered to help finish the project. Isn't that fabulous?"

Justin wanted to laugh but knew from experience that doing so would intensify the headache.

"It's brilliant, is what it is."

Abby visibly relaxed before dropping a gentle kiss on his cheek. "We're going to do this," she said for his ears only. "And it's going to be beautiful."

He caught her hand before she could step away. "You're amazing, you know that?" he murmured.

"I'm just a girl, standing in front of a boy, asking him to please stay in his chair."

No longer able to hold back the mirth, Justin laughed through the pain. "I can do that."

"Good," she said. "Let me know if you need anything, okay?"

Shooing her away, he watched his partner divide the new recruits into teams, assigning two to each flower bed. Another team would transport the plants across the roundabout, while a final group was in charge of watering. Within minutes Abby set the entire operation into motion, joining Thea to tackle the front left quadrant.

One perk of Justin's position came to light right away, as Abby knelt with her bottom in the air, providing a show he'd happily admire all day long. And then Thea bent down to place the first plant, revealing a startling amount of cleavage, and he immediately searched for an alternate view.

Justin had never been much of a people watcher, but the pastime helped alleviate his boredom. When his phone rang an hour into the day, he appreciated the distraction.

"Hello?" he answered, following doctor's orders and not looking at the screen first.

"We've hit a speed bump," Q said in a panic-stricken voice.

Thanks to the accident, Justin hadn't thought about the real estate deal since Friday, when Q had volunteered to compile a list of possible investors.

"Gee, I'm fine, buddy," he replied. "Thanks for asking."

"Why wouldn't you be fine?" Q asked, clueless as usual.

With a sigh, Justin said, "No reason. What's your speed bump?"

"They want more land."

"Who wants more land?"

"Royce-Upton. They're out of Memphis but looking for deals around Nashville."

Score a point for Q. "Sounds like a good lead."

"But they say the parcel isn't big enough," he repeated. "We need to add more land before they'll commit."

Then they'd definitely hit a wall. "There isn't any more land. It's plus or minus six acres. I told you that would be our biggest obstacle."

Q's voice became muffled. "I'll be there in two seconds, babe."

Assuming that statement wasn't directed at him, Justin said, "Who are you talking to?"

"A pretty little thing named Becky," the other man whispered. "I think she really likes me."

Justin didn't recognize the name. "Good for you."

The Culpepper matriarch had already chased off two potential daughters-in-law in the last two years. If this Becky person made it home to meet the family, he'd bet his Infiniti she'd be back in Tennessee within days, with a Manolo Blahnik shoe print on her derriere.

"So what are we going to do about the deal?" Q asked.

Accepting reality was their only choice. "There's nothing we can do. It was a long shot to begin with, and now we know the tract isn't viable for the development needed to make an investment worthwhile. It's time to look for another option. I hear east of Nashville is booming. Try something along I-40, towards Knoxville."

A female voice chimed from Q's end of the call, and he said, "I need to go. But I'm not ready to give up on this."

"It is what it is, man. The potential was good, but the land isn't there."

"We'll see about that."

The call cut off and Justin shook his head. Slowly and with very little force. At some point in the last few days, landing a big deal had lost its appeal. He no longer cared if Chesterfield ever begged him to come back. If the call came tomorrow, Justin would turn it down. All because of the pretty brunette who'd just spread dirt across her forehead.

A sense of peace quieted his headache as the truth dawned. Everything Justin wanted was right here in Ardent Springs. His family, his roots, and the woman he loved. He'd return to the development world, but on his own terms and definitely not in Chicago. Maybe that would be their next venture together. AJ Developers had a nice ring to it.

In addition to her deepening tan, Abby had gained new respect for manual labor. Landscaping turned out to be an excellent workout, and she didn't even mind scrubbing dirt out of her ears at the end of the day. Between the daily dose of vitamin D, her newly toned bottom, and watching the flower beds come to life, she felt quite confident in her unorthodox career change.

Since Tuesday she and the garden society had put the finishing touches on three of the four beds at the center of the square. Justin had given up his position as patient observer by the end of the day Wednesday, assuring Abby that she no longer needed him watching over the project. Going to work without him on Thursday had been nerve-racking, but the crew didn't seem to notice his absence.

By the time they broke for lunch on Friday, the last flower had gone in, two teams had moved to the smaller beds that would accent the outside of the roundabout, and word had arrived that the large planters they'd ordered would be delivered the next day. That would leave them just over ten days to fill fifty-six four-by-two-foot planters—a daunting task that Justin had assured her could be done.

"Where do you want this?" Cooper yelled to Abby from inside his truck.

She excused herself to Thea and pointed to the opposite corner of the square. "Far right parking space in front of the barbershop. I'll meet you over there."

Her twin did not look happy, though he hadn't complained the day before when she'd asked him to pick up the mulch for a noon delivery. If he didn't want to do it, he should have said so.

Abby sprinted across the street to reach the parking space at the same time Cooper did.

"You got somebody to help me unload this mess?" he snapped, slamming his truck door.

"The average age of my crew is sixty-eight," she informed him. "You're stuck with me."

He dropped the tailgate with a thud and snagged a set of work gloves from his back pocket. "You aren't lifting fifty-pound bags of mulch. I've got it."

She'd spent ten years lifting humans that weighed far more than fifty pounds. Abby grabbed the bag closest to her and hauled it to the back edge of the space. "Remind me not to ask you for any more favors."

"I told you I didn't mind," Cooper said, elbowing his way past her with two bags at once. Abby didn't know what his problem was, but her typically affable brother had something on his mind.

"You want to tell me why you're acting like a jerk?" She tossed a smelly bag over her shoulder.

Jaw tight, he said, "I got a call from Tanner Drury this morning."

Cooper had gone to work at Tanner's garage back in high school and eventually saved enough pennies to buy the business from him a few years ago.

"What did he want?" she asked.

Dropping two more bags on the asphalt, he returned to the truck, barely winded. "Someone made him an offer on the land."

Still in the dark, Abby said, "What land?"

"The land the shop is on. The garage sits on property that goes back more than a hundred years in Tanner's family. He didn't want to hand that over, so I bought the buildings and everything that went with them. He kept the deed to the land."

"Okay." Dragging another bag her way, she pointed out the obvious. "If he wouldn't sell the land to you, what makes you think he'd sell to someone else?"

"He doesn't want to, but his wife is pushing for it." Cooper leaned on the tailgate. "I guess his retirement isn't stretching as far as they'd expected, and Diana is scared. I can't really blame her, but dammit, I've put everything into that business. If they sell, I'll have to close down or move."

Heart aching for her other half, she said, "You don't know that for sure."

"The buyer is a developer." He sighed. "There's no way they're going to let me stay."

Abby tried to come up with a solution. "Maybe there's another way for Tanner to make some money."

Cooper shook his head and loaded up two more bags. "He's seventy-four years old, Abbs. His knees are shot, he can barely hear, and the only thing he knows how to do is fix cars. Even that he can't do anymore. The technology passed him by."

Accepting defeat, she squeezed his arm. "I'm really sorry, but we'll make it work, right? There has to be somewhere around town where you can relocate. We just have to find the perfect spot."

"I can't think of one, but maybe you're right." Two more bags hit the pile. "If I do have to move, Hal and I will need to put off the wedding."

As far as Abby knew, they hadn't even set a date. "Did I miss a memo?"

Cooper propped his hands on his hips and surveyed the center of the square. "Nothing specific, but we were hoping for maybe Christmas. Guess not now." Gesturing toward the mound across the street, he said, "That looks really good."

Abby ignored the undercurrent of surprise in his tone. "Thanks."

"Do the locals have any idea how bad this place is going to smell once you get this mulch down?"

"Not a clue," she laughed, adding her bag to the stack. "We could have an angry mob on our hands, depending on who ends up downwind, but I highly suggest not eating at any outside cafés for at least a week."

"That reminds me." Cooper tugged on her ponytail. "Payment for this favor is a thorough truck washing. I expect this baby to be smelling like roses by the end of the weekend."

"You mean you didn't do this out of the goodness of your heart?" she asked, feigning innocence.

"Nice try, sis. A deal's a deal. Sunday. My place. You, a sponge, and a big bucket of suds."

She'd hoped he wouldn't make her pay up. "Fine. But don't tell Haleigh that I'm making her help me."

Two more bags filled the parking space. "My lips are sealed."

Chapter 21

One week later than intended, Justin resolved to answer all of Abby's questions. While he'd still been in the hospital, she'd told him about the bacon-coated meatloaf and the candles that had gone to waste thanks to the factory fire, so he'd set out on that Friday afternoon to re-create the scene. Knowing his limitations, he'd called in backup on the meatloaf.

At precisely fifteen minutes before Abby was scheduled to walk through the door, Mom delivered the main course, while Justin had the candles in place and the wine ready to pour. None of which had required heavy lifting, bending, or eyestrain, so she couldn't scold him for doing too much.

When he heard her car pull into the garage, Justin leaned against the kitchen island with a wineglass in each hand. Technically, his contained water, since he couldn't mix alcohol with the pain meds—which he, thankfully, needed less and less of—but the fancy glass kept up the romantic look he was going for.

Unfortunately the mouthwatering scent of bacon could not compete with the barnyard odor that followed Abby through the door. He'd forgotten today was mulch day.

Abby froze just inside the kitchen, barefoot, wearing nothing but her skivvies, and filthy from head to toe. "Hi," she said, green eyes apologetic. "I stink."

Justin set the glasses on the counter as his eyes watered. "I noticed. Did you spread the mulch or swim in it?"

"Turns out members of the garden society aren't cut out for carrying fifty-pound bags of anything," she explained. "Sweet Dorothy Jane tried to help, but she couldn't hold up her end, and I went down face-first."

Do not laugh. Do not laugh.

"I see," he snorted, clearing his throat. "That sounds, um, gross."

Her face contorted. "It went in my mouth."

He wanted to hug her, but not until she'd showered. "Come on, honey." Justin looked for a clean spot to touch and settled for one bare shoulder. "You'll feel better after a hot shower. Though I suggest you brush your teeth first."

On their way through the kitchen, Abby spotted the table. "You lit candles." Sniffing the air, she asked, "Is that bacon?"

How she smelled anything over her own odor, he didn't know.

"The meatloaf will be ready when you come out."

Her abrupt halt caused him to run into her. A typically pleasant experience. Not so much in that moment.

"You're making the dinner we missed. That's so sweet."

"That's me," he said, nudging her forward. "Sweet. Now go take a shower so we can get this evening started."

Abby picked up her pace. "I can do that." At the door to her bedroom, she paused to glance back his way. "I love you, Justin."

He would never get tired of hearing that. "I love you, too, Abby."

She disappeared out of sight, and Justin hurried in to check the meatloaf. The bacon bubbled, and the smell drove the stench from his sinuses. After turning the oven down to 250, per his mother's orders, he pulled up the music on his new iPhone. The previous one had been found in tiny pieces next to his car.

Twelve minutes later Abby returned to the kitchen wearing the same white dress from the night at the hospital and a wet knot of hair atop her head. His body clenched at the sight of her.

"You look gorgeous," he mumbled in hushed tones, drinking her in.

"Not sure about that," she said, dismissing the compliment, "but I definitely smell better."

Justin pulled her close. "When I say you're gorgeous, you say thank you. That's how compliments work."

Pressing against him, she wrapped her arms around his torso. "Saying thank you implies that I believe you."

Locking her chin between his thumb and forefinger, he forced her to hold his gaze. "You're the most beautiful woman I've ever met, Abigail Williams. If it takes the rest of my life, I'm going to make you believe that."

Rising to kiss his lips, she squeezed him tight. "The rest of your life? That's a long time."

He nibbled her earlobe. "Not nearly long enough."

Their mouths met and the whole world fell away. Soft hands dipped under his shirt to slide up his back as his knee slid between her thighs to press against her core. Before long they were breathless, clinging to one another in a tangle of arms and tongues and murmured promises. The moment he lifted her off the floor, which prompted a moment of vertigo, but Justin was too far gone to care, the timer on the oven went off.

Abby broke the kiss, her legs still tight around his middle. "We should probably eat," she panted.

"We can eat later." Justin covered the few feet to the stove, shut off the timer and the oven, and then carried Abby down the hall. "This can't wait."

She didn't argue as her body writhed against his. In the sunlit bedroom, they toppled onto the bed, and Abby's dress lifted to reveal an arousing lack of panties. He slid two fingers along her folds and her hips rose to greet him, hot and ready, and Justin didn't hesitate to strip her bare.

He knelt above her, suckling a tightly puckered nipple as she dragged his T-shirt up his back. Breaking contact long enough to release the material over his head, Justin lifted one arm at a time until the shirt hit the floor. At which point he took the other nipple between his teeth. Her husky purr made his dick twitch.

"Help me take these off, baby," he said.

Abby pushed against his chest until he was upright and reached for the buttons on his jeans. When they were all undone, she slid her hands behind the denim as she kissed his abs, licking lower. Justin lifted off the bed with a growl, shoved the pants to the floor, and grabbed a condom on his way back onto the mattress.

Legs spread and eyes dark with desire, Abby offered him everything in that moment. And he needed to give everything in return.

Holding her gaze, he pulled her down the bed until his tip touched her opening. Hands fisted on the blankets, she licked her lips and lifted for him, pleading with her body. Begging him to take what he wanted. What they both wanted.

"I love you, baby," he murmured, teasing her just enough to make her moan.

Abby nodded and rolled her hips. "I can't wait any longer, Justin. Please. I love you. Please."

Power surged through him as he took her mouth the same moment he buried himself in her heat.

Abby clung to his shoulders, meeting every thrust with one of her own. The fever built, spiraling up her spine and blazing through her limbs.

Justin whispered love words in her ear before driving faster until neither could find enough air to speak.

He circled her nipple with his tongue before biting down, drawing a cry of pleasure from her throat. Her nails dug into his skin as she pressed hot kisses and bites along his broad shoulder, getting drunk on his taste and scent. The feel of him, thick and hard, pulsing inside her, sent her over the edge.

As she called his name, Justin tensed against her, muscles tight until the tremors took over. She rode out the orgasm with her hands in his hair, a thin sheen of sweat covering them both. Mouths lingered a breath apart, their lungs desperate for air but neither willing to leave the other to get it.

One last burst of pleasure shivered through him before Justin collapsed next to her on the damp sheets. "Amazing," he sighed, nuzzling against her neck. "The no-panties thing was a nice touch."

A satisfied smile curled her lips. "I thought you might like that. I was going to tell you halfway through dinner, just to see what you'd do."

Justin leaned up to look into her eyes. "Now I'm almost sorry we skipped the food."

Abby laughed. "I'm starting to think we aren't meant to eat meatloaf."

"At least this is a better reason for missing it than the last time."

"Much better," she agreed, kissing the healing bump on his head. "You probably shouldn't be exerting yourself this much."

"Sex heals everything. You're a nurse. You should know that."

"*Was* a nurse," she corrected. "Now I'm a landscaper. And I had the mulch in my bra to prove it."

Scooting up onto the pillow, Justin cradled her against his chest. "I bet you're ready to strap on the scrubs again after this week."

He couldn't be more wrong. "No more scrubs for me." Abby twirled a wisp of hair around her finger. "I can't wait for you to see the square. I haven't been this proud of anything in a long time."

"Do you mean that?" he asked.

Abby nodded. "I do." She looked up into his face. "What about you? Do you ever want to go back to your other career? Go back to Chicago?"

Tucking his free arm behind his head, he sighed. "Before I answer those questions, I need to answer some other ones. Like the one about what happened to send me back here."

After his accident, Abby had been content to focus on the future. Whatever happened in his life before the night of her kitchen fire didn't have any bearing on the future they would build together. Ironic that once she'd let go of his past, Justin decided to share it with her.

"Is this story going to make me want to beat someone up?" she asked.

"Just me." He chuckled, kissing the top of her head. "You know that Q is an old college buddy, but you don't know that we also worked together at Chesterfield Developers. That's the company I worked for in Chicago," he clarified. "Bringing Q on board was my idea, and, unfortunately, not my best one."

Abby hummed to let him know she was listening.

"Q might not seem like it, but he's a numbers guy. Brilliant at math. Not so brilliant at everything else. But his biggest weakness is his trusting nature. There isn't a cynical bone in the poor guy's body."

"That doesn't sound like a fault to me," she confessed.

Justin tucked a lock behind her ear. "In most cases it wouldn't be. But in the world of high-dollar development, you need a little cynicism. Enough to check and double-check the numbers to make sure you aren't building a skyscraper on an empty promise."

The picture became clear. "So Q didn't double-check?"

"No," he confirmed, his chest rising and falling as his heart beat out a steady rhythm beneath her ear. "But neither did I. Another buddy of ours tried to use our project to save his dad's dying construction business and convinced Q that Rockwood Contractors could do the work. Needless to say, they couldn't."

Sitting up, she said, "How could they blame you if he lied?"

"Because it was my job to make sure that everything was cleared, and anyone who looked at their financials would have seen the truth. I trusted that Q had done his due diligence, but I didn't do mine. The project fell apart, and Chesterfield fired us both."

Justin had been wrong. Abby definitely wanted to beat someone up. "Then this Chesterfield person is an idiot. You made one mistake. No," she corrected, tucking the sheet beneath her arms. "Two other people made mistakes, and you paid for them. That's bull . . . mulch."

"I appreciate your support, but I should have checked those numbers."

"If that's the case, then so should Chesterfield."

Hazel eyes narrowed. "He put me in charge of the project so that he wouldn't have to check them."

Following his line of reasoning, she pointed out what Justin was clearly missing. "What he did was delegate. In turn, you did the same. That's how things get done. A hospital runs the same way. If I had taken a vital sign wrong, or administered an incorrect dosage of medicine, I would have been the person to answer for the mistake. Granted," she added, "I could have killed someone and not simply delayed a building project, but still. Iva wouldn't have been fired because of my incompetence, and you shouldn't have been fired because of Q's. Or whoever the other guy was."

"Howie," Justin supplied.

"Fine. Howie," Abby repeated. "If the blame had to go all the way up the chain, then Chesterfield was as responsible as you were. More so, in fact, since his name is on the door."

Staring as if she'd grown a third eye, he shook his head. "Your brain works in amazing ways, but your logic doesn't change the facts. To anyone looking in, a major deal collapsed under my watch. Like anything, the developer business is a small world. Once Chesterfield made sure my name was tied to that failure, no one else would touch me. And that's why I came home. To regroup until I could figure out how to redeem myself."

Taking his face in her hands, Abby said, "*You* do not need redemption. Do you hear me? Any man who fights fires and helps sweet old ladies fill their town with flowers does not need redemption."

Removing her hand from his cheek, he placed a kiss in the center of her palm. "You're right," he whispered, rolling until she was pinned beneath him. "I don't need redemption. All I need is you."

Pulling him down for a kiss, she replied, "You have me, Justin. You'll always have me."

⌒

"Thank heaven meatloaf is good cold," Abby mumbled with a mouth full of bacon. "Remind me to ask your mom how she gets that extra kick. Mine doesn't have that."

Licking the grease from her fingertips, Justin shifted her on his lap. When they'd finally left the bedroom, he'd refused to let her out of his reach, even to eat.

"She'll tell you it's a secret, but it's really hot sauce," he revealed. "Mom puts hot sauce in everything."

Abby dipped a piece of meat in ketchup. "In everything?"

Justin nodded. "If she ever offers you pancakes, run the other way."

"Stop telling lies about your mother," she scolded.

"I'm not lying," he defended, biting her shoulder. "Don't say I didn't warn you."

Swinging her leg, which twitched her bottom against his groin, Abby said, "At the risk of pushing my luck, there's one more detail about your past that I'm curious about."

Reaching for another slice of bacon, Justin said, "I'll tell you anything you want to know."

"That day that we had dinner at the fire station, you said you almost got married once. Will you tell me about that?"

Justin debated his answer, buying time by popping a large bite of food into his mouth. To her credit, Abby waited patiently.

"There was a girl in Chicago. She came from money and liked fancy things. Something we had in common."

She stopped chewing. "You like fancy things?"

"Have you not seen my car?" he asked.

"One shiny car doesn't make you a collector of fancy things."

"No," he admitted. "But a storage unit filled with obscenely overpriced and utterly useless possessions does."

Distracted, Abby straightened. "Now I have to know what's in it. Can I see?"

"Not without a trip to Chicago. Do you want to hear my story or not? It isn't pretty, so I can stop now with no problem."

Contrite, she settled back down. "Sorry. Continue."

"Where was I?" he said, feigning deep thought.

"Fancy things," Abby reminded him.

"Right. We both liked fancy things, and like an idiot, I thought that was enough to build a marriage on."

Abby grew serious. "You didn't love her?"

At the time he'd believed he did, but now Justin knew better.

"What I felt for Victoria never came close to what I feel for you. She was beautiful and connected and had all the same ambitions that I did. We were going to throw the most talked-about dinner parties in our million-dollar penthouse." Trailing his thumb along Abby's jaw, he added, "When I think about it now, I can't believe that I was ever that guy."

Always ready to soothe, Abby put her arms around his neck. "There's nothing wrong with wanting nice things," she said, her green eyes soft. "I've been eying a dress in Virgil's Boutique window all week that is very fancy and very expensive. I'd never have a reason to wear it, but that doesn't stop me from drooling every time I pass by."

He loved that she equated a dress with a million-dollar penthouse.

"The point is, she turned out to be someone I not only didn't love, but didn't like very much." Seeing no need to share the part where Victoria slept with Q—as there was only so much humiliation a man would own up to in one night—he ended the story there. "And now I have a girl that I like a lot. She's sexy, even when she smells like a cattle truck." Justin turned Abby until she was straddling his hips. "She's way smarter than I am," he added, placing a kiss below her left ear. "And being with her makes me a better man."

Pressing her breasts against his chest, she said, "You really know how to make a girl feel good."

Caressing her bare ass, he murmured, "I'll make you feel better than good, baby. Way better."

Abby pressed down against his erection. "I think dinner is over now."

Dragging his hands up her back, he nipped at her bottom lip. "Time to move on to dessert, then. What do you think we should have?"

Hot fingers slipped behind the band of his boxer briefs. "I want this," she said, freeing him from the material.

"Your wish is my command." Releasing his hold, Justin held his breath as Abby lowered to her knees in front of his chair.

Chapter 22

Abby's alarm had gone off much too early for a Saturday morning. Especially considering how little she'd slept. Not that she'd change a moment of the night's sexual debauchery, but the sun could have had the decency to allow the exhausted lovers an extra hour or two of shut-eye.

Thanks to a Donovan family reunion in Franklin, Abby would be handling the delivery of the large street planters on her own. Justin had offered to skip the gathering, but she knew full well that Karen would never forgive her if he did. At least today would not require heavy lifting. All she had to do was point, pace off, and point again.

After the second time she'd paced wrong, requiring the poor deliverymen to pick up and move the misplaced planters to the proper locations, Abby took advantage of her proximity to the bookstore to grab a cup of coffee. The moment she heard a woman at the counter ask for Justin Donovan, her mind came fully awake.

"Who are you again?" asked Bruce.

"Victoria Bettencourt," the woman answered, her voice bold and confident, as if these two words alone could move mountains. "I'm Justin's fiancée."

Amazing. Justin finally shared the woman's name, and, like magic, his confession seemed to summon her to town.

"I've got this, Bruce," Abby said, strolling to the counter. "So you're Victoria. I thought you'd be . . . taller."

The pixie wore four-inch heels, yet they stood eye to eye. She also screamed high maintenance. The clothes were more fit for an art gallery function than the Bound to Please bookstore, and the purse and shoes had designer written all over them. If Abby guessed right, the whole ensemble cost more than her car.

Steel-blue eyes squinted her way, indicating a bit of vanity at play. Heaven forbid she ruin her makeup by wearing glasses.

"Do you know Justin?" she asked, slightly less cordial than she'd been with Bruce.

"I do," Abby confessed. "I know him very well."

"Then you must know where I can find him."

"Oh, you won't find him around here. He's out of town."

Perfectly lined lips parted to reveal pearly white teeth. "Is he in Chicago? That would be just like him to come back to me right when I've come to retrieve him."

Her choice of words pricked a nerve. *Retrieve him.* As if Justin were one of her fancy purses.

"Justin won't be going back to Chicago. And he won't be going back to you, either."

The petite blonde closed the distance between them, sizing up her opponent with a bloodred sneer. "You must be the country bumpkin Q told me about. What was it? Agnes?"

Abby refused to take the bait. "He told me about you. How you like dinner parties and fancy things. Justin has moved on from that now. You're wasting your time coming down here."

"After living with the man for three years, I think I know him a little better than you do." That detail threw Abby off. She hadn't expected the revelations regarding his shallow fiancée to be so long in coming.

Victoria smiled the moment Abby flinched. "Men like Justin don't change, Miss Agnes. They get a little distracted sometimes," Victoria explained, "but always find their way back."

"It's Abby," she corrected. "And I didn't say he changed. I said he's moved on from you. I'm sure you had a good run, but there's nothing here for you to *retrieve*."

"You're feisty," she said. "I admire that." High-dollar perfume wafted in the air, making Abby long for the simplicity of her flowers. "Justin doesn't move on from me, my dear. Regardless of what he might have told you, this isn't anything we haven't been through before. We have a little misunderstanding, he goes to his end of the apartment and I go to mine, but we always make up. This time he ran a little farther, but no matter how far he strays, Justin knows that I'm the only woman for him."

Victoria's confidence ignited doubts in Abby. The man she described sounded nothing like the man Abby knew, which brought Haleigh's warning to mind. Though he'd told her about Victoria, Justin had clearly skipped some crucial details.

"Let me guess," the other woman pressed. "He told you that our engagement is off." Victoria shook her head with a knowing smile. "Our last fight was more serious than usual, but I'm still wearing his ring, and he's still paying for our apartment, so I wouldn't take those claims too seriously."

Anger simmered in Abby's chest. As much as she wanted to believe he hadn't lied to her, she couldn't ignore her own instincts. In fact, she'd done that far too much where Justin was concerned. In her desperation to find love, Abby had given her heart to a man she knew very little about. Sharing a hometown wasn't enough. He'd had a full life in Chicago, the details of which he'd glossed over at best. And the only reason a man continued to pay for an apartment in another city was if he intended to go back.

Pride alone kept Abby from admitting defeat.

"I'll say this one more time," she growled. "Justin isn't going back to Chicago, and he isn't going back to you. This trip was a waste of your time."

Bruce, who still lingered behind the counter, cleared his throat. "You have your answer now, ma'am. It's time for you to go."

Victoria didn't spare him a glance.

"I'm not leaving until I talk to *my fiancé*," she announced, squeezing the life out of her little black clutch. "I know he lives above this store. You can't keep me from seeing him."

Bluffing, Abby said, "He lives with me."

Technically, most of his wardrobe resided upstairs, but Justin had slept at Abby's house every night since leaving the hospital, and though petty, she wanted the woman to know exactly how far he'd strayed.

"Enjoy him while you can," Victoria snarled. "Because once he sees me, Justin won't remember your name."

With impressive grace, the dolled-up elf marched out the door in a cloud of obnoxious eau de toilette.

Coming to stand beside Abby, Bruce said, "She doesn't seem like his type."

"She's got three years and a ring that says differently," Abby replied.

Letting out a low whistle, he patted her on the back. "Looks like our Mr. Donovan has some explaining to do."

Yes, she thought. *Yes, he does.*

Loaded down with various samples from the Donovan Family Dessert Drive, Justin fumbled into the house, eager to tell Abby about his day. On the way home he'd decided to start with the bicycle story, featuring Uncle Willard and his pet squirrel, before rolling into the real entertainment of the afternoon, when Truline had displayed impressive pugilist skills up against cousin Wanda Jane.

Colt Thompson should have been the one getting the beating, since he'd been stupid enough to show up with Truline, and then swap spit with Wanda Jane behind the barn.

At times like these Justin found great peace of mind in the fact that Donovan blood did not run through his veins. Although his adoptive status had also led to more than one awkward pickup line at the buffet and an overexuberant good-bye kiss from Aunt Jezebel, who came by her name honestly.

"Hey, baby," he called from the foyer, dropping his keys on the side table. "I come bearing presents." Justin found Abby in front of her laptop at the table. "I grabbed a slice of pecan, like you asked, though I almost had to arm wrestle Uncle Moody for it."

Abby continued to stare at the screen. "You never seem to tell me the whole story," she said, voice even. Emotionless.

"What are you talking about?" He set the foil-covered paper plates on the table. "What story?"

A glance over her shoulder revealed the headline *Bettencourt Engagement Called Off—Infidelity Suspected.*

Slowly, Justin lowered into a chair. "Why are you looking at that?"

"She's beautiful," she said, ignoring his question. "A little too made up for my taste, but I can see why you chose her."

"I told you about Victoria last night. Why are you acting like this is a surprise?" He closed the laptop. "Look at me, Abby."

Like a robot, she turned his way. "You didn't tell me that you were still paying for your apartment in Chicago."

"The lease isn't up until October, but how do you know that?"

"I should know it because you told me, but instead I heard it from your fiancée. She showed up at the bookstore looking for you today," Abby explained. "Your Ms. Bettencourt said she'd come to retrieve you. Like a rebellious puppy who'd gotten out of the fence."

Justin had underestimated his former fiancée. "She isn't my any-thing, and I'm not interested in being retrieved." The second half of the headline lit like a neon sign in his mind. "Let's get to the point here, Abby. You aren't pissed because of a rent check. You think I cheated on her."

"*According to a source close to the couple, infidelity played a major role in the split*," she said, clearly quoting the article. "During our conversation today, Victoria let me know that no matter how far you *stray*, you always go back to her. Interesting choice of words, don't you think?"

Holding his temper in check, he said, "I'm not a dog, Abby. And I sure as hell don't stray."

"Did your engagement end because of cheating or not?" she asked.

Knowing what conclusion she'd drawn, he replied, "Yes, it did. And you assume the cheater had to be me."

Green eyes glowed with unshed tears. "What else am I supposed to think, Justin? Why else would you conveniently leave out that part of the story?"

"I've done nothing to make you doubt me. Nothing!" he bellowed, rising fast enough to send his chair flying. "You want to know the whole story?" he said, leaning over her. "Then I'll tell you. I walked into my apartment on a sunny March day to find my fiancée fucking Quintin Culpepper in my bed. That's why I left that part out. Forgive me for choosing to keep the humiliation to myself."

Abby sprang to her feet. "That's why you didn't tell me? Because you were embarrassed? What did you think I would do?" she asked. "Laugh at you? Justin, this can't work if you don't trust me with the truth."

"Trust?" he snapped. "You just accused me of being a cheater, and you want to talk about trust?"

"If you had told me everything, I wouldn't have been blindsided by Victoria Bettencourt. But this is what you do," she charged, stabbing a finger into the table. "You never tell me the whole story. Like why, if Quintin slept with your fiancée, are you helping him find property around here? Is that even why he's really in Ardent Springs?"

"I won't be interrogated," Justin said, heading for the front door.

Abby followed after him. "Why won't you answer me? Why won't you tell me?"

"Because not everything is your business," he snapped, drawing her up short.

"Wow," she mumbled. "I'm sorry you feel that way, because I can't live with all these secrets, Justin. I won't do it."

"You don't have to," he said, snatching his keys off the foyer table. "Because this is over." Without another word, he slammed the door behind him.

⁓

Abby didn't think she'd ever stop crying. Her sinuses throbbed, her throat felt raw, and she'd already progressed to her second box of tissues. By the time Haleigh responded to her sobbing message and rushed through Abby's front door, night had fallen, casting the living room in darkness.

"Abbs, honey, where are you?" Haleigh called as she switched on every light in the house.

"I'm here," she whimpered from her position on the living room floor.

Abby had cried at the table long enough to soak the cloth place mat before moving to the couch and sobbing all over her new throw pillows. As the sun went down, she descended with it, until her bottom hit the floor and her head dropped to her knees. That's where she'd been ever since, tears creating dark circles on her jeans.

Haleigh dropped down beside her and lifted Abby's head. "What happened?" she asked, reaching for a tissue to dab her friend's cheeks.

"I met Justin's fiancée today," Abby blubbered. "And she made me think he'd cheated on her."

"Whoa," she replied. "Justin has a fiancée?"

"Had," Abby corrected. "At least that's what he says, but he's still paying for their apartment in Chicago."

"That isn't a good sign."

"I know." She blew her nose before continuing. "If he'd told me the truth, that she'd cheated on him, I never would have accused him of being unfaithful."

Haleigh put an arm around Abby's shoulders. "This girl sounds like a real winner."

"She's gorgeous," Abby confessed. "Young and perky and totally sure of herself. Nothing at all like me."

Squeezing her shoulders, Haleigh said, "I don't care how gorgeous and perky this chick is, she has nothing on you." She slid the hair out of Abby's face, and then held her cheeks, looking into her eyes. "Take a breath now. In and out."

Abby hiccupped as she fought to calm down, but the tears continued to fall.

"I don't know how to fix this, Hal. I don't know how to make it right."

"Like you said, if he'd been up-front about everything, this might not have happened. Maybe you don't need to make it right."

"Please don't say I told you so," she sniffled. "I need you on my side right now."

"I'll always be on your side, honey." Her oldest friend kissed her cheek. "But half-truths aren't enough to make a relationship work. If he can't be totally honest, then he isn't the guy for you."

"I'm just not meant to have a happy ending," Abby lamented.

"Don't say that," Haleigh ordered. "There will be other guys. And if for some reason the right one never comes along, you can still be happy. Your life is wide open, Abbs. You can take all those trips you've dreamed about. Snap a selfie in front of the Eiffel Tower and Buckingham Palace. And you can take your best friend to the movies when she needs a break from the little ones."

Leaning away, Abby said, "How many are you planning to have?"

"Cooper wants four, but I'm still negotiating for two."

"We *are* twins," Abby reminded her. "You could get pregnant twice and still get four."

Shoving her friend away, Haleigh rose to her feet. "Are you trying to curse me?"

Grabbing the box of tissues, Abby rose with her. "No half-truths, remember?" After a deep breath, she said, "Thanks for coming over."

"Anytime. Do you feel better?"

"Sure," she said, lying to keep her friend from worrying.

Haleigh shook her head. "No, you aren't. But you will be. Do you want to come home with me?"

"No, I'll stay here," Abby said. If a miracle happened and Justin did come home, she wanted to be there. As stupid as that was.

"You sure?"

With a nod, she walked Haleigh to the door.

"Positive."

Abby stayed at the door long enough to watch the silver Ford Focus fade in the distance. On her way through the house, she switched off the lights, pulled a fresh box of tissues from the hall closet, and stopped at her bedroom door. Staring at the bed, a well of pain opened in her chest.

Without a word, she carried on to the spare bedroom next door and crawled under the covers to cry herself to sleep.

Chapter 23

"Explain this to me again," Justin ordered Q, who rode in his passenger seat. "You just happened to find an available piece of land next to the exit parcel?" The man had insisted that they make this drive today, which required Justin to sacrifice his lunch hour.

"All I had to do was check the public records," he explained. "This Tanner Drury guy has fifteen acres, including the land his house is on. We don't need all of it, so he gets to keep his home, and we make the investors happy." Pointing ahead, he said, "Pull off right up here."

Justin parked the Infiniti on the shoulder and climbed out. The edge of the original plot of land sat to his right, a field of tall grass sprawled to his left, and a narrow dirt road split the two.

"I don't see a sign," he said. "How did you know this land was for sale?"

"It wasn't," Q replied, rounding the front of the car. "I took a chance and called the guy up. Made a lowball offer, way under the price per acre we'll be paying for the first tract, but an amount this dude's probably never seen in his lifetime."

He wasn't about to let Q extort land from a local. "How lowball are we talking?"

"Almost twenty grand less per acre." He smacked Justin on the arm. "It's a steal, man. This solves everything."

It was a steal. And if they moved forward, Justin would make sure the price per acre went up significantly.

"How far does it go?" he asked, strolling down the side of the highway.

Q gestured toward the horizon line. "Just over that rise." Continuing down the road another thirty feet, they crested the modest hill and a building came into view. "The edge is about an acre past that garage."

Squinting, Justin made out the sign on the building. "That's Cooper Ridgeway's shop."

"Guess so." His friend shrugged. "But it won't be for long. The buildings will have to be cleared once we get rolling."

Justin shook his head. "Has he agreed to sell his part of the land?"

The jackass snorted. "That's the beauty of it. The Cooper guy doesn't own the land his business is on. When he bought the setup, Drury wanted to keep his land intact, so the moron bought the buildings and pays rent for the land." Q shook his head with a smile. "Gotta love these small-town hicks."

Snatching the man up by his offensively bright shirt, Justin snarled, "We aren't hicks, and you aren't taking this land."

"What are you talking about?" Q squirmed, his feet barely touching the ground. "This makes the deal, man. Who cares about one stinking garage? The dude can fix cars somewhere else."

"That's not the point," he ground through clenched teeth, shaking the worthless sack of shit with every word. "You don't get to ride into this town and start ripping lives apart. These are real people, you son of a bitch. Not collateral damage for your stupid land deal."

Justin released his hold, stirring dust when Q landed on his ass.

"This is *our* land deal," he said. "And I'm not giving it up because of a stupid garage. Get your head back in the game, Donovan. This is going to be huge. You know what we can do with fifteen acres. We'd be crazy to pass this up."

"Then I'm crazy," Justin said. "The deal is off. Take your ass back to Chicago and stay the hell out of my life."

Justin stomped back to the car, leaving his passenger on the side of the road.

"Hey!" Q yelled. "You can't leave me out here."

"Watch me," he mumbled and climbed behind the wheel.

⌒

"I'm not sure that's the right blue," Abby's mother said, changing her mind for the fifth time in the last hour.

"It's the blue you said you wanted," Haleigh reminded the older woman, growing as frustrated as Abby was.

They'd all gathered at Haleigh and Cooper's house to work on wedding details. Since Abby preferred to avoid the bookstore lest she encounter Justin, the location of the wedding became the obvious place to meet.

"Maybe we should go with the darker blue. I don't want Bruce to feel like I've turned this into a girlie affair. It's his wedding, too."

Abby flashed Haleigh an *I'll handle this* look. "We don't have enough of the dark blue to make all the bows, remember?" The plan was to put a bow on the first and last chair in every row. "This blue does not look girlie, and Bruce isn't going to care two bits about the decor so long as you meet him at the end of that aisle."

Mama sighed. "I guess you're right. If we don't have enough, then that one will have to do."

Rubbing her temples, Abby offered to make her mother happy. "Do you want me to pick up more of the dark blue tomorrow? There's plenty of time to make more bows."

"I don't want to put you out, honey."

A lie if Abby had ever heard one.

"I have to make a trip for the chalkboard anyway." Thanks to a wedding planner website Mama had found, guests would be directed throughout the day by chalkboard signs. "It won't be a problem to throw some ribbon in the basket."

Cheeks dimpled by a grin, Mama said, "That'll be good, then. I really do like the darker blue."

Haleigh rolled her eyes and Abby switched ribbons to begin the bow again. They continued to work in companionable silence, which had been the case for most of the day, since ignoring the subject of Abby's imploded love affair seemed to suck all the oxygen from the room.

She'd sent Justin a text on Sunday, letting him know she would gracefully back out of AJ Landscaping. There was no question that they would no longer work together, at least on her part. Justin hadn't bothered to answer, but she knew that he'd shown up on Main Street this morning to pick up where she'd left off.

Abby had also contacted Thea. Justin wouldn't stand a chance of completing the project on time without the garden society's continued assistance. Though their breakup had not played out in public, the gossip would commence once those who reported on such things noticed that the two were no longer spending time together. She didn't know or care what conclusions they'd make, but in case public opinion fell in Abby's direction, she wanted to make sure the older ladies didn't withdraw on her behalf.

"Have you decided what you're bringing to the cookout?" Haleigh asked, referring to the rehearsal dinner Friday evening. With the wedding being held in their backyard, it only made sense to turn the dinner afterward into one of Cooper's legendary cookouts.

"Not yet," Abby replied. Truth be told, she hadn't turned on her oven since the night Justin had made her meatloaf. Cooking for one didn't require much, and her loss of appetite at least meant she was keeping the weight off that she'd lost working on the flower beds.

"You should bring that pasta salad with the almonds in it," Mama suggested. "I liked that one."

As the salad didn't require heat, other than boiling water, which Abby could actually do without causing major damage, she said, "I might do that."

"I'm going to kill him," Cooper roared, tearing into the house like a man on fire.

"Kill who?" Haleigh asked, hopping out of her chair at the kitchen table.

Abby's brother pointed at her. "Your little boyfriend is going to pay for this."

She blinked, clueless what Justin could have done to Cooper. "Pay for what? And he isn't my boyfriend anymore."

"Good," Cooper snapped. "Then I won't feel bad about killing him."

Mama put down her glue gun. "There will be no killing of anyone. Now what are you ranting about, son?"

"The offer to buy Tanner's land came from a developer. A small company going by the name of Culpepper and Donovan." Gripping the seat back across from Abby, he fumed at her. "Sound familiar?"

"I can't believe it," she said, rising to her feet.

Cooper picked up the chair and slammed it down. "Believe it, because I saw the paperwork. That piece of shit is going to take my business to build some outlet mall. Who the hell needs an outlet mall up here?"

Abby didn't have an answer. Limbs numb, she collapsed back into her seat. All this time he'd been working with Q behind her back. Plotting to destroy her brother's life while sleeping in her bed. And she'd felt sorry for hurting him. Had been crying her eyes out over a man she clearly never knew.

A buzz replaced the numbness, as if she'd grabbed hold of a live wire. "We can't let this happen," she said, eyes staring straight ahead. "We have to stop them."

"It's too late," Cooper huffed. "Tanner plans to sign the papers tomorrow. They're undercutting him on the price per acre, but it's still more than he can pass up." Leaning against the counter, her brother's head dropped. "I don't know how long I have, but the deal is done. I'm going to have to move the business."

"To where?" Haleigh asked, rubbing a soothing hand along his arm.

Cooper shrugged. "I don't know. There aren't any standing options in town. If I want to keep it going, I'll probably have to build, and I don't have the capital for that."

"Bruce can help you," Mama offered.

Green eyes cut her off with a glare. "No," he said. "I'll figure this out on my own."

"Honey, maybe you should think—"

"I'm not taking charity," Cooper barked, stomping from the room.

The women exchanged worried glances before Haleigh said, "If you two come up with a solution for this, let me know. We cannot let him lose that garage." A second later she darted from the room to go after him.

"You have to fix this," Mama said. "Find Justin and make this right."

Abby stuttered. "Mama, I . . . I don't know how. You heard Cooper. The deal is done."

"Figure it out," she ordered, stepping out from behind the table. "You're the only hope your brother has."

Once this street project was finished, Justin was boarding a plane, and he didn't care where he landed as long as it was far away from Ardent Springs.

Everywhere he looked, he saw Abby. Even his own bed above the bookstore. Two nights on the ancient couch had done as little for his temper as for his back. His headaches returned, probably due to spending the morning lifting bags of dirt to fill the planters.

Not that he had a choice. Abby had backed out, likely concerned about rubbing shoulders with a known cheater, and though the garden ladies were still with him, Justin would burn in hell before he'd let one of them pick up a fifty-pound bag of dirt.

As he packed another bag into his third pot of the day, an all-too-familiar voice cooed behind him.

"Surely you haven't chosen manual labor over coming back to Chicago," Victoria chimed.

Justin was starting to hate the name of that damn city.

"Why are you here, Victoria?"

"For you, of course. Why else would I be in this hellhole?"

What had he ever seen in her?

"Then you've wasted a trip."

She released a long-suffering sigh. "You've made your point. I screwed up."

"You screwed Quintin," he corrected.

"When are you going to stop throwing that in my face?"

Taking a break, Justin leaned on the shovel handle. "We aren't talking about you breaking my favorite mug or scratching one of my records. You had sex with someone else in our bed. Someone who was supposed to be my friend."

"That was nothing," she quipped, brushing away reality with a hundred-dollar manicure. "I was upset that you'd been away so much. I was lonely."

"Then get a dog, Victoria. Or, here's an idea, a job."

His former fiancée had been brought up very much as Q had, only she'd never felt the need to step out on her own. Why bother when she had her daddy's credit cards to keep her in the lifestyle to which she'd become accustomed? In fact, Justin doubted he could have afforded to keep her happy for long, since those credit cards would have been the first thing to go.

"I have a job," she defended.

"Hosting nightclub parties is not a job."

Hot-pink lips flattened in a pout. "You don't get to criticize how I make my money when you're standing on a street corner playing in dirt."

Justin almost felt sorry for her. Victoria would never know the satisfaction of a job well done. Unless one considered twerking a job.

"There's no point in arguing," he sighed, wiping his forehead on his sleeve. "Go back to Dearborn Street and forget I ever existed."

"But Justin—"

"Victoria, I don't want you," he blurted, patience spent. "We're over. Move on."

Blue eyes turned to ice. "Like you did?" she asked. "I met your little country mouse the other day. Or maybe I should say cat, since she showed me her claws."

Justin returned to his work. "Stay away from Abby."

"Why? Afraid I'll tell her all your bad habits? Maybe scare her off?"

Playing the only card he knew would get her out of his life, he said, "How about if I call your daddy and let him know about that little cocaine habit he's been supporting?" When her eyes went wide, he added, "Yeah, I know about that."

She fidgeted, her bravado faltering. "I don't do it all the time."

"You do it enough," he said. "Just go home, Victoria. And consider getting yourself some help."

"You're going to miss me," she snapped, clicking up the sidewalk on her pointy heels.

"I'll do my best to muddle through," Justin murmured. Leaning forward, he wiped the sweat from his eyes on the bottom of his T-shirt. When he opened them again he spotted Abby crossing the street toward him. "This is not my freaking day."

Abby hadn't been able to hear what they were saying, but the look on Victoria's face indicated a less-than-friendly encounter. She'd nearly chickened out, hiding behind a sandwich sign in front of the Latte Love Café until the former fiancée had moved on. The only reason she forced herself to cross the street at all was the echo of Mama's words in her ear.

You're the only hope your brother has.

Which meant Cooper had very little hope at all. She would attempt to reason with Justin. Ask him not to buy the land, but remembering his comment about redeeming himself, she assumed her pleas would fall on deaf ears.

Still. She had to try.

The moment she stepped onto the curb, his eyes locked with hers. She'd been too busy avoiding traffic to realize he'd seen her coming. The sight of him released butterflies in her stomach, and for a second she hoped he might grace her with one of his smiles. The wicked ones that curled one side of his mouth higher than the other and always let her know how happy he was to see her.

But Justin didn't smile. "What do you want?" he asked.

Drawing on the bitter taste of betrayal, she said, "I need to talk to you."

"I'm talked out," he said, driving the shovel in his hands deep into the planter.

Determined, Abby stepped closer. "This is important."

"You know?" he jeered. "There were things that were important to me. Like trust. Loyalty. Respect. But every woman I meet throws those things back in my face. So forgive me if I'm not real interested in what you think is important."

Abby felt her chance slipping away. "I know I hurt you, Justin, but we need to talk."

"Dammit," he exploded. "What is it with you women? What part of *not interested* is so hard to comprehend?" Lifting the shovel from the planter, he slammed it against the sidewalk with a clang. "I don't need to listen to anything. I heard all I needed to hear when you revealed how little you think of me. Now, if you don't mind, *I* have work to do."

Catching several curious stares from passersby, Abby backed away, choking on humiliation and regret. Lies. The promises and the sweet words had all been lies, and she'd fallen for every one of them. As she walked away, the butterflies felt more like a swarm of killer bees, angry and painful and fighting to get out.

By the time she reached her car, the tears flowed unheeded, blurring her vision. Abby found napkins in the glove compartment and wiped her eyes. Both Haleigh and her mother had told her to fix this, and not only had Abby failed, she'd let Justin make a fool of her in the middle of the street. Starting the engine, she merged into traffic with a new mission in life.

To stay single for the rest of her days.

Chapter 24

By five o'clock, Justin had hit his bullshit limit for the day. As if his drive with Q and the sack-kicking visits from Victoria and Abby weren't enough, two of the new garden planters fell apart the moment he poured the dirt, making a mess all over the sidewalk.

This Monday could go suck a lightbulb. Justin was going home.

"Despite the setback," Thea said, catching him as he loaded the shovels into Pop's truck, "things are looking quite promising."

These planters had been special ordered and taken two weeks to come in. He didn't have two weeks to replace the defects.

"I'm glad you think so," he spouted, too tired to be polite. Sleep had been fitful at best since he and Abby had fallen apart. "If any more planters collapse on us, this street will be far less colorful than we'd planned."

"There are always compromises," she replied, seemingly unconcerned. "I saw you chatting with Abby earlier. She didn't look very happy when she walked away."

So far, Thea had maintained a professional distance. Justin didn't see any reason to change that now.

"She wanted to talk," he explained. "I didn't."

Removing her flower-covered orange gloves, Thea shook her head. "I thought you kids were going to make it, but I guess this was inevitable, with you sweeping Cooper's land out from under him like this."

"Excuse me?" Justin said, certain he'd misheard. "Me sweeping what?"

"The whole town is talking about it. At first most folks thought that bit of trouble who'd been asking about you was to blame for the breakup, but then we heard about you buying Tanner's land and forcing Cooper to move his business, and the truth was easy to guess."

Justin ripped off his gloves. "I'm not buying anything."

"There's no sense in denying it." She shrugged. "Your name was right there on the paper, next to that troublesome Culpepper fellow's. No one in town knows what to make of that boy."

Rubbing his face, Justin struggled to keep up. "Thea, I'm not buying anything, and I told Quintin this morning that he needed to go home and never come back."

"Really?" she said. "Are you sure?"

Sucking on his teeth, he nodded. "Yeah. I'm sure. What paper are you talking about? And what trouble is Q causing?"

Thea leaned on the truck bed. "Other than him being part of buying that land," she said, "he's taken up with Becky Winkle, who had been seeing Frankie Beckham until your friend came along."

Now Justin knew his ears were failing. "Frankie was dating Becky Winkle?"

"He quite liked her, too. Just this weekend he had a little too much to drink at Brubaker's Bar and let all in attendance know that if he caught Mr. Culpepper—he didn't refer to him so politely, of course—in a dark alley, he'd show him what happened when a fellow jumped another man's claim."

If Q did make the mistake of wandering into Frankie in a dark alley, he deserved whatever he got. Provided Frankie could see him. Justin was more interested in the land deal.

"The paper, Thea. What paper is my name on?"

She tapped the gloves against her leg. "The official offer on Tanner Drury's land. It's a shame he's having to sell. That farmland has been in his family for five generations."

This must have been why Abby came to see him. She thought he was putting her brother out of business.

"Did you see which way Abby went? Did she go to the bookstore?"

"She drove down Main, darling. I assume she went on home."

Justin raised the tailgate on the truck. "Thanks for the information," he said, swiping the keys from the truck ignition and locking the doors. He needed to reach Abby in a hurry, and the way he planned to drive would turn the shovels into weapons of mass destruction. "I'll move this later." Two steps toward the bookstore, where his Infiniti sat in the alley, he turned around. "Do you have Tanner Drury's number?"

"Oh, I don't . . ." she started.

"I never agreed to buy that land, Thea. Help me make this right."

She nodded. "I'll text it to you."

Justin gave a wave of gratitude as he sprinted past gawking pedestrians. He felt the phone vibrate in his pocket and kept on running.

"I tried," Abby pleaded for the third time. "He wouldn't listen to me."

Haleigh threw her hands in the air. "You should have made him listen."

"Well I didn't. So now what do we do?"

Cooper had returned to the garage more than an hour ago, and Mama had gone back to the bookstore to talk to Bruce. Her brother may be too prideful to accept charity, but family backed family, and in less than two weeks, Bruce would be part of theirs.

"What if we helped Tanner out?" Abby asked. "If we can get them money some other way, then they won't have to sell the land."

"Short of buying the land ourselves, I don't see how we could do that," Haleigh said, pacing her kitchen.

Maybe that was the answer. "Then that's it. We'll buy the land."

Brown eyes pierced her to the wall. "Do you have a quarter million dollars sitting around?"

Abby's house didn't even cost that much. "That's what Justin is paying him?"

Haleigh rolled her eyes. "He has *investors*," she spat. "This deal won't cost that little pecker a penny."

Name-calling seemed a bit much, but then her friend had every right to be furious. Cooper's whole life was on that land, including a collection of old cars he'd planned to restore. They would likely be the hardest items to relocate.

"What about an injunction?" she asked. "Shouldn't the town have a say in what they put out there?"

"Tanner's land is beyond the city limits. They'll need permits through the county, but that's only once they start building. They can buy any land they want if they have the money."

Her fallout with Justin had been a heartbreak for her alone. Abby had dealt with loss before and survived, and she would do so again. But this was an attack on her family. An outsider invading their territory and taking down one of their own.

With every fiber of her being, Abby wished that Justin had never come back from Chicago.

Haleigh continued to pace as Abby's phone chimed from her purse. Assuming it was Mama with an update, or possibly a solution, she checked the screen.

"It's Justin," she whispered, as if he might hear her.

"Give me that phone," Haleigh growled, snatching it from Abby's hand and accepting the call. "You listen to me, you little two-bit weasel. You've screwed with the wrong family. And if you think you're going to call my best friend just to make her cry again, you're more of an idiot than I thought you were. We're going to fight you on this, and we're going to win. So piss off."

In shock, Abby stared at her cell spinning where Haleigh had thrown it on the floor. "We're going to fight him?" she said.

"Of course we are." If she paced any harder, Cooper would need to replace the kitchen tile along with his garage.

"How are we going to do that?"

"I don't freaking know," Haleigh said, taking a seat and dropping her head onto the table. "That was the anger talking. Gah!" She snapped upright. "I want to punch him in the throat for doing this to Cooper. I mean, I'd kick him in the balls for you, but that noise they make when you get a good blow on the windpipe is really satisfying."

Abby opted not to ask how Haleigh knew that.

"I wouldn't mind kicking him myself, but daydreaming about the way we could inflict pain on Justin Donovan isn't getting us any closer to an answer."

"I know. Still," she said. "I'd like to snatch a knot in his ass."

Patting her friend's hand, Abby sighed. "We all would, sweetie. We all would."

Thanks to Haleigh—at least that's who Justin believed had called him a two-bit weasel—intercepting his call, Justin still had no idea where to find Abby. He'd been on the way to her house and wasn't surprised to find the place empty. Since Haleigh was a doctor, he tried the hospital, but once he arrived, Justin had no idea where to look for them.

A quick check of the cafeteria turned up nothing, so he'd asked a passing nurse for the maternity floor. When he arrived at the desk, a chipper nurse in Disney-themed scrubs let him know Dr. Mitchner was not on duty.

Running out of time, he changed tactics and pulled up Thea's text. One touch and he waited through four rings before Tanner Drury picked up.

"Hello?"

"Mr. Drury, this is Justin Donovan. I understand my colleague, Mr. Culpepper, had been in touch with you."

"Yes," responded a creaky voice. "He has."

"This is going to seem like an odd question, but are you sure you want to sell your land?"

A weighted pause echoed down the line. "I don't know that 'want to' plays into it much, Mr. Donovan."

Exactly what Justin figured. "What would have to happen for you to turn down Mr. Culpepper's offer?"

"I thought the offer came from both of you."

"Not quite. Please, Mr. Drury, what would make you change your mind?"

A hum traveled down the line. "We need the money, plain and simple. I've got diabetes now, and the medicines aren't cheap. Diana needs that knee replacement . . ."

Ah, yes. The good old American health care system. "What if you received another offer? One that wouldn't result in the land being developed?"

"I don't know," he said, understandably skeptical. "What are we talking about here?"

Justin did some quick math and guessed at what Q had offered. "Would two hundred thousand cover it?"

Another hesitation. "That's fifty thousand less than the other offer."

Damn. Still ridiculously low compared to the other plot for sale, but just out of Justin's price range. Unless he found a way to come up with a little more money.

"I might be able to match that. Mr. Drury, can you give me twenty-four hours?"

Indecision was clear in his voice as he said, "I'm supposed to sign with Mr. Culpepper in the morning. Not sure I want to jeopardize the deal."

"Just twenty-four hours," Justin bargained. "I know that Mr. Culpepper is very anxious to take your land. Tell him that you want one more day to think it over. If I don't call you by this time tomorrow evening, you can sign the papers Wednesday morning and nothing changes."

Justin held his breath.

"And you say if you buy it, nothing gets put on it?"

"That's right," he agreed.

"Then what do you want it for?"

"A gift," Justin said, watching the sun set behind the hospital. "I want to buy it as a gift for someone."

"Well," chuckled the man on the other end. "That's a mighty big gift, but if you've got the money, I sure would like to see it stay the way it is now."

Eyes closed with relief, he said, "You and me both, Mr. Drury. I'll be in touch."

Ending the call, Justin leaned on the steering wheel, exhausted as if he'd been running a marathon. His savings didn't quite measure up to the funds needed, and twenty-four hours wasn't much time to find another investor. Of course, he'd then have to explain to said investor that he or she would never see a return on their money. Not likely to go over well.

Sitting back, he stared at the shiny Infiniti symbol pressed into black leather and knew what he had to do.

The mood over dinner was somber, at best. In a show of unity, Bruce closed the shop early so that he and Mama could join Abby, Haleigh, and Cooper for dinner at her brother's house.

"This is good chicken," Mama said, repeating the sentiment for the second time.

"Thanks," Haleigh replied, the same response she'd given five minutes earlier.

Watching the people she loved most in the world act as if the apocalypse were imminent, Abby set down her fork and took charge.

"We've moped long enough," she said, drawing everyone's attention. "Yes, this sucks. Cooper's going to have to move his business. But this isn't the end of the world. We can handle this."

"*We* aren't handling anything," Cooper argued. "This is my problem to fix."

"Horseshit," Mama said, startling them all into silence. "We're a family, and families stick together. Back when you bought that garage, we all had a hand in cleaning it up. Organizing and making it yours. And we'll do it again."

"That's right," Abby said. "And now we have two more family members to join the team."

Cooper dropped his fork with a loud clang. "I shouldn't have to move in the first place. I spent two hours this afternoon searching for a new location, and there's nothing."

"What about the old gas station way up Fifth?" Bruce asked. "On the corner there, right before it turns into Hillsboro. That's been empty for a couple years now."

Shaking his head, her brother said, "They razed it. I drove by there today."

"Then maybe you can build there," Haleigh suggested.

"Maybe," he said with little enthusiasm.

Abby hit her limit. "Is this what I've been like for the last two years?" she asked, pointing at Cooper. "And if it is, how did you all not smack me before now?"

"Don't be a smart-ass, Abbs," growled her twin.

"Language," Mama corrected.

Cooper's face turned red. "You said *horseshit* two seconds ago."

Stabbing her chicken, his mother said, "That was different. You made me mad."

"And she made *me* mad," he stated, channeling his inner toddler.

"Let's all get a grip," Haleigh shouted, tapping a fork against her glass. "Fighting isn't going to help." When the Ridgeways fell silent, she continued. "Abby is right. At the risk of sounding clichéd, it doesn't matter if you get knocked down. It only matters that you get back up. Moving a business happens all the time. It's the reality we're facing, and we'll deal with it."

A hush fell over the table as everyone returned to eating.

"Have you contacted Ronnie Ottwell yet?" Bruce asked, referring to a realtor they'd all used before. "He might know a place."

Cooper nodded. "I'm meeting with him tomorrow afternoon. I was hoping Tanner would call and say he'd changed his mind, but that was wishful thinking on my part."

"With all this going on," Mama said, "maybe we should put off the wedding."

"Oh, Linda, no," Haleigh cut in, followed closely by Cooper.

"Nothing is getting in the way of this wedding. Besides, I've already bought twenty pounds of ribs, and Spencer is bringing another twenty pounds of pulled pork. No sense in letting it go to waste."

It was Bruce's turn to drop his fork. "Son, that's a lot of meat."

With a humble shrug, Cooper smiled. "It was supposed to be a surprise. A gift for the happy couple."

Even Abby didn't know about the generous spread. "We'll be eating pork for weeks." She laughed, relieved to see her loved ones smiling again.

"Not with one hundred and twenty on the guest list," Haleigh chimed in.

"Linda!" Bruce cried, nearly choking on his drink. "You promised you'd get it down to less than a hundred."

"I tried, honey. I really did." Mama's grin eliminated any chance of her looking remorseful.

"Have you invited the whole county?" her groom asked.

"Oh, Bruce," she chuckled. "They aren't all from this county."

Haleigh burst out laughing, while Cooper covered his mouth to keep from spitting chicken across the table. Abby opted to console her future stepfather.

"Just think of all the presents you'll get," she said, patting his arm. "And remember, enduring Mama's overzealous guest list will pay off when you're spending a week alone with your lovely new bride in the mountains of Gatlinburg."

Appeased, he sighed. "That is something to look forward to." Digging back into his dinner, Bruce said, "Just so you know, I left notice on the apartment door above the store. He has a week to vacate the premises."

"You didn't have to do that," Abby said.

"Yes, I did. That boy is hurting my family. He needs to go."

Though Bruce had been in their lives for over a year, he'd always seemed like an outsider. The guy in Mama's life but not necessarily Abby's and Cooper's. Until that moment.

Cooper locked eyes with his sister, and they both nodded. As twins, they often didn't need words to communicate.

For the rest of the meal, the Ridgeways and their significant others tossed around ideas for Cooper's new and improved business. And for the first time in a long time, Abby didn't feel like the odd one out. She may not have her own significant other, but she had people who loved her, and that was enough.

Chapter 25

"Are you sure you want to do this?" Pop asked, bouncing one knee.

Justin didn't have to be told to know that his father was uncomfortable. Surrounded by luxury machines and salesmen wearing suits that likely cost more than the old Chevy had new, the man in the overalls was definitely out of his comfort zone.

"Much like Tanner Drury," Justin muttered, "I don't want to but I have to."

"I told you we can sell the tractor. It's worth nearly twice as much as your car."

The '85 Case was Pop's pride and joy. If anyone was going to part with something they loved, it would be Justin.

"We've done that dance and you aren't parting with your tractor."

Harrumphing with annoyance, Pop kicked a pebble at his feet. "I don't see why we're here. There's no reason you should lose something you worked so hard for just to help Cooper Ridgeway out of a jam."

"Because I put him in that jam," Justin stated simply. "If Q hadn't followed me down here, none of this would be happening. I should have kept a better eye on him."

Pop snorted. "You aren't the boy's keeper, son. His sins are not yours."

True, Justin thought, but this particular sin would cause more damage than a lost job and fiancée. It was one thing for Q to mess with his life, quite another for him to mess with Abby's family. But there was another reason Justin was taking such drastic action.

"I appreciate your support, Pop, but I might not deserve it. The fact is, a year ago I probably would have done the same thing that Q is doing now. Close the deal by any means necessary, without a thought to the collateral damage left behind. I'm not proud of that, but it's who I was."

Not a flicker of disappointment shone in the older man's eyes.

"One of the benefits of growing old—maybe the only benefit—is knowing more today than you did yesterday. Or thirty years ago, for that matter." Ken Donovan relaxed into the small leather sofa. "When your mom said we should adopt, I was hesitant. 'You never know what you're going to get,' I thought. What if we got a bad seed?"

Unsure where this was going, Justin said, "It's a toss-up for sure."

"Nearly thirty years later and I wouldn't have any other child. You're a good man, son. You always were. A little ambitious, but that's a good thing. I never had to worry that you'd take up residence on our couch long beyond the time came for you to be on your own." Tapping the side of his nose, he winked. "I like to cuddle with your mom in the evenings, and you'd have been in the way."

"Maybe that's why I tend to fall for a woman so fast. I'm trying to find what you and Mom have."

"You'll find it," he said, squeezing Justin's knee. "Don't be too hard on yourself, son. Being young means making mistakes. So long as you learn from them, you'll do all right."

The last few years had been filled with enough mistakes for a decade. The wrong girl, the wrong friends, the wrong approach to life. The only mistake he hadn't made was coming back home, yet he'd still managed to mess that up in the end. Abby may have jumped to the wrong conclusion, but if he'd been up-front with her from the beginning instead of protecting his all-too-delicate pride, they might have had a chance.

"We've got the paperwork all drawn up, Mr. Donovan," said the young saleswoman who'd welcomed them nearly thirty minutes ago. "I'll give you a few minutes to look this over."

Taking the document, Justin's eye went straight to the bottom line. Slightly shy of what he'd been hoping for, but a sound offer and likely the best he'd get on such short notice.

"I don't need to look it over," he said before she could walk away. "I'm ready to sign."

"Great. Just follow me then."

As she led them across the showroom, Pop put his hand on Justin's shoulder. "I'm proud of you, son. I want you to know that."

For once in Justin's life, words failed him. In stunned silence, he stepped into the tiny windowed office to sign his baby away.

∽

The Safe Haven Women's Shelter, a passion project for Carrie Farmer, established with the help of Haleigh and her mother, had opened the previous December, but Abby had never had a reason to visit.

Until today.

Not long after dinner the night before, Carrie phoned with an invitation to lunch. Only instead of meeting at one of their usual haunts, she'd asked Abby to drive out to the shelter. Considering she didn't have a job, and sitting around waiting for the call that Tanner had signed would only make her crazy, Abby had agreed.

"So how do you like the facility?" Carrie asked at the end of the unexpected tour.

"It's nice," Abby replied, impressed by both the welcoming decor and the homelike atmosphere. "When we were kids, Cooper and I came up here for a few summers when this was still a camp, and I never imagined it could look like this."

"Because of what our residents have endured before they arrive, we put a lot of focus on calm, clean, and cozy."

Curious, she asked, "Is there a limit to how long they can stay?"

Carrie shook her head. "Not at all. We provide resources to help them transition out, but there's no point at which we force them to leave."

Speaking of transitions, Abby marveled at the woman before her. Two years ago Carrie could have been best described as a mouse. Timid, skittish, and quiet. Today she served as a powerful advocate for the abused and underserved. A confident, courageous woman in her own right, and a force of nature when it came to her beloved shelter.

"What about the men?" Abby asked, dancing around a delicate subject. "What if they come looking for them?"

"That was probably our biggest dilemma—how to keep every-one safe once they were here," she said, leading Abby from the main entrance back to her office. "Thankfully, Dale Lambdon provided a solution by convincing local law enforcement officers to volunteer on their days off. Between the sheriff's office and the Ardent Springs police department, we almost always have armed security on the premises."

"Wow," she said. "That's really generous."

"But not surprising," the other woman added. "In my experience, police officers and firefighters are the best when it comes to caring for others." As if realizing what she'd said, Carrie backtracked. "I mean, most of them. Not all."

Abby held up a hand. "It's okay. Justin doesn't care any less about his fellow man than he did before we broke up. He only cares less about me."

"I doubt that's true," she soothed. "He'll come around."

"He might," Abby agreed. "But it's too late to go back now. Not with him brokering the sale that's forcing Cooper to move his business."

"Cooper is moving his business?" Carrie asked.

"Maybe the gossip lines haven't stretched this far out yet," she quipped. "It's a bit complicated, but Justin and one of his friends offered to buy Tanner Drury's land in order to put an outlet mall, and who knows what else, out by the interstate. Though Cooper owns the business, he was paying rent to stay on the land. That won't be an option once the sale goes through."

Leaning back in her chair, she said, "That's awful. Is he doing it to get back at you?"

"That's the kicker," Abby said, tapping the arm of her chair. "The deal was in the works before we split up."

Carrie's jaw nearly hit the desk. "You're kidding."

"I wish," she sighed. And she hated herself for it.

Even now, with all the evidence staring her in the face, a little voice buried deep in Abby's heart insisted that the man she fell in love with wouldn't do such things. That if given the chance, Justin could explain everything, the land would be safe, and they could go back to the way things were.

Before she broke his heart.

And he broke hers.

"I'm really sorry," Carrie said. "Now I feel awkward about why I brought you here."

"Why?" Abby asked, baffled about why their location would make things awkward.

Carrie flattened her palms on the desk. "It's time to confess. I didn't really ask you here for lunch."

Confused, she said, "That's funny, because you fed me." They'd had delicious sandwiches hand delivered by Carrie's boyfriend, Noah.

"Okay. Not *only* lunch. I was hoping that you might come to work for us."

Too shocked to speak, Abby stared, certain that her face reflected the classic deer-in-the-headlights look.

"I wasn't sure if you were even looking for a job," Carrie continued, "but Haleigh told me that you weren't working with Justin on the landscaping anymore, and though you're ridiculously overqualified, I'm hoping you'll still consider the offer."

Stunned didn't begin to describe this moment. Just last night she and Haleigh had discussed Abby's future and come to the conclusion that she would most likely have to commute at least an hour each way in order to find a new nursing position. Maybe longer.

At the mention of her best friend, she grew suspicious. "Did Haleigh put you up to this?"

"I actually haven't talked to her about it," Carrie confessed. "I meant to, but she canceled our meeting yesterday due to some family emergency that I assumed she'd tell me about later." Revelation dawning, she said, "That was the issue with Cooper's business, huh?"

Abby affirmed her suspicions. "That was it. If she could have gotten her hands on Justin yesterday, he'd be walking with a limp today, if he was able to walk at all." Returning to the topic at hand, Abby proceeded with cautious optimism. "As far as the offer goes, what should I be considering?"

"I'm calling it a resident liaison. The reality is, many of our residents arrive battered and bruised. A trip to the ER is dangerous, as we can't protect them as well there, and adds to the humiliation they already feel. We've begun the process of improving our small clinic, but we need someone to run it. A medical professional who would not only treat them as patients, but as human beings. Equals, even."

Though not as creative as designing flower beds, Abby couldn't imagine a more ideal position. Her entire motivation for becoming a nurse had been to help people, but by the time Iva had let her go, her job had felt more like a thankless routine. The patients came and went, and she'd been too locked in her own pity party to make a real connection with any of them. Which meant the hospital had never been the problem—Abby was.

In the role that Carrie described, she could help heal not only the physical wounds of the women and children who walked into the shelter, but the wounds that couldn't be seen as well. With compassion and a friendly smile, Abby could be the light in someone else's darkness.

And she liked the thought of that very much.

"I'll take it," she said, riding a wave of enthusiasm.

"You will?" Carrie chirped, rising from her chair. "But we haven't talked about pay or benefits or anything."

Abby tapped out a happy beat on the desktop. "We can work those out later. When should I start?"

Caught off guard, Carrie shuffled a stack of folders to check her calendar. "Will next Monday be too soon?"

"Not soon enough." Bolting to her feet, Abby leaned over the desk to drag Carrie into a hug. "Thank you so much. This is exactly what I needed."

Carrie beamed. "Excellent. But for the sake of full disclosure, it isn't always going to be sunshine and rainbows," Carrie warned. "Many of our residents have trust issues and don't warm up easily. It may be a battle at first to get through to them."

If nursing had taught her anything, it was how to gain someone's trust.

"I'm ready." She nodded with renewed purpose. "And grateful for the opportunity."

"Alrighty then," Carrie said, hurrying around the desk. "Welcome to the Safe Haven family, Ms. Williams. Let's go meet the rest of the staff, shall we?"

Abby grinned like a loon. "I have no place else to be." She laughed and motioned toward the hall. "Lead the way."

At five after six Tuesday evening, Justin placed the call he'd promised to make.

"Hello," answered Tanner Drury in his rusty tone.

"Mr. Drury, it's Justin Donovan again."

"Well," the landowner said, "I wasn't sure whether I'd hear from you."

His lack of confidence was understandable. If a stranger called offering a quarter million dollars out of the blue, Justin would be dubious as well.

"I'm assuming you asked Mr. Culpepper for the extra time?"

"I did," came the reply. "He wasn't happy, but didn't withdraw the offer over it."

Cutting to the chase, Justin said, "I have the money to match the original offer." In addition to selling the Infiniti, he'd drained both his savings and his 401(k), but sacrifices had to be made. "Do you want an offer in writing this evening, or would you rather wait until morning?"

Unaccustomed to the sleep habits of septuagenarians, Justin didn't want to keep the man awake if he didn't have to.

The line went silent, Mr. Drury presumably deciding how much he trusted his new benefactor.

"Would you mind coming by the house tonight?"

Assessing the few boxes he had left to pack, Justin replied, "Is seven thirty too late?"

"Not at all. Do you need the address?"

Justin kept the amusement from his tone. "I have it, sir. I'll see you in a bit."

"Sounds good."

"You should not have to do all this," his mother grumbled as soon as the call ended. The way she was packing his coffee mugs, he'd be lucky if any remained intact. "People should know that you wouldn't do these horrible things. The whole town thinks you're some land-grabbing monster. It's nonsense."

Kissing her cheek, Justin removed the Cubs mug from her angry grip. "My name is on the paperwork, Mom. That's all they know."

"But *you* didn't put it there," she insisted. "I have half a notion to tell that prissy Linda Ridgeway that her girl is the mean one. Calling you a cheater. The nerve of her."

Having learned his lesson regarding half-truths and whole stories, Justin had disclosed all his dirty secrets to his parents, tossing his bruised ego at their feet and hoping for the best. That they supported him wholeheartedly came as no surprise, but his mother's righteous indignation had been the cherry on top. When she'd heard about the eviction notice, which Justin hadn't for a second considered challenging, Mom had to be forcibly subdued from charging after Bruce Clemens and telling him exactly where he could stick his precious apartment.

"Women can be a challenge," Pop said, packing the books from the windowsill. "You never know when they're gonna turn on you."

"Don't judge us all by that Ridgeway girl," Mom scolded.

"Williams," Justin corrected.

Blue eyes rolled. "Seems to me, if a man gives a woman his name, he should stick around instead of traipsing all over the world."

Father and son exchanged a questioning glance.

"The boy was in the army, Karen," Pop reminded her. "He wasn't traipsing anywhere. He was serving his country."

"You served *your* country and I went with you."

Returning to his packing, Pop said, "A year in Greece in the eighties was different. They're sending these soldiers into war zones. What was he supposed to do, strap her to his back and head out?"

Conceding her husband's point, Mom said, "I don't suppose so. But she must have been sick with worry. All those years of not knowing where he was or if he was okay. A woman shouldn't be left in the dark, is all I'm saying."

Justin never flew off into battle, but he had run into a burning building without her knowing where he was. Abby had most likely been angry at first, when he stood her up without so much as a text, but at some point the worry must have set in. All the old fears creeping up from the past, taunting her with the worst-case scenario.

Another woman might have walked away. Chosen sanity over constant dread. But not Abby. She'd not only stayed, she'd been there when he woke. A lifeline out of the darkness. An angel by his side. And he'd let her go. Let anger and pride ruin the best thing that ever happened to him.

"If she hadn't hurt my boy, I'd almost feel sorry for her," Mom added, dragging Justin from his thoughts.

"No," he said. "The last thing Abby would want is your pity. She's stronger than anyone gives her credit for, and heaven knows I never deserved her."

Wadding the newspaper in her hand, his mother jumped to her son's defense. "She accused you of cheating, Justin."

"And if I'd told her the truth before Victoria got to her, things would be different now. Just like if I'd told *you* the truth, your reaction when Q called would have been different. To think," Justin said, reaching for a Blackhawks mug, "all of this might have been avoided if I hadn't been so determined to protect my ego."

For once his mother didn't argue, but his father's words broke the silence and the tension.

"Welcome to manhood, son. We're all idiots here."

Chapter 26

Wednesday morning the deal was done. Or at least secured. Justin had submitted an official offer to Tanner Drury to buy fifteen acres of land for $250,000, and Tanner had accepted. By Wednesday afternoon, Q learned that his *steal of a deal* had indeed been stolen, Royce-Upton retracted their interest in the project thanks to a phone call from Justin's lawyer back in Chicago stating his client was not and never would be in business with one Quintin Culpepper, and Justin had officially moved back in with his parents.

Temporarily, of course.

Thursday had been duty at the fire station, which made Friday the big day. Justin pulled the old pickup onto the premises of Cooper's Total Auto Care and hoped the big man would let him talk before throwing a punch. On a good day he could hold his own in a fight, but his chances were greatly diminished with his concussion.

Stepping onto the pavement, Justin spotted Frankie first. Since they'd shared duty the night before and Justin had disclosed his recent activities, he had at least one ally in his corner. Which was good, since the next face he saw looked set on murder.

"You've got some fucking nerve," Cooper growled, charging across the drive.

"Step off, brother," said Frankie, standing his ground at the edge of the garage. "Hear him out before you do something stupid."

Green eyes so much like Abby's bored through Justin's skull. "I'm not interested in anything this shithead has to say."

"I don't need to say anything," Justin stated, squaring his stance. "I only came to deliver something." He held the folded document in the air.

"What's that?" Cooper spat. "My marching orders?"

Shaking his head, he kept his voice even. "Just read it. That's all I ask."

The mechanic snatched the papers from Justin's hand, and flipping to the first page, he skimmed the contract. "What is this?" he asked, brows drawn. "You and your buddy are charging me rent?"

Taking the opening, Justin explained. "I was never involved in the original deal with Quintin Culpepper. We used to be friends and colleagues, and he used my name without my permission. I'd never heard of Tanner Drury until Monday morning, when the deal was already in motion."

"But he sold to you," Cooper said. "For your fancy development scheme."

"Again, not my scheme. I was in on the legwork on the six acres for sale closer to the interstate, but that's where my involvement ends." Encouraged that he'd gotten this far without losing any teeth, Justin continued. "The only way I could stop Quintin's deal was to buy the property myself. Your friend Mr. Drury needed the money, so I made sure he got it."

Shuffling, Cooper returned his attention to the document. "So now you're charging me rent?"

Knowing Ridgeway would never accept the land for free, Justin had devised the next-best solution.

"This garage and its outbuildings sit on a quarter acre, which is worth ten thousand dollars in the current market. At two hundred dollars a month, you'll have the property paid off in less than five years."

Slapping the contract against his leg, the man stared hard, as if uncertain whether to believe his sudden good fortune. "What are you going to do with the rest of the land?"

"Tanner has approved possible leasing for livestock, but otherwise, the rest of the parcel will remain untouched." Justin left out the part about possibly building a house on it someday, as that remained a distant dream pending future developments, and not of the real estate kind.

With one simple word, Cooper cut to the heart of the matter. "Why?"

Justin cleared his throat. "I have my reasons." Gesturing toward his new tenant, he said, "That's your copy. You're welcome to have it reviewed and under no obligation to sign, but if you do, my number is on the last page."

Climbing into the truck, he heard the man closing in behind him.

"You're doing this for Abby," Cooper charged, as if he'd solved a puzzle. "You still care about her."

"Like I said before." Justin closed the truck door and started the engine. "Always have. Always will."

The rehearsal dinner was only a week away, and Abby had yet to decide if she really wanted to take pasta salad. Something as special as her mother's rehearsal dinner deserved a bit more effort on her part.

Lorelei would supply the desserts, which eliminated the need for a second attempt at a cake. Having just gotten her house back together, the idea of setting it on fire again did not appeal.

Nor did she want a certain fireman charging in to save her. Not that he would.

She'd been through four cookbooks so far—casseroles, Crock-Pot, five-ingredient, and quick and easy. As far as Abby was concerned, not a single recipe in the last one looked quick or easy. Though all included delicious-sounding meals, not one hit on the key element she needed.

A recipe she could actually pull off.

But positive Abby would not give up and moved on to cookbook number five, the classic *Cooking for Dummies*. Clearly this book was written with her in mind.

"Oh, shish kebabs," she said aloud. "I bet I can do that. How hard could it be to slide meat and veggies onto a stick?"

"Abby, where are you?" hollered Haleigh from the front door. Before she could get out of her seat, her best friend sprinted into the kitchen. "What the hell, Abbs? Why aren't you answering your phone?"

Checking her cell, she spotted six missed calls. As part of her new job, Abby had met with the shelter board that morning and must have forgotten to turn her ringer back on.

"I didn't hear it," she said, panic rising. "What's the matter? Is something wrong?"

"Absolutely nothing," Haleigh chimed, dragging Abby from her seat and twirling her around the kitchen. "It's all fixed. And you aren't ever going to believe how."

More than a little confused, she twisted out of the crazy woman's arms. "Did Cooper find another garage?"

Like a kid on a playground, Haleigh leaned forward and said, "Even better," before jumping in place. "And the best part? It was all for you." Fearing she'd fallen off the wagon, Abby leaned close enough to smell Haleigh's breath and got her nose swatted. "Stop it, you dork. I haven't been drinking. I'm just happy. For both of us."

Confusion growing, Abby crossed her arms. "You aren't making any sense. What is fixed, and what does it have to do with me?"

"You'd better sit down for this." Haleigh pulled over a chair and placed it behind Abby's knees. "Go ahead," she said, waiting. "Sit."

"Just tell me already."

With a resigned sigh, she started at the beginning. "Justin showed up at the garage today." Abby's butt hit the chair. "I tried to warn you. Cooper, of course, was going to kill him on sight, but Frankie made him stop and listen."

"Lucky for Justin that Frankie was there."

"Eh. That firefighter training isn't for sissies. He might have survived with minor fractures."

Brows up, Abby stared her back to the point.

"Right. He handed Cooper a rental agreement. Apparently that Culpepper guy used Justin's name even though he wasn't involved. He didn't even know who Tanner Drury was until earlier this week."

She was lost again. "If he wasn't involved, then what was the rental agreement?"

"That's the best part. Justin bought the land out from under Culpepper, and he's going to let Cooper rent the property that the garage sits on until he's bought it outright. A rent-to-own type of deal."

"So he isn't going to develop the land? Or is he letting Cooper stay and putting the outlet mall around him?"

"No development," she answered. "There might be some cows on it eventually, but they'll be far enough away not to bother the garage."

Struggling to wrap her head around the story, Abby bounced back to her feet, walking and talking at the same time.

"Justin spent a quarter of a million dollars on a piece of land, and he intends to do nothing with it?"

Haleigh grabbed her by the shoulders. "Don't you see? He did it for you. And for Cooper, but mostly for you."

"You don't know that," Abby whispered, afraid to get her hopes up. "He just hates Q. Justin didn't want him to win."

"Uh-uh," she corrected, wiggling a finger in the air. "To make sure this is all legit, Cooper called Tanner. He shared the whole story. After Justin promised that he'd never develop the land, Drury asked him why he wanted to buy it. He said as a gift." Shaking the stuffing out of Abby, she added, "A gift for you, woman. He still loves you."

"No," she snapped, rejecting the possibility. "Maybe he felt bad and didn't want Cooper to lose his business. Or maybe he wanted to get back at Culpepper for sleeping with his fiancée. Whatever reason Justin has for doing this can't possibly have anything to do with me."

Calming, Haleigh navigated Abby back to the chair and forced her to sit before cradling her cheeks. "Listen to me, Abby Lou. When Cooper accused Justin of doing this because he still cared about you, he said, 'Always have. Always will.' Honey, that boy has loved you for a long time. And nobody knows better than I do how much men like that are worth."

"Do you really think he wants this to work?" she asked.

"I'd say dropping a quarter million dollars is a sure sign, yes."

Pressing against her best friend's palm, Abby said, "But what if you're wrong?"

With a tender smile, Haleigh replied, "What if I'm not?"

An ember of hope glowed warm in Abby's chest. "Should I try to talk to him?"

"I'll never forgive you if you don't."

"Well, then," she sighed. "I guess I'd better go."

Slender arms pulled her up into a protective hug. "Go get your happy ending, Abby Lou. You definitely deserve it."

Tucking her head into Haleigh's shoulder, Abby let the smile shine through. "This is really scary."

The taller woman pulled away. "You can do this. Love makes you stronger, remember?"

Abby took a deep breath. "Right. I can do this."

"Yes, you can," she cheered, waving invisible pom-poms.

Reaching for her purse and keys on the table, Abby shook her head. "Don't do that."

Haleigh followed her to the garage. "Too much?"

"Way too much." She turned to place a wet kiss on the blonde's cheek. "Wish me luck."

"You don't need luck. You have love."

Hitting the button to open the garage door, Abby shook her head. "You should get a job writing greeting cards with that one. Don't forget to lock that."

As she climbed behind the wheel, Haleigh did as ordered, pulling the door shut behind her. "I didn't have to come here, you know," she snipped, sashaying past Abby's car. Smacking the trunk, she yelled, "Pick up some condoms on the way."

Laughing as she put the car in gear, Abby decided she *would* be making a stop on the way, but for something much less predictable.

"You've got a lot of nerve coming here, missy."

This was how Justin's mother answered the door. It seemed like an odd thing to say to a pizza delivery person.

"I just want to talk to him, Karen," Abby replied, and Justin bounded off the couch before his mother did something crazy, like slam the door in her face.

"I've got this, Mom," he cut in, catching the door before it closed. "Give us a minute, okay?"

Mom's lip curled up in a snarl. "Don't you hurt him again, girlie. He's been through enough because of you."

Stepping onto the porch, he closed the screen door behind him. "We should probably talk out here."

"That seems best, yes," Abby replied, taking a seat on the porch swing. Once he joined her, she held silent, staring at the envelope in her lap.

Justin took the opportunity to drink her in. The way her lashes created little shadows on her cheeks. And the lock of hair that tumbled over her right eye, hiding her expression. He assumed she'd talked to her brother by now, but he hadn't made things right with the expectation that she'd come back to him. He wanted her to know that.

"About your brother's garage—" he started, but Abby cut him off.

"I got a job," she said, as if they were old friends catching up.

"That's good," he replied. "Are you going back to nursing?"

"Sort of." The corner of the envelope bent beneath her nail. "I'll be working at the Safe Haven Women's Shelter as a sort of liaison with the residents, especially when they first arrive. Addressing medical needs or just helping them get settled."

Off balance, Justin said, "You'll be good at that." Which she would. Abby was a natural caretaker. "I'm glad you found something you think you'll like."

"The thing is," she continued, "I thought creative meant drawing or painting, but it really means making something that didn't exist before. With the shelter, Carrie has created a safe place for women who desperately need one, and I'm looking forward to helping her bring her full vision to life."

Justin started to worry. He hadn't heard from Cooper yet. Maybe Abby had been sent to throw the rental agreement in his face.

"Is that what you came all the way out here to tell me?" he asked, cutting his eyes to the horizon because not touching her was driving him mad. "That you got a new job?"

She toed the swing into motion. "Not only that, no. I heard about what you did for Cooper."

He hadn't done anything for Cooper, but Justin didn't correct her. "Are you here to give me his answer?"

The swing stopped. "What answer?"

"Whether or not he's going to sign the agreement."

"Of course he's going to sign the agreement," she said, as if this were a foregone conclusion, "but that's not why I'm here."

Justin met her gaze and nearly lost himself in her eyes. The green depths held no anger. No judgment or reproach. Only hope. An emotion he'd been fighting to contain all day.

Stretching his arm across the back of the swing, he repeated the question. "Why are you here, Abby?"

The seat swayed from side to side this time. "I thought there might be a reason to come. That there might be a chance."

Giving in to temptation, Justin twirled a lock of hair between his fingers. "A chance for what?"

Eyes lowered again, she whispered, "Us."

One word that allowed him to dream again.

"There is for me," he murmured. "How about you?"

Abby took a deep breath and let it out slowly. "I think so. But I need to say something first." She traced circles on his denim-clad thigh with one warm fingertip. "I shouldn't have accused you of cheating, and I don't blame you for being angry with me."

"I should have controlled my temper," he admitted. "And told you the truth from the beginning. I didn't realize the damage that keeping secrets could do."

A sad smile curled her lips. "No more secrets, then?"

Justin nodded. "The whole story. Every time."

"I guess we've both learned some hard lessons in the last few weeks." Abby clasped her hands around the envelope in her lap. "Since we've been apart, I've learned another one."

Praying for the right answer, he asked, "What's that?"

"That I can be happy alone."

Like a punch, Justin felt the declaration reverberate through his chest. Drawing his arm off the bench, he leaned forward with his elbows on his knees.

"I've been so busy being unhappy," she went on, "that I forgot how to live. To enjoy the moment and stop wallowing in what I don't have." She tapped the envelope against her chest. "I mean, I'm enough all by myself, you know? I have dreams and ideas, and I don't need a man in my life to be fulfilled."

Why didn't she set him on fire already?

"You are enough, Abby." Justin rose from the swing. "Sounds like you're all set to have a nice life."

"Where are you going?" she asked, following him to the door. "Don't you want to hear the rest?"

"What do you want from me here? My blessing? Do you want me to say 'good for you'? Because I've got nothing. I don't want to wish you well and wave good-bye. I want to be by your side to watch you chase those dreams, and listen to all of your ideas while you're lying in my arms." He swiped a hand through his hair. "I guess that's not what you want."

Taking his hand, she said, "You didn't let me finish. I know now that I don't need a man to be happy, but that doesn't mean I don't want one. That I don't want you."

If this was her idea of playing hard to get, Justin didn't think he had the strength for it.

"So you don't need me, but you want me?"

Abby tugged him back to the swing. "Exactly," she said, pulling him down beside her before withdrawing what looked like two plane tickets from the envelope. "I have a long list of places I plan to see, and I'll go alone if I have to. But I'd much rather take you with me. Our first stop is London. What do you say? Can we try this again?"

Lifting her into his lap, Justin took her mouth with his, answering her the only way he knew how.

When they finally came up for air, Abby breathed, "Is that a yes?"

"Yes," he laughed, holding her tight. "I'll go anywhere with you, Abby girl. Just promise to never leave me again."

"Never," she said, curling against him. "Never again."

Chapter 27

Abby leapt to safety in time to avoid being run over by the reckless driver.

"Watch your toes," called Ian O'Malley as he chased after the two outlaw toddlers in the pink princess car. "I didn't know these toys could go so fast."

The young mechanic picked up his pace, followed closely by Noah Winchester.

"Let off the gas, Molly!" ordered Noah, smiling and not winded in the least. The toy car slowed to a stop, little-girl curls blew in the summer breeze, and four wide eyes looked up as if to say, "What did we do?" Though Emma looked more stunned than innocent, as if being in Molly's passenger seat had been more excitement than she'd expected.

Ian lifted the redhead into his arms. "Jess will have my butt if you get hurt, munchkin."

Jessi had fallen hard for Ian O'Malley, one of Cooper's employees, shortly after moving in with Abby the year before. Most men Ian's age, barely twenty-one, wouldn't have looked twice at a girl down on her luck and toting a newborn, but he'd surprised them all and stepped up for the young mother. Now the pair shared a small apartment over his parents' garage, and lucky Emma had two doting parents instead of one.

"She gets prettier every day," Abby chimed, running a hand over bright red curls.

"Just like her mama," Ian beamed.

Molly lifted her arms as Noah approached, and he lifted her straight onto his shoulders.

"Might be time to let the car rest," he said, holding the child with one hand and moving the toy to the side with the other. Along his forearm, Abby spotted a tattoo she hadn't seen before, featuring two familiar names tucked beneath a soldier's helmet.

If that didn't say forever, she didn't know what would.

The men marched back to the party, bundles in hand, and Abby followed them down the sidewalk leading from Cooper's back door to the elaborate spread in his backyard. The wedding had been a beautiful affair. Mama and Bruce swayed in the middle of the makeshift dance floor, surrounded by several couples twirling through a two-step. Spencer led Lorelei into a spin that any professional would envy, while Caleb and Snow chose a more simple turn.

Cooper, who fancied himself the best two-stepper in town—though he'd never held a candle to Spencer's skills—tugged Haleigh reluctantly around them all. She kept looking at her feet, and Cooper kept tipping up her chin to share a *trust me* smile. No matter the approach, they all looked madly in love, and Abby finally knew exactly how they felt.

"I missed you," Justin said, stepping up behind her and wrapping her in his arms.

"I was gone less than five minutes," she pointed out.

"That was four and a half minutes too long."

Since the day she'd arrived on his parents' doorstep asking for a second chance, Abby and Justin had spent every minute together, aside from his nights at the firehouse. Abby had been happy with Kyle, but in a different way. He'd made her feel safe. Protected. But the ever-present fear for his safety had locked her into a cocoon. In order to support him, she'd had to become all but invisible. To be the one thing he never had to worry about.

Justin offered the opposite. With him in her life, Abby could do anything. Chase any dream, walk any wire, and know that he'd be there beside her, every step of the way. She would never forget or stop loving Kyle, but the time had come to end the mourning and embrace the new future she'd been given.

"Do you think your mother is ever going to forgive me?" Justin asked.

Regardless of the fact that he'd saved Cooper's garage *and* made her daughter exceedingly happy, Linda Ridgeway continued to hold a grudge. Intentionally or not, Justin had brought Quintin Culpepper to Ardent Springs, and furthermore, committed the greater offense of making her little girl cry.

Abby patted Justin's arm. "Give her time. She'll come around." Turning to face him, she rubbed a thumb along his jawline. "I still can't believe you sold your car for us."

"For you," he corrected. "A car can be replaced. You can't."

Sharing a secret, she whispered, "Cooper is already looking for a replacement. For the car," she clarified. "He's determined to do at least that much to thank you."

Justin dropped a quick kiss on her lips. "I got everything I wanted, and I'd do it all again in a heartbeat. Haven't you figured out yet that it was always you? All those flower deliveries back in the day were an excuse to see that smile of yours. The night you set your kitchen on fire I wasn't even on duty." He laughed.

Abby blinked as her hand dropped to his shoulder. "You had a crush on me when you were eighteen?"

"A major crush," he admitted. "The day I heard you tell the other nurses that you'd gotten married, my world ended."

"That sounds very dramatic for an eighteen-year-old boy."

"I was an old soul." Justin squeezed her tight. "I admit, I tried to move on. I gave myself to other women."

Laughter bubbled up and her cheeks ached from smiling. "No one could blame you for that. I *had* broken your heart, after all."

"Shattered it into pieces," he embellished. The man had missed his calling for the stage. "But you put it back together again, too. And now it's all yours."

"Always has been? Always will be?" Abby asked with a teasing tone. Those had been the words that brought her back to him. The words that made all the difference.

"Exactly." He nodded, leaning down for a longer kiss, but they were interrupted by the sound of silverware tapping a glass.

Abby glanced over her shoulder to see Mama waving a knife in the air. "It's time to cut the cake," she announced.

"Remember where we left off," Justin murmured, leading her back to their table near the front.

On the way, they passed the last couple she'd expected to see today. As one of Cooper's longtime employees, Frankie had been invited to the wedding. And thanks to the exile of Quintin Culpepper, who'd been fetched home by his high-society mother, Becky Winkle was once again on Frankie's arm.

A development that had taken most in attendance by surprise.

"Could I talk to you for a second?" Becky said, catching Abby by the wrist.

Shocked by not only the contact but the gracious tone from the typically caustic blonde, Abby said, "Um . . . Mama and Bruce are about to cut the cake."

"This won't take but a second," she assured.

Seeing no reason to be rude, Abby surrendered. "Okay, then. Let's talk."

Becky smiled at Justin before saying "Excuse me, honey," to Frankie and tugging Abby away from the crowd. Once they were alone behind a blooming crepe myrtle, the other woman halted, eyes anxious and hands clasped. "I know that you don't like me, but I hope you'll hear me out."

Unwilling to lie, Abby didn't correct the first part of her statement. "I'm listening."

"Well," she started, darting a glance back toward the table they'd just left. "I like Frankie. I like him a lot."

There had to be a hidden camera in this tree somewhere. "That's a little hard to believe when you recently ditched him for a stranger."

"I know. I'm an idiot." Who was this woman and what had she done with Becky Winkle? "I'm a sucker for a slick talker, and I know I should know better by now. I mean, I've been married enough times you'd think I'd have learned my lesson. But I want to change, and Frankie thinks you could help me do that."

Dazed, Abby lost her tact. "You've been hateful since high school, Becky. Heck, you were hateful in grade school. You made Lorelei's life miserable when she already had enough grief to deal with, losing her mom, and just last year you were horrible to Jessi when you learned she was your sister."

"Half sister," Becky corrected.

"Which proves my point. You aren't a nice person. You never have been."

Pale blue eyes narrowed before closing completely. Taking several deep breaths, the woman mumbled to herself before responding.

"I'm a spoiled brat, okay. Daddy poisoned me against Lorelei from a young age, but that's no excuse for my behavior. I know that. But you can't deny that I've always been the one left out. I know that people call me names. That y'all make fun of the way I dress and do my hair."

Her wedding attire included a chartreuse skirt with a sunny yellow blouse, and her hair had been teased into submission, most likely held in place by an entire bottle of hair spray. A despairing look to say the least, but then making fun of the woman's poor fashion sense didn't make them any better than she was.

"You have to admit," she said, searching for a noninsulting descriptor, "the outfits are a little loud."

Smoothing the skirt, Becky said, "I like attention. I guess this is how I try to get it."

Talk about a missed approach. "Try being nice instead. Smile once in a while, and not that sneer thing you do, but a genuine smile."

"See," Becky said. "That's the kind of advice I need. I'm willing to put myself in your hands and do whatever you say. Within reason, of course."

"Are you suggesting that I give you a makeover?" Abby asked.

Becky's eyes twinkled with excitement. "That's exactly what I'm asking."

The obvious question had to be asked. "Why? You've never given the impression you wanted to change anything. So why now?"

Chewing the inside of her cheek, the tiny blonde shifted from foot to foot.

"When Frankie takes me places, no one will talk to him. It's like he's walked in with the plague. I knew that I wasn't the most popular person in town, and that was fine when people were only avoiding me, but now they're avoiding Frankie, and I hate that. He took me back after the Quintin mess, and he says he doesn't care what other people think, but for his sake, I do.

"I don't want to be the spoiled brat anymore, Abby. I want to be a woman that Frankie can be proud to have on his arm. Will you help me do that?"

She would likely regret this, but Abby said, "I guess we can try." Knowing this was a job for the professionals, she added, "We'll get you into Gertie's first thing next week, and I'll call Virgil about helping with your wardrobe."

"Virgil Lexington?" Becky asked, a look of distaste twisting her lips.

"Yes, Virgil Lexington. If you have a problem with that, the deal is off."

"It's just that the dresses in his windows are always so . . . subtle."

Abby nearly burst out laughing. "Embrace the subtle, Becky. You don't need these crazy outfits to stand out. If you care enough about Frankie to even ask for help, there must be a good person hiding in there somewhere. We need to let her do the talking instead of the clothes."

Wringing her hands, she said, "If you're sure."

"I am. Now let's get some cake before it's all gone."

⁓

"What was that about?" Justin asked as Abby returned to her seat with a large slice of cake.

"You aren't going to believe this," she said, settling a napkin in her lap, "but I just agreed to make over Becky Winkle."

His fork lingered inches above his plate. "You're kidding. Are you hiding a magic wand in that dress?"

"I know, right? But she's doing it for Frankie, so I caved."

Justin watched the bearded man tuck the blonde under his arm. "They have to be the oddest couple ever."

Abby followed his gaze. "I don't know. They're kind of cute."

"In a King Kong sort of way," he suggested. "If the gorilla wore thick glasses and the woman dressed like a Vegas marquee sign."

"Be nice," she scolded. "That's my Cinderella you're talking about."

"What were you doing with Becky Winkle at the cake table?" Haleigh asked, slipping into the chair on the opposite side of Abby.

"She's adding fairy godmother to her résumé," Justin answered, earning a jab to his ribs.

Haleigh scoffed. "Please. Fixing that look would take more than fairy dust."

"Stop it," Abby hissed. "Becky has the courage to want to change, and I'm going to help her. We're *all* going to help her."

"We're what?" Haleigh said.

"We who?" Justin asked at the same time.

Abby sat back and crossed her arms. "We all like Frankie, do we not?"

"Sure, but—" he started, only to be cut off.

"No buts. We like Frankie and Frankie likes Becky. She's taken the first step by asking for help, and now we're going to be the bigger people and grant our assistance."

"Did you spike her drink?" Haleigh asked him.

"Maybe your friend Lorelei added something to the cake," he replied.

"You two can joke all you want," Abby said, sitting forward and scooping a bite onto her fork. "But I've recruited you whether you like it or not. We have a near thirty-year reputation to undo, and that's going to take the whole team. Buckle up, because I have a feeling this is going to be an interesting ride."

Stating the obvious, Haleigh whispered, "But we don't like her."

Abby shrugged. "Maybe we don't know her."

"Didn't you all go to school together?" Justin asked, not the least bit surprised by the new development. Abby was a born caretaker, and when Frankie had asked if she might help Becky out, the answer had been an easy one.

"Yes," Haleigh responded. "And she's always been a bitc—"

Abby slapped a hand over her best friend's mouth. "No one deserves to be judged by their past mistakes. Right, Haleigh Rae?" One thin brow arched. "That's what I thought. If she reverts to her old ways, then at least we'll know we tried. Until then, no more insults. Understand?"

The blonde nodded her agreement seconds before licking her friend's hand.

"That's gross," Abby said, wiping her palm on her napkin.

The party was once again interrupted by the clinking of a glass.

"All the single ladies to the dance floor," called Lorelei. "It's time to throw the bouquet."

Neither Abby nor Haleigh moved.

"What are you waiting for?" Justin asked. "You're both single."

"I'm engaged," Haleigh replied.

"I don't see a ring," Justin argued.

"Your boyfriend's being an ass," she said to Abby.

"Abigail Louise, get your butt up here," the bride ordered. "You, too, Haleigh Rae."

Justin smirked, earning a smile from his better half.

"You know what it means if I catch this, right?" she asked.

He most certainly did. "What it means is going to happen eventually anyway, but a little insurance from the universe never hurts."

Abby rewarded him with a slow, wet kiss before strutting to the dance floor, all blue chiffon and delicious curves. When Becky joined the group, Abby welcomed her with a smile, and less than a minute later a dozen women reached for the flowers, but only one came down with the prize.

Becky Winkle.

Justin was likely the only person who saw Abby bump the bouquet toward her new project with her elbow and wasn't surprised when the resulting applause lacked enthusiasm. In her excitement, Becky went from hugging Abby to hugging Haleigh, who looked as if she'd been accosted by a bear, the expression on her face priceless.

Color high on her cheeks, Abby returned to the table with pride in her eyes.

"You did that on purpose," he whispered.

She returned to her cake. "I don't know what you mean. I gave that my best shot."

Once again, Justin wondered what he'd ever done to get this lucky.

"I love you, Abigail Louise," he murmured, kissing her temple. "I don't deserve you, but I love you."

Leaning into him, she said, "That's good. Because I love you, too. And I plan to keep loving you for a very long time." She slipped a bite of cake between his lips before pressing her own against them.

Staring into her gorgeous emerald eyes, Justin had only one thought. Life didn't get much better than this.

Acknowledgments

Because I somehow made this year even more complicated than normal, the people who support me in this crazy career were forced to go above and beyond to keep me together. As always, huge thanks to my agent, Nalini Akolekar, who never lost faith in my ability to pull a rabbit out of a hat. Or rather, a book out of thin air. She's a rock and a bulldog and a friend I wouldn't want to take this journey without.

Thank you to my editor, Alison Dasho, and the entire team at Montlake Romance, including Ahn Schluep and Jessica R. Poore. You make me smile, are always there when I need you, and by some higher power believe in me and my books. You're my publishing fairy godmothers, and I'm blessed to have you on my side. Thank you, also, to Krista Stroever. This book is far better thanks to your patience and guidance.

To my daughter, Isabelle, who never blinks when waking for school to find her mother hasn't been to bed yet, and to my writing buddies who talk me off the ledge more often than I'm willing to admit—Fran, Maureen, Marnee, Jessica, and Kim. To my street team, Team Awesome, for not minding constant neglect, and to every reader who has picked up one of my books. You're by far the best part about this job.

About the Author

Photo © Kimberly Rocha

Award-winning author Terri Osburn fell in love with the written word at a young age. Classics like *The Wizard of Oz* and *Little Women* filled her childhood, and the romance genre beckoned during her teen years. In 2007 she put pen to paper to write her own heart-melting love stories, and just five years later she was named a 2012 finalist for a Romance Writers of America Golden Heart Award. Her debut novel was released a year later. Terri resides in Middle Tennessee with her teenage daughter and a menagerie of high-maintenance pets. To learn more about this international bestselling author, visit her website at www.terriosburn.com.